REUNION

REUNION

—

A NOVEL

ELISE JUSKA

HARPER

An Imprint of HarperCollins*Publishers*

REUNION. Copyright © 2024 by Elise Juska. All rights reserved. Printed in the United States of America. No part of this book may be used or reproduced in any manner whatsoever without written permission except in the case of brief quotations embodied in critical articles and reviews. For information, address HarperCollins Publishers, 195 Broadway, New York, NY 10007.

HarperCollins books may be purchased for educational, business, or sales promotional use. For information, please email the Special Markets Department at SPsales@harpercollins.com.

FIRST EDITION

Art by komkrit Preechachanwate/Shutterstock, Inc.

Library of Congress Cataloging-in-Publication Data has been applied for.

ISBN 978-0-06-334676-5

24 25 26 27 28 LBC 5 4 3 2 1

For Jake

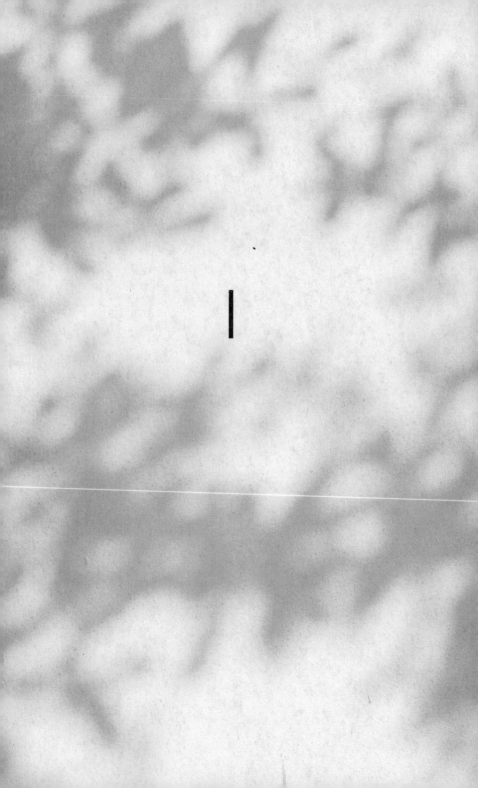

ONE

HOPE

"I could have sworn you knew this was coming up," Hope said, carrying a stack of dinner dishes to the kitchen sink. "It's right there." She stopped to nod at the refrigerator, where beside the kids' most recent school pictures, the calendar was turned to the month of June. "See?"

A year ago, a different calendar had hung in that same spot, a different month of June, the one that had vanished. The squares had remained filled with canceled graduation parties and end-of-year class picnics, day camps and trips to the Jersey shore. Now, the boxes had filled up again, assuming their hopeful new shapes: Izzy's eighth-grade dance, Rowan's indoor karate classes. Ethan's end-of-semester faculty reception. *Reunion*. One year later, a different event.

Ethan was still at the kitchen table, wearing the blue T-shirt, blue sweatpants, and bald leather slippers he changed into at the end of every workday online. "Reunion? What reunion?"

"My college reunion. My twenty-fifth—well, twenty-sixth, technically."

"I thought that was canceled."

"It was," Hope said lightly. "That's why it's happening now."

He tunneled his fingers through his hair and frowned, as if questioning her math.

"We talked about this," Hope said, but kept her eyes on the dishes as she scraped the uneaten noodles into the garbage disposal. It was technically true. They had talked about it, back in April, when the email arrived in Hope's inbox announcing her reunion had been rescheduled. Ethan had been sitting in that same spot, drinking coffee and reading something on his iPad, while Hope stood by the counter, waiting for Rowan's waffles to finish toasting and scrolling on her phone. When she saw the invitation—*A Celebration with Classmates, Long Overdue*—she'd read it out loud to confirm that it was real.

"Kind of melodramatic, isn't it?" Ethan had said.

"Is it?" Hope had replied. "Oh, I don't think so. I think it's kind of moving, actually."

"On Zoom?"

"No, no. On campus."

"So you'll go?"

"Of course!" she'd said. "I mean, assuming people are going."

And then—what? Izzy had texted from her room that the wireless router needed to be reset again or Rowan had raced into the kitchen declaring he was starving or Ethan had evaporated into another meeting, and they hadn't resumed the conversation, not then and not ever. Hope had written it on the calendar, but Ethan never noticed the calendar, much less consulted it for information. To him, it was purely decorative, as dated as a rotary phone. In the past year, he'd become even more reliant on technology, AirPods nestled in his ears and his bedside charging station drooling wires. His schedule existed solely in the cloud.

Now he blinked at the calendar, as if waiting for a more reasonable explanation to present itself. Appropriately, it was the Walthrop one that the school sent Hope each year for donating to the alumni fund. The photo for the month of June showed the quad in early summer—classic redbrick dorms, flowering pink trees—and the squares beneath it were crowded with Hope's handwritten notes and reminders. If Ethan ignored wall calendars, Hope relied on them, the ink-filled squares evidence of the fullness of their lives. She was a planner by nature; for her, the shapelessness of the past fifteen months, the inability to look forward, had been one of the hardest parts.

"And this is happening tomorrow?" Ethan said.

"Right." Hope turned on the faucet, holding a finger under the tap until the water ran hot.

"I'm assuming I'm not going," he said. "Or did you forget to mention that, too?"

"Oh—I figured you wouldn't want to," Hope said, knowing this was true. Ethan had gone to previous Walthrop reunions but never appeared to particularly enjoy them, and had never attended his own reunions, or even seemed to see the point. Maybe because he now worked in academia, he was no longer able to summon any nostalgia for his own alma mater, a tier-one university fifteen times the size of Hope's cozy liberal arts college. His relationship to higher education had become largely managerial: a history professor turned dean of the Humanities Department, chair of the Academic Crisis Task Force last spring.

"But you're taking the kids?" he said.

It was more a statement than a question, and the part of the conversation Hope had been dreading most. "No, actually," she said, doing her best to sound casual as she pulled open the dishwasher. "Just me."

Ethan pinched one arm of his glasses, a square two-toned pair Izzy had chosen for him online, and resettled them on his face. "What?"

"I just thought it would be simpler."

He gave a short laugh. "For whom?"

Hope had rehearsed her reasons. "It's too big an event to bring them to," she told him, rinsing a handful of forks. "Too much too soon. And your semester is officially over, right?"

This was all true, too. Though things seemed to be—finally, thankfully—getting back to normal, and the college was taking plenty of precautions, she could argue it was still safer to leave the kids at home. And in theory, Ethan now had some room in his schedule. The week before, he'd attended a modified version of commencement, addressing the graduates and their guests, who sat sprinkled across the football field.

"It is," Ethan said. "But I was planning to get back to working on my book."

Hope concentrated on slotting plates in the dishwasher, wanting to point out that Ethan was always working on his book. That Ethan was always working, period. As soon as the academic year wound down, there was the book, a history of global transportation, perpetually urgent and perpetually unfinished. Admittedly, in normal times, Hope didn't mind that Ethan was so busy: he worked on campus and she stayed home. It was a lifestyle made possible by the generosity of her parents, who had quietly helped them out with down payments and private school tuitions and three years of fertility treatments. Of course, taking care of the kids and house was hard work, too (more so than Ethan ever seemed to realize), but Hope was aware of the perks that came with it: the moments of solitude on a weekday—a glass of pinot grigio, a midday TV show, an hour spent curled with a book in the sun—pockets of stolen peace and pleasure in exchange for keeping everything running.

In the past year, of course, that alone time had disappeared. The separate parts had all merged: work and home, Ethan's life, her life. They'd never spent so much time together, not even when they were first dating, Hope prying Ethan away from his research for happy hour with her coworkers from the PR firm or takeout at her Center City apartment. Now Ethan was deeply around, yet deeply absent, most days spending fourteen hours in his office upstairs, emerging irritable and exhausted and leaving Hope to deal with everything else. So, as much as Hope wanted to take offense when he objected to her leaving for the weekend, the truth was that she *had* purposefully waited to tell him, afraid that to mention it sooner would complicate her plans.

"I'm sorry," Hope said. "I really thought you knew about it." She perched the wineglasses in the upper rack of the dishwasher. "But it should be an easy weekend. I already went to the store." Not that she could remember the last time Ethan had shopped for groceries. Even last year, it was always Hope who braved Whole Foods, waiting in the carefully spaced-out line that wrapped around the parking lot before entering the building. She'd made sure then to stock up on all of Rowan's favorites, and for this weekend, she'd bought many of those same things—fruit snacks (bunny-shaped), chicken nuggets (dinosaur-shaped)—before swinging by Target for Lucky Charms (nuggets of processed sugar, but in desperate moments, they worked). For Izzy, whose help Hope knew she would rely on for the next few days, she'd picked up vegan ice cream and a case of coconut La Croix.

"I also made that taco casserole Rowan likes," Hope continued, pouring detergent into the dishwasher. "It's in the fridge. It just needs to be reheated."

Ethan typed something into his phone, scratching at his beard. For their first fourteen years of marriage, he had always been clean-shaven, but in the past year he'd grown a thicket of bristles. "And when will you be back?" he asked without looking up.

"Sunday."

"Yes, but when Sunday?"

"In the evening," Hope said, quickly adding, "I didn't want to fly." Which, if not the complete truth, was certainly credible. The flight to Portland, Maine, was just ninety minutes, but Hope didn't relish the thought of sitting elbow to elbow in a small, enclosed space. Mostly, though, she liked the prospect of the solo drive—leaving early with her tumbler of coffee, cruising by the service plazas of New Jersey and the shimmering silhouette of New York City and on into New England, where the landscape would exhale, the sky widening and roadsides softening with trees.

"You're driving?" Ethan said with the perplexed look of someone who had spent the past decade researching transportation and knew this was the least efficient option. "Why?"

"It's not that far." Hope shrugged. "I'm used to it." She'd done the drive many times in college, first with her parents and later when she took her Jetta back and forth to school. "And Izzy will be here. She'll help with Rowan." Now that Ethan had been debriefed, Hope could let her daughter know about the reunion and ask her to pitch in. The dishwasher pinged, and she pressed the Start button and shut the door, heard the weary slosh of the wash cycle begin. "She just has that dance on Friday night—don't worry, she's getting a ride with Lacy—but other than that she'll be around. I'm sure at some point you could sneak off to campus. The only thing you really need to remember is OT on Saturday morning."

Ethan glanced up. "Online?"

"In person," Hope replied, plucking the sponge off the sink. Ethan had not seen Rowan's occupational therapist, in any format, since his initial evaluation, six weeks before the world shut down. The two of them had perched on child-sized chairs in a brightly colored playroom while Ellen, a kind, fit woman around Hope's age—*I'm a parent, too*, she told them—spelled out what she'd observed about their son, the sensitivities and anxieties that, since then, had grown only more acute.

"I think it could be nice," Hope continued, sweeping the sponge along the faucet. "You've been working so hard. And I know Rowan wants to spend time with you. It could be good for you to—"

"Please," Ethan interrupted. "I don't need you telling me what's good for me." He took his glasses off and slid them onto the table. "It's exhausting."

Hope stood still, sponge in hand, heartbeat ticking in her chest. Maybe it was because she'd be leaving soon for her reunion that for a moment she zoomed out and observed her husband at an objective distance, as she would a person she hadn't seen in years. His hair was still more brown than gray, but noticeably thinning, and his hairline was receding. His eyelids looked heavy, probably from fatigue, and his glasses had left two shiny red dents on either side of his nose. But what struck her most was his expression: annoyed, impatient. She thought again about the beginning, when Ethan had seemed so grateful for her stepping in to organize his life, when his dedication to his work had reassured her. She'd mapped out a plan for their future: a tenure-track position for him (East Coast, not too far from her parents), a wedding (August, at the Jersey shore), a baby (before age thirty-four). And for the first few years, it had happened just as she'd envisioned. She recalled her conversation with Polly—her college roommate, herself the mother of a five-year-old by then—when Hope decided to hold off on going back to work after having Izzy.

A stay-at-home mom? Polly had said. *Is that as thankless as it sounds?*

Then from upstairs, Rowan shouted: "Mom!"

Hope tipped her head toward the sound of his voice. "Yes, Ro?"

"I need you!"

She paused to note his tone, gauging the intensity of the issue: urgent, but probably not serious. He couldn't find Gray Rabbit. His toothbrush tasted funny. His pajamas were inside out.

"It's an emergency!"

"What's the emergency, Ro?"

"I just need you," he repeated, and, serious or not, Hope could tell from the tremble in his voice that things could escalate quickly.

She fought to sound airy and untroubled as she called back: "Be right there!" though she felt like bursting into tears. Then she returned the sponge to the sink and looked at her husband, and he looked at her, and for a moment Hope feared something would give way, the churning dishwasher might gape open and flood the room, but she only smiled. "It's just one weekend," she said.

In April, when the possibility of going to the reunion alone first crossed her mind, Hope had dismissed it out of hand. After her family's months of constant togetherness, she couldn't begin to picture it, felt guilty even considering it. Rowan needed her too much. But when she called the charming inn across the street from campus (an inn so charming it didn't have online booking), Hope heard herself asking for just one room.

Since then, she'd been texting about it with Polly and Adam

and had joined the Walthrop 26th Reunion Facebook group, where she tracked the RSVPs. From her class of nearly four hundred, there were a respectable 122 yesses, not including people like Polly, who weren't on Facebook. She received notifications every time someone posted an old photo, setting off a cascade of comments about the plaid flannels, wind pants, and overalls that were so popular in the nineties. Hope had dug out her college album so she could upload her favorite picture of herself and Polly and Adam, standing outside Fiske Hall: Polly in her too-thin leather jacket, wearing a grudging smile; Adam in a striped wool hat pulled to his eyebrows, midlaugh; Hope between them, head level with their shoulders, smiling happily, wearing her beloved Fair Isle sweater.

Still, the reunion weekend had felt somewhat abstract, knowing Ethan needed to be reminded. But now Hope had told him. She was going. Once she finished packing, she would ask Izzy about helping out. Rowan she'd talk to in the morning; she worried that knowing too soon would make him needlessly anxious. She'd never been away from Rowan for an entire weekend—and in the past year, scarcely more than a few hours—but she'd frame this as a treat for him: extra snacks, TV shows, time with Dad. She was sincere in her belief that this weekend would be good for the two of them. For all of them. The past year had been a test for everyone's marriage—who *couldn't* use a few days apart?

As she hoisted her suitcase onto the bed and unzipped the shiny titanium shell, Hope felt buoyant. Tomorrow, at this hour, she would be back on campus. The forecast wasn't ideal for an outdoor reunion—there was a 40 percent chance of rain on Saturday morning—but the rest of the day looked clear, warmish even. She pictured how her classmates would congregate on the quad on Saturday afternoon, drinking summer ales, shedding jackets and sweaters, before piling on the layers again for the lobster bake that evening. Giddy, Hope turned to face the walk-in, then considered her reflection in the mirror on the closet door.

The past fifteen months had exacted a toll on bodies: no one had emerged looking the same as they had going in. People had shrunk or expanded. They'd gotten in shape. They'd let their hair go gray. Ethan looked a little trimmer, even though he barely left his study. Hope, despite her failed attempt at committing to an online yoga class, had gained at least ten pounds. After the new year, she'd stopped checking her scale, stashing it in the basement and resolving to go easier on herself—it was an extraordinary time. Once inside Whole Foods, she couldn't resist grabbing a few pandemic indulgences, sea salt caramels and gelatos and exotic cheeses, before taking the long route home just to be alone for a few extra minutes, listening to music, or to nothing, until she worried the frozen foods might melt.

If her shirt pinched under her arms, palazzo pants felt snug across her hips—well, so be it. Hope had grown up with a sister and mother who were effortlessly skinny, while she'd inherited her father's broad shoulders and solid thighs. *Stocky*, a pediatrician once described her, something no self-respecting children's doctor would say in 2021. But Hope had the self-esteem to withstand this kind of thoughtlessness. As a child, she'd even been recruited for few local commercials; her face was *appealingly symmetrical*, they said. It was the same face, she reminded herself now, smiling in the mirror—she was a believer in the power of smiling—but couldn't help noticing the wrinkles that feathered around her eyes. The sunspots sprinkled along her jawline. Her hair had lost some of its fullness. She regularly picked strands of it from the shower drain, packing them into tiny blond snowballs and tucking them in the trash. Biting into a pita chip one day last summer, she'd felt a twang of pain on one side of her skull, like a gong had been struck. *Cracked*, the dentist had confirmed, practically shouting to be heard over the roar of the ventilator in the corner, wearing headgear that looked like it belonged in outer space. She'd been grinding her teeth in her sleep, he explained, weakening the enamel and splitting a molar down the middle. *I've never seen more cracked teeth in my career.*

At least the tooth was concealed on the inside of her body, part of an assortment of ominous tweaks and twinges—soreness in her lower back, stiffness in her right wrist, the sprig of nerve endings that flowered occasionally in the sole of her left foot. In the past year, she'd lie in the dark at night just staring at the ceiling, intimately aware of the workings of her anatomy, the steady effort of her lungs and heart, trying to imagine how and when things would get back to normal, cycling through increasingly dire what-if scenarios, until she drowned her nerves in the dull light of her phone.

Hope vowed that, for the next three days, she would banish all such thoughts from her mind. She wasn't letting anything interfere with her reunion. Besides, all things considered, Hope looked fine—more than fine! She could dress to hide her belly, and her grays were disguised by highlights in a natural-looking blond. She'd always been good with makeup, and her skin was still relatively firm, with the exception of her neck. She flattened one hand beneath her chin, something she'd seen her mother do when she was a girl, watching the subtle way her face lifted, and years melted away. When Hope let the hand drop, her entire face sank a few degrees. She might have passed for forty, even younger when she put in the effort, if the neck didn't give her away.

"What are you doing?" Izzy asked, materializing in the doorway.

Her daughter had a talent for appearing at Hope's most embarrassing moments: sobbing at a Google commercial, or nibbling frosting off the inside of a cupcake wrapper, or poring over an article about eyebrow threading like she was cramming for a test. Izzy had been that way ever since she was a baby, studying Hope with her wide, all-seeing eyes, as if she were on to her, and it wouldn't be long before she was in charge. In the delivery room, Hope had declared her baby girl would be called Isabel, but a nurse had called her Izzy, and Ethan had repeated it, and to Hope's dismay it had stuck.

"Oh, nothing," Hope said, turning from the mirror. "Well, no. Not nothing, actually. I'm packing."

Izzy frowned, pushing her hair behind her ears. It was currently white-blond, with an inky dark part down the middle, like she was aging in reverse. "For what?"

"My college reunion is this weekend. In fact, I was just about to—"

"In Maine?"

"In Maine," Hope said, adding, "It isn't that far."

Her daughter eyed the suitcase suspiciously. "How long are you staying?"

"You have to overpack," Hope said. "The weather is unpredictable." As if to illustrate her point, she turned back to the closet and slid two sweaters from their hangers, a light cardigan and a chunky cable-knit.

Izzy still looked dubious. Below her thick and furrowed brows, her lids were coated a garish neon green. Hope understood this kind of eye makeup was in fashion. Izzy and her friends seemed offended by the very notion of trying to look pretty or feminine, and while Hope supported this in theory, she felt sure that neon eyeshadow was one of those trends, like leg warmers in the eighties, that would one day be looked back on with regret.

"I'm not going, am I?"

"You have your dance tomorrow."

"It's a social."

"I stand corrected," Hope said. A week ago, she had made the mistake of asking who Izzy was going with, opening herself up to a lecture on how her generation was so regressive about dating and everybody went to things like this in groups. "But actually, Iz, I wanted to ask you—" she began, when Izzy interrupted: "Dad's not going either?"

"Of course not," Hope said. "He's staying here with you."

Izzy folded her arms across her stomach, bare between her cropped sweatshirt and giant sweatpants, rolled deliberately at the waist. "Because you didn't want him there?"

"Because he has work to do," Hope said, tucking the sweaters into her suitcase. "And because he doesn't like reunions."

Her daughter fixed her with that knowing stare. Given any hint of conflict between her parents, Izzy would always side with her father. Hope had come to expect and accept it. Ethan was less available, so naturally Izzy sought out his approval. Meanwhile, Izzy was skeptical of all things where Hope was concerned. Her Spotify list. Her low-carb bread. Her Facebook posts—too frequent, too obviously curated—why was she even *on* Facebook? Her overuse of exclamation points. Her leather tote. Sometimes Hope secretly wondered if Izzy had become a vegan primarily to get on her nerves.

"Dad wouldn't want to be there," Hope reasserted, turning to her dresser and opening up her jean drawer. "Plus, families don't necessarily attend reunions. This year especially. Remember my friend Adam? His wife isn't coming either."

Granted, Adam was in a different situation, bringing his kids along because his wife had plans of her own. *A restorative yoga retreat*, Adam had texted. Hope had replied with an enthusiastic row of prayer hands—*Good for her!!!*—though she could imagine few things worse.

Then Izzy's phone dinged, and she dropped to the foot of the bed, producing it from the folds of her sweatshirt sleeve. As her daughter smiled at the screen, Hope wondered, as she often did, what went on in the depths of Izzy's phone. She wondered the same thing about Izzy's sessions with Sandra, which took place online on Friday afternoons. It was Izzy herself who in seventh grade asked for a therapist, though what prompted this Hope didn't know—problems with friends? Stress about grades? Hope remembered her own teenage self, her meltdown over the B-minus she got on Professor McFadden's twentieth-century American lit midterm freshman year of college. When Polly found her crying in their room in the middle of the afternoon, she thought someone was dead. *A B-minus?* Polly had said, her tone amused but kind. *I'm pretty sure that in real life, this won't matter at all.*

Now Izzy surprised her by saying, "That friendship seems so random."

Hope deposited an armful of pants on the bed and looked up at her. "Me and Adam? What makes you say that?"

"He's a guy, for one thing."

"And?" Hope said. "I have plenty of friends who are guys—men." She did, even if they were the husbands of her female friends, all men she would lose in hypothetical divorces.

"Also, it seems like you have literally nothing in common," Izzy went on, typing rapidly as she spoke. "He's kind of crunchy, isn't he? Doesn't he live in the woods or something?"

"He lives in New Hampshire. The town is kind of charming, actually," Hope said, though the one time she'd gone to visit Adam there, shortly after his twins were born, she *had* been surprised by how rustic it was. A big, unkempt farmhouse, in a town with four stoplights. Hope had taken pains to get there—the four of them were in Boston, visiting Ethan's sister, and while Izzy went sightseeing with her aunt and father, Hope and Rowan took a day trip to New Hampshire, bearing two big bags of hand-me-downs. She didn't know Andrea well—Adam hadn't met her until his late thirties, and then they eloped, to Hope's disappointment—but quickly deduced that she was the kind of mother who used cloth diapers and made her own baby food and would never let her children wear clothes branded with Marvel superheroes.

"Is Polly going?" Izzy asked then.

Hope was pleasantly surprised; Izzy rarely showed any interest in her life, especially her life before Izzy's birth. She tended to regard any details of Hope's experience in college—the presence of fraternities or the gendered term *freshman* or the literature anthologies on their bookshelves filled with straight dead white men—with a disbelief verging on scorn. "Yes, thank God," Hope said, rolling up a pair of skinny jeans. "She hasn't been there since the five-year."

"She's the one we saw that time in New York?"

"She is," Hope said. It was less than two years ago, but felt like another lifetime. Ethan had been speaking at a conference—it drove Hope mad that they scheduled academic conferences around the holidays—so in an attempt to make lemonade, she'd decided they'd all join him on his trip to the city. See *The Nutcracker*, the Christmas windows, the iconic skating rink. They'd met Polly and her son at Rockefeller Center, though the place was so crowded it was hard to catch up properly. Plus, Rowan was only four, so naturally he was fussy. Jonah was a sullen sixteen.

As if reading her mind, Izzy asked, "What about her son?"

"What about him?"

"What's his name again?"

"Jonah," Hope said.

"Oh, right," she said, with an exaggerated nod. "Is he going, too?"

Ah, Hope thought. Now her interest in the reunion made sense. On the New York trip, Jonah had slumped by the skating rink, pierced and disaffected, the kind of brooding teenage boy whom twelve-year-old Izzy might have nursed a quiet crush on. She'd been going through an awkward stage, her hair frizzy and chin pimply. She'd insisted on wearing the same shark-tooth necklace every day. Jonah kept touching the dime-sized circles yawning in his earlobes; Hope found it painful even looking at them. When she tried engaging him, his replies were short, borderline rude; he'd kept both feet planted on his skateboard, rolling it back and forth beneath his heels as if he might take off at any second. He didn't touch the nine-dollar hot chocolate she bought him. He called his mother Polly instead of Mom.

"They're driving up together, apparently," Hope said. This was a recent development, which Polly had texted her about just the day before; she was dropping Jonah on Ledgemere Island, thirty minutes from the college, a detour that would no doubt make her late. But this was Polly: there was always some complication, some unforeseen drama, a combination of poor planning and impulsivity and bad luck. In college, she'd finish a paper at the last minute only to realize the printer was out of ink. Senior year, she worried about finding a job after college but blew off her appointments with Career Services. Before Hope's wedding, she'd called to ask if she could bring Jonah—*What else am I supposed to do with him?*—as if people didn't find babysitters, as if a formal wedding were a personal affront. Jonah, age three, had ended up sitting at the head table, dressed like a pirate, wearing a patch over one eye and dragging a plastic scabbard around the dance floor. He'd popped up in dozens of pictures (because wedding photographers loved kids, and who could resist a kid in a costume?), scowling in every one; as far as Hope could tell, he'd been scowling ever since.

"But he's not coming to the reunion," Hope said, folding a pair of black pants into her suitcase. "He's staying with a friend." At least she hoped that was still the plan; she didn't want him putting a damper on things.

Izzy was typing again, two-thumbed, chin burrowed inside her sweatshirt collar. "Will it be weird seeing Polly?"

Hope paused. "Why would it be weird?"

"I don't know. You don't seem that close."

"What?" Hope said. "We're very close."

Her daughter arched her brows. Even with the neon eyelids, she managed to exude a kind of moral certitude. "Oooo-kay."

"We are," Hope said.

"Then how come you're getting defensive?"

"I'm not getting defensive. I'm clarifying the facts."

"You're doing that thing with your hands," Izzy said, and Hope squeezed them into fists. It was a new and unfortunate habit. Last spring, when they were all stuck in their houses, she'd stopped wearing her rings—nobody ever saw them, except when lifting a glass of wine on Zoom Moms' Night Out, so what was the point? But when she slid them back on a year later, they bothered her. They felt too small. Too constricting. She fussed with them, twisting them in circles. She regretted not following the example of her mother, who never took her rings off, no matter the activity—sleeping, showering, kneading meatloaf—and, on Hope's wedding day, had advised her to do the same.

Now she said, "I'm just trying to explain how close we were," and returned to the closet, scanning her shoe cabinet. She wanted to be prepared for any kind of weather—what was that famous line about weather in Maine? "We were roommates for all four years. We were practically inseparable."

"But that was in college. When's the last time you, like, spoke?"

"What—the exact date?" Hope said, grabbing a pair of suede booties. Wedge sandals. Hunter rain boots, just in case. "I don't know exactly. It's been a strange time for being in touch with people," she said, which was and was not true. They'd lost in-person gatherings, but if anything, Hope had had more regular contact with more people since last March. Usually, she would reach out to Adam and Polly anytime something from their shared past came up—the item in the alumni bulletin about Maddie Davis winning a MacArthur Genius Grant or the Spin Doctors song that had been ubiquitous senior year playing in a Starbucks—but during lockdown, they'd checked in all the time.

Admittedly, Hope couldn't remember the last time she and Polly had actually spoken. But was this so unusual? It wasn't like years ago, when, besides snail mail, phone calls were the only option. It was also how life went. Polly had Jonah; Hope got married, had two kids. Friends grew older, and their lives changed, and the people they talked to most were the ones who were in their worlds every day.

"It's been a while since we spoke," Hope conceded, jamming

the sandals in a side pocket. "But it doesn't matter, honestly. That's the thing about college friends. Some people you're just close to, no matter what." This, she thought, was 100 percent true. Even if they didn't talk regularly, even if they seemed to have nothing in common—the experience *was* the thing they had in common. Twenty-five years later, Hope still considered Polly and Adam her closest friends, the ones who knew her best.

But when she looked up from her suitcase, ready to launch into an explanation, she found Izzy was texting again, thumbs flying. Hope decided to take advantage of the distraction, changing the subject. "Listen, Iz," she said, "about this weekend"— then was stopped by the expression on her child's face. Beneath the gaudy makeup, the two-toned hair, Izzy looked so sad. Hope felt a deep wash of remorse. Would Izzy have *wanted* to go to the reunion? It hadn't even occurred to her. But these kids had been through so much. Maybe she'd have liked to get away at the end of the school year. It had been forever since the four of them had gone anywhere together—and this was Maine. *Vacationland!*

"I'm sorry," Hope said. "Did you want to come this weekend?"

"God, no," she said. "I literally couldn't care less."

"Oh." Hope laughed, though her comment stung a little. "Well, then."

"Sorry." Izzy glanced up. "No offense. I know you're obsessed."

"Obsessed?"

"With Walthrop."

"I'm not *obsessed*," Hope said. "I happen to love where I went to college. Which I happen to think is very lucky. When you're older, you'll understand," she added, but Izzy had resumed peering at the screen, face bathed in a private glow. "Actually, Iz," Hope tried again. "I need to ask a favor."

Izzy winced. "Oh God. What?"

"While I'm gone," Hope said, "will you help out with Ro?"

Her text sailed into the ether with a loud swoosh, and Izzy sighed, blowing a column of air upward and fanning out her bangs. Hope recognized this exasperation was partly for show. Rowan was the one person for whom Izzy had endless reserves of patience. If he was dysregulated, she remained unflustered, sensing just the thing he needed—Theraputty, finger fidgets, a few minutes in the "calming corner" of the living room. That she was more comfortable than Ethan in these situations went without saying.

"Fine," she said.

"Thank you."

Izzy shrugged. "No big deal."

"I'll tell him in the morning. I didn't want him—"

"Right," Izzy said.

"I'll bring you a sweatshirt," Hope added. "Or how about a pair of joggers?"

"Do *not* bring me any more Walthrop stuff. I'm serious," Izzy said, then paused, pressing her finger to her chin. "I *could* use a new iPad, though."

"Nice try," Hope said, but Izzy proceeded to mount her case.

"You know mine's been dying," she said. "It made school so much harder. Even though, let me remind you, I still made honor roll. Every marking period. Straight As."

One day, she thought, Izzy would make an excellent litigator, like Hope's own father. Hope realized that giving in would set an unwanted precedent, but over the past fifteen months, she'd given herself permission to abandon her better judgment when it came to certain things. Chores. Junk food. Screen time. There were too many bigger battles being waged. *You can only do what you can do*, said the moms on the weekly Zoom call. It had become a kind of mantra, one Hope had taken to heart. She took faith in the articles about how this unprecedented time would have a positive impact on their children, make them more resourceful and resilient. It had been hard, but they'd gotten through it. For the moment, Hope cast her mind forward only as far as the weekend, watching it play out in her mind—the luxurious drive, the room at the charming inn, her old friends gathering on the sun-dappled quad—and said yes.

TWO

ADAM

It was the same duffel bag he'd carried through four years of college, blue canvas with white straps that had frayed and faded to an ash gray. As a teenager, Adam had piled this bag onto the team bus for high school track meets, hauled it on camping trips to Hammonasset Beach with his friends, mashed it into the backseat of his parents' car to unpack as a freshman in Fiske Hall. Thirty years later, he tossed it between two booster seats in the backseat of the Subaru, littered with Zbar wrappers and orphaned Legos, then walked back inside his house.

The three of them were cuddled on the bed together, Zachary and Sam nestling on either side of Andrea. They were watching a movie on the iPad, a sick-day indulgence. The boys clutched sippy cups of ginger ale, maraschino cherries waiting in the bottoms, the dog asleep at their feet.

"How are you feeling?" Adam asked them.

"Better," Sam said. They were both shirtless, wearing plaid pajama bottoms, their hair the color of reddish wheat. Only June, and their chests were already faintly sunburned. In her leggings, sweatshirt, and fuzzy wool socks, Andrea looked as if she were living in a different climate.

"I'm glad," he said. "I'll really miss you."

"We'll miss you, too," Andrea said. "But we'll have fun, won't we, guys?" She hugged them around their necks.

"You'll go easy on Mom, right?" Adam asked, and the boys both nodded, curled on their sides like two pink seahorses, eyes glued to the screen.

Standing in the doorway, Adam again debated bailing on the reunion. Why was he going? He shouldn't be, not without the boys. As of yesterday, they'd been coming with him. He thought it would be fun. He would take it easy at the parties, have a few drinks and pack it in early. Maybe on Saturday he'd drive them to Ledgemere Island—he'd loved going out there in college, roaming around the cliffs and beaches. At his favorite spot, near the end of the island, the rocks formed a natural staircase, perfect for smoking and thinking what, at nineteen, had seemed like deep thoughts. Then last night they'd started throwing up: first Zachary and then Sam, the order in which they'd been born and in which they'd since done just about everything. By that morning, they'd both seemed better, but obviously they were staying home, and Adam assumed he was, too.

But when Andrea had discovered him stuffing the duffel back into the closet in the mudroom, she'd looked surprised. "You're not going?"

"It's no big deal," he said, attempting to cram the bag onto a shelf piled with winter hats and mismatched gloves.

She hesitated, then said, "Adam—"

"It's okay. Seriously. I'd rather stay."

"You don't have to."

"It's just a college reunion," he said, knocking down an umbrella.

"Adam," she said quietly, touching the small of his back. "Go. I think you should."

He turned then, clutching the deflated canvas bag. His wife's face looked pale, her freckles extra bright against her skin. But her expression was firm. Resolute. Maybe she wanted to prove she could manage without him. Maybe, in his absence, progress would be made.

"Last chance," Adam tried once more from the doorway. "I really don't need to sit in weekend traffic," he added, though he doubted the roads would be congested. June was still early for tourists, and there were fewer commuters now.

Andrea gave him a knowing look. "Don't worry about us," she said. "We're good. Have fun." Then she smiled, a smile that relaxed her entire face. He'd missed it.

"Bye, Dad," the boys murmured, cheeks resting on their palms, looking so content that for a minute Adam wondered if they'd managed to get sick on purpose.

He kissed their heads, their hair smelling like grass and sweat. "I love you guys," he said, then kissed his wife. "I love you, too," he said, then left the room, grabbed his keys, and walked outside.

At first, Adam had allowed himself to entertain the possibility that Andrea might actually come with him. He liked having his wife by his side in social settings: a reminder of his other life, his real life, at home. He'd partied too much in his twenties and then well into his thirties, spent long hours as a junior partner at a firm in Boston, followed by late nights and early five-mile runs along the Charles. While the lives of his peers grew fuller, adding kids and cars and houses, his grew faster. The women he went out with were quick and witty, vaguely competitive, able to go toe-to-toe with him at a pool table at one in the morning. But when he met Andrea—they were set up by one of the legal secretaries, whose son was in her preschool class—it was as if life shifted into a different gear. He'd suggested they meet for coffee, thinking this could allow for a quick but polite getaway, but as soon as she sat across from him—apologizing for being late, one of her students had been stung by a bee—Adam didn't want to leave. He'd never met someone who wore their emotions so comfortably, so legibly. When she talked about this kid, her whole face crumpled with sympathy. When Adam confessed that the legal secretary was fed up with his relationship choices, she laughed, warm and light. When he told her his father had died suddenly when he was a freshman in college, her eyes filled with tears. He learned she was close to her parents. An only child. They both loved hiking and fantasized about moving to a cabin in the woods. When he left, he called her from the taxi, and that Friday, they met for a real date that lasted three days.

To his surprise, Adam found himself opening up to Andrea. About his childhood—his father's temper, his alpha-male older brothers, his mother's chronic headaches—stuff he never talked about, psychic baggage he'd had no idea he was still dragging around. Telling her actually felt easy; it calmed him. When he told her so, she reminded him she taught preschool. *Full-body listening*, she explained. A technique she taught her four-year-olds: *eyes, hands, mouth, ears.* In the years since, he'd witnessed her have this same effect on other people, even his famously reserved mother, who spent much of her life in a dim bedroom and died of a stroke before the twins were born. On one of their rare visits to Adam's childhood home in Connecticut, he found his mother showing Andrea old family albums, confiding in her about her unhappy marriage. *He wasn't an easy man*, she whispered, as if Adam's dead father might overhear. At Adam's twentieth reunion, Troy Abernathy had asked Andrea: *How much do I owe you?* after she'd listened with genuine compassion to his lengthy, beer-breathed monologue about his divorce. After the past year, the thought of her coming with him to this reunion—a corrective, a do-over, a return to something—had made him so happy that, though he'd known deep down there was no chance it would happen, he'd let himself hope.

When the pandemic first hit, he and Andrea had been partners, working together to keep their boys happy and engaged. It was easier, living where they did now. Five years before, the day they found out Andrea was pregnant with twins, they'd decided to leave the city for somewhere less crowded. More green. Adam immediately gave notice and started transitioning his work to colleagues; Andrea tearfully told the preschool she wouldn't be back that fall. They broke the lease on the apartment they'd rented in Beacon Hill. In college, he'd had a reputation for taking off abruptly from parties—*ghosting*, it was called now. Polly and Hope had given him a hard time about it. But with Andrea, the suddenness felt acceptable, even noble: a mission statement on parenting, a commitment to a better life. He found a job in New Hampshire, a small practice focused on shoreline protections. They bought a turn-of-the-century farmhouse—big sun-filled rooms, a kitchen woodstove, a wraparound porch—on two acres of grass and wildflowers. It wasn't a cabin in the woods (in fact, the house was far bigger than they needed), but in spirit, it was close. Andrea put in raised garden beds, and Adam repaired a broken stair, a leaking faucet. With the help of YouTube, he found he could fix most things himself.

And during lockdown, their move had never seemed like a smarter idea. While Adam worked on the porch at an old barn-door-turned-desk, Andrea ran an ad hoc preschool, taking Zachary and Sam exploring in the yard equipped with buckets and magnifying glasses. The boys jumped in mud puddles and watered the vegetables and assembled leaves and acorns into gluey self-portraits. *The planet got sick, but it will get better,* Andrea told them, smoothing their hair from their brows, and they accepted this. Whatever stress their parents were feeling, they seemed reasonably sheltered from it, even Sam, the more sensitive of the two. At the end of each blurry evening, after putting the boys to bed and collapsing on the couch, Adam felt accomplished. He and Andrea had made it through another day. They drank a beer. They had sex almost nightly, even though they had never been so tired. Life was hard, but somehow sweet, distilled into only what mattered most.

Then sometime in April, as they sat in the living room after dinner, Andrea said, "Honey. Read this."

It was the usual evening tableau. Andrea and Adam were stretched out on the couch, her socked feet tucked under his thighs, while Zachary and Sam sat on the floor playing Legos. For the past month, the boys had been working on the same project: The Tunnels, an elaborate underground network of connected roads and bridges that had overtaken the first floor of the house. Andrea was reading on her iPad; in the absence of a TV, they caught up on the day's news on their devices. When the boys were in earshot, they usually refrained from discussing current events—or chose vocabulary that sailed over their heads—but that night she thrust the screen in his face. "Look," she said.

The photograph at the top of the article was jarring: a boy of eight or nine standing before a sweep of technicolor, acid-toned sky. He was looking directly into the camera, his expression both sorrowful and accusatory. The headline beneath his chin read: "We Knew Generation X, Y, and Z—Meet Generation ???"

Adam felt Andrea watching him as he scrolled down the page. The site was focused on parenting and wellness, crowded with pop-up ads for purportedly nontoxic playmats and organic sunscreens, but the article was based in scientific fact. It quoted climatologists on the grimness of the crisis, the uncertainty this generation would be facing. It described how recent improvements to atmospheric quality were only temporary, how over the next twenty-five years the health of the planet would worsen dramatically. Adam found it harrowing but, sadly, not new.

"It's terrible, isn't it?" Andrea said.

"It is," he said, with a glance at the boys.

"This is their future, Adam. This is what they're going to inherit."

Sam looked up from the Legos, always alert to shifts in the emotional weather.

"How about we table this for later," Adam said.

"But it's so"—she looked down at her lap, at her curled hands—"so undeniable. *Unambiguous.*"

"What's unambiguous?" Sam asked, and Zachary looked up, too. They didn't know the word, but they understood their mother's tone.

"Just something on Mom's computer." Adam closed the screen and set the tablet aside. "Now tell me what's going on in The Tunnels," he said, sliding onto the floor and diverting them with questions about the half-built ocean liner that was submerged in the dangerous waters off the porch.

Later, after the boys were asleep, he found Andrea in bed, staring at the article again. "I know. I shouldn't have said anything in front of them," she told him. "I couldn't help it. I can't stop thinking about it. The world they're going to grow up in."

"I get it," Adam said. He climbed in beside her, threaded one of his legs around hers. "It's scary. But we've talked about it, right?"

They'd had many talks, before Andrea went off birth control, about the ethics of bringing children into a world that was self-destructing. Ultimately, she concluded she didn't want the future to keep them from living in the present—that felt too much like giving up hope—and Adam agreed. They would be good and loving parents. They would give their children happy lives.

"We have two amazing kids," he said. "And they're doing great, despite everything."

"They are," she said. "But sometimes it's all just too much."

Adam turned onto his side and kissed her shoulder. "Surrender the iPad," he said, and she expelled a sigh but set it on her bedside table. "It's been a long day," he said. "It'll feel better in the morning." He reached for her under the covers, and she rolled toward him, pressing her chin into his chest.

But Andrea became fixated on this story, and this story was followed by other stories: the drought withering the West Coast, the fires sweeping through Brazil, the bleaching in the Great Barrier Reef. Sometimes she'd look at the boys and start to cry, tears slipping quietly down her cheeks. Adam began to notice she was keeping them indoors more often, drawing or doing puzzles, despite the arrival of gorgeous spring weather. The flowers were bursting, the backyard vivid with color. Maybe he just hadn't been paying as close attention, but Adam couldn't ever remember a spring so beautiful before.

One afternoon in mid-April, Adam found Andrea standing by the bedroom window. It was gray and blustery that day, the leaves on the birch trees twitching in the wind. She clasped her elbows tightly and watched the sky, as if waiting for a cyclone to come funneling toward them. "We should keep the boys inside," she said.

"They're in the living room," Adam said, glancing at the window. "This is supposed to blow through by dinner."

"I meant I don't think they should go outside."

He chuckled. "Ever again? That seems extreme."

"Adam," she said, and he could tell by her tone she wasn't kidding. "We don't know what's going on. We don't know how far it travels—we don't know anything."

Adam wasn't sure exactly what she was saying and was too afraid to ask. He might not know much about what was happening, but he knew he couldn't confine two four-year-olds to the house unless under direct orders from the surgeon general himself.

"The boys need to go outside," he said, gently cupping her shoulders, which felt a little bonier than usual. "Run. Play. Besides, we're not exactly tripping over our neighbors, right?"

It was part of why they'd moved there, the big yard with space for the kids to roam. But as Adam gazed out at the clouds gathering and the clothesline flapping, what had once felt like an oasis looked like a minefield. "We need to keep going," he told her.

She kept her eyes on the yard, spoke quietly but firmly. "I can wait," she said.

Something was shifting, something Adam didn't understand. Andrea had had brief spells of sadness before—for weeks after the boys were born, she'd been a little restless, and weepy—but she'd always pulled herself out of it. She'd meditated and practiced yoga, but over the past month had quit doing both. Some days she mostly stayed in bed. He canceled meetings, explaining his wife was ill, but didn't offer details, occasionally having unnerving flashes of his own mother disappearing into her room. Andrea avoided prescription medication, so he called the natural foods store in Keene and ordered lavender, magnesium, valerian root, which the owner left in a bag on their front porch with a kind, contactless wave. The remedies didn't make much difference, but Andrea didn't seem concerned. She was sad, she said. Worried about the big picture. She just needed time.

But for Adam, there was no big picture. He was driving a car at night, focused only on the six feet of highway that were visible in the headlights' glare. It was on him to keep things going until Andrea was herself again. To maintain some consistency, some normalcy—some *fun*, even! In college, he'd had a reputation for being fun. He was the guy who'd once woken up on the roof of Fiske Hall in a blizzard. The guy who initiated impromptu drives out to Ledgemere Island, or the diner three towns over that served one-pound cheeseburgers, or the twenty-four-hour L.L. Bean flagship store, where he'd once dragged Polly and Hope at two in the morning. They'd crawled inside a tent in the Camping & Fishing section and hung out until dawn. Twenty-five years later, he reached into his old bag of tricks. He popped a tent in the backyard, where he and the boys camped out with s'mores and flashlights. He went out for groceries one afternoon and came back with a rescue dog. He made pillow huts and tree forts and introduced the boys to the original *Star Wars* trilogy. He delighted them by growing an unruly pandemic beard. He read them books about legendary disasters, prehistoric animals, sea creatures, gnarly specimens that slunk around the ocean's bottom. Adam found them oddly soothing, a bizarre alternative universe running parallel to his own.

Andrea had given in on Zachary and Sam going outside—maybe sensing that Adam would draw the line—though she herself barely left the house. It was Adam who took them to the playground or out into the yard. The three of them wandered around the neighborhood, Sam's fist wrapped around the dog's leash and Zachary's binoculars knocking against his skinny chest. Adam jogged beside them, in a pale imitation of his old five-milers, trying to field their unanswerable questions: Why did the president make fun of people? When would the sickness be gone? When he felt frustrated, he was determined not to let it show. As a kid, he'd been an expert at interpreting the sound of his father's footsteps, gauging whether he was pissed off (hard, fast) or quietly stewing (hard, slow) or in that rare good mood. The upshot, as an adult, was knowing exactly the kind of father he didn't want to be. Above all, he wanted his kids to feel safe and loved. But sometimes Adam sensed it, that low simmer of anger, like the night he was speeding home from the grocery store, listening to an NPR interview with a celebrity who described how nice it was to have a break from the Hollywood rat race, to enjoy being with the children she never got to spend time with—they were all learning to knit—which made him say out loud: *Fuck you.*

He didn't tell anyone about Andrea, not that he had anyone to tell. There were his four coworkers, people he'd once chatted with around the office, but no one he would confide in about something real. Besides, everyone was stressed. Everyone was dealing with it. Andrea's parents were in their eighties, alone in Michigan; he wasn't going to add to their worries. His own parents were dead, not that he'd have told them anyway, and he and his brothers weren't close. It wasn't until early May, a random Friday in the hour between eleven and midnight—the one hour each day Adam had to himself, provided he didn't have work to catch up on and Zachary wasn't up late reading and Sam wasn't having a bad dream, the hour during which he sat on the couch and drank a beer or two or just stared at the iPad and didn't do a fucking thing—that he'd told Polly and Hope.

In normal life, he and his college friends were sporadically in touch. They all lived in different cities. They'd met Andrea only a few times; by the time they got married—in their apartment with a bagel tray, two witnesses, and a justice of the peace—Polly and Hope both had kids. During Andrea's pregnancy, they'd gone to New York—riding in the Amtrak quiet car, spending a weekend in the city, the kind of trip that was now impossible to imagine on any level—and met Polly and her son at a museum. And Hope had come to New Hampshire once, after the twins were born. When Adam and Andrea were first getting to know each other, she'd been surprised to hear his friendships with Hope and Polly had always been platonic, but outside of one sloppy make-out with Polly freshman year, this was true. Polly and Hope had been like sisters to him. It was their door he'd shown up at when he found out his father died, their room where he'd retreated to study when he was on academic probation and needed to pull up his grades.

During lockdown, it felt natural to be in touch with them. A comfort, to lapse back into their old roles. Hope remained the caretaker, the organizer, initiating their text messages as she once had their lunch plans in the dining hall. Polly was as blunt as she'd been sitting on the quad thirty years before, comparing notes on their shitty dads. Now, they texted about their kids. Their health. How they were coping with it all. Hope's one-pot dinners, and Polly's students and their struggles. They teased Adam about his life in the sticks, his lumberjack beard. Still, he'd hesitated to tell them about Andrea, but that night for whatever reason—the isolation, the exhaustion, the memory of their past closeness—he found himself typing into his phone: *Things are pretty rough here.* And after that he couldn't stop, a gut-spill of worry—about Andrea, and the boys, and the pressure he felt to not screw things up.

A year later, Adam couldn't remember most of the details, only his gratitude for their compassion, and the relief he'd felt, knowing that they knew. So when Hope's text appeared telling them to check their email—the reunion was rescheduled and they were going, *no excuses!!!*—it felt important that he see his old friends in person.

"We could go together," he'd proposed to Andrea. "The four of us."

This was May, fourteen months after lockdown and one month after Hope's heads-up about the reunion, and life was in some ways back to normal. Zachary and Sam were going to preschool three days a week in person. Adam had shaved off his beard. The boys played soccer on Saturdays, went to outdoor playdates and birthday parties, and Adam drove them wherever they needed to go. He now worked partly from home. Andrea, though, still left the house only when really necessary. She didn't seem to miss socializing. It was as if the world had shrunk around her, an island of her own making, and she was content there.

That morning, it was still chilly enough for a fire in the wood-stove. The boys were sleeping in for once, so he and Andrea were alone in the kitchen. It was big—almost half the size of their Beacon Hill apartment—but cozy. A breakfast nook, a farm-house sink, the wallpaper a tacky pattern of oranges and lemons that Andrea had insisted on keeping. Adam was making coffee as Andrea heated the teakettle. She was dressed in her usual sweats, hair tied back in a limp ponytail. Adam had been waiting for the right morning to bring up the reunion; Andrea was better in the mornings. Happier. Softer. The sky was a delicate pink, the grass glittery with dew. She hummed a little as she sliced bread for toast. But as soon as he spoke, she stopped and looked at him.

"It's last year's reunion," he said. "It was rescheduled."

Her lips parted, confusion on her face.

"It's all outdoors, of course," he added hurriedly. "But I was thinking we could stay up there for the week." He took her hand, which was light and cold. "We could turn it into a vacation. Rent a little house near the campus. Ledgemere Island," he continued, talking faster now, and she looked alarmed, but he couldn't stop. "There are these great hiking trails, and rock beaches where the boys can play. Think how beautiful it would be," he said, the image enfolding him like a cocoon, the four of them on the misty Maine coast.

Andrea squeezed his hand, then released it. "You go," she said. "I think I'll just stay here."

The kettle was rumbling, the kindling crackled. She resumed cutting the bread, dropped the slices into the toaster, and lifted two chipped plates from the rack.

"I want you there, too," he said.

"You'll have your friends to catch up with."

"But they'll want to see you," he said. "Polly, especially."

Andrea's face softened, and he knew she was thinking of that weekend in New York. After the museum, the three of them had gone to dinner, and over too many cocktails, Polly had gotten uncharacteristically emotional—telling them about things that had happened in her twenties, things Adam had never known. He'd been useless that night, drunk and dumbfounded, but Andrea had reached across their empty glasses, round belly pressing against the table, and taken his old friend's hand.

Remembering his wife's kindness, he stepped closer, wrapping his arms around her waist and speaking into her hair. "They'll miss you too much," he said.

She laughed a little. "They barely know me."

"Well, I'll miss you. How's that?" he said, and felt her body relax a little. The kettle was rumbling, but she didn't move to pick it up. Instead, she turned around and kissed him. Adam felt a sharp stirring of desire. Whenever they had sex these days, it was he who initiated. Now she smiled, touching his eyebrow, the one with the scar running through it. "You'll have more fun without me," she whispered, and slipped out of his arms.

Adam watched as she turned back to the counter. Picked up the kettle, filled her mug with steaming water. As if this were a normal conversation. As if her going had ever really been an option.

"Andrea," he said, hearing a slight hoarseness in his own voice. "I really think we need this."

She didn't say anything at first, but set the kettle back on the burner and looked out the window. The yard was alive with green, the clothesline slicing across the dawn, now a deep gold. Adam felt a small surge of hope. But when she turned to him, her eyes were wet. "Please don't press me," she said quietly. "I can't."

Something collapsed inside him then. His pitch was over, the one he'd been building up to, the fantasy he'd let himself create even though he knew it wouldn't happen, but needing it to happen, and now a tendril of panic awoke in his chest.

"But you go," she said. "We'll be fine here. Me and the boys."

As she returned to her tea, Adam's disappointment was overwhelmed by a fresh strain of worry. He hadn't let himself consider a scenario where Andrea wasn't going, but faced with the prospect of leaving the boys with her at home, he wasn't sure he could.

"Or," he said, "I could just bring them."

She shook her head lightly. "You don't have to."

"But I could. I mean . . . it'd be okay. It's all outside." He paused. "I mean, I think I probably should, right?"

She looked at him then, her face blighted with sorrow. What they both knew but didn't say was that he wasn't comfortable leaving the boys with her for an entire weekend. She nodded, accepting it. "Whatever you think is best," she said, just as the boys came scuffling into the kitchen, as if sensing her sadness and knowing their presence would make her feel better. They bumped into her waist, towheaded and sleepy-eyed, one burrowed at each hip.

So that had been the plan: Adam would go to the reunion with Sam and Zachary. There were plenty of things for kids to do—he had a vague recollection of a bouncy house at the last one, before he had kids and would have registered the deep significance of a bouncy house. Hope's son wasn't coming, but he was sure at least a few other classmates would bring kids. Not that it mattered. The boys had each other. They could all sleep in his old dorm. It would be sort of like camping. He packed the duffel bag for all three of them, Sam's stuffed monkey and Zachary's binoculars and a weekend's worth of clothes.

Then, last night, Zachary called out that his stomach hurt. In the hour between eleven and midnight, he threw up twice. By dawn, Sam had thrown up, too. But no coughs, no fevers. It wasn't like before, when the slightest symptom would have sent Adam into a tailspin. Still, he scheduled a telemed appointment with the pediatrician, who confirmed it sounded like the twenty-four-hour bug that was going around. *Just a garden-variety virus*, she said. *We still have those, too.*

Now, as Adam drove away from his cozy house, his simple life, he felt a roaming sense of unease. Guilt that he was leaving. Worry about Andrea. About the boys. But more than anything, he felt the basic strangeness of being apart from them, the miles adding up between them, as he watched the road in front of him and drove north.

THREE

POLLY

Polly had gotten on the road at ten thirty, which meant they'd now spent the last six hours in the cramped front seats of her thirteen-year-old Toyota Corolla. The Corolla: a handy car for parallel parking, a lousy car for long road trips. Still, it felt good to be in motion. In fifteen months, she and Jonah hadn't left New York.

It was a plan that had materialized at the last minute, the two of them heading up to Maine. A week ago, Polly had been adamant that she wasn't going, then Jonah spotted the Walthrop flyer in a pile of junk mail and proposed a joint trip: Polly could go to the reunion while he visited Charlie, his old bunkmate from Camp Elmwood, whose family had a summer house on the island near the college. It had been so long since Polly had seen her son excited about something.

"Can you pull over?" he asked.

"Sure," she said. "Hungry?"

"Bathroom."

It wasn't a full-fledged rest stop, just a Quick Mart next to an off-ramp in northern Massachusetts, a few gas pumps and benches, a concrete ashtray with wrinkled butts buried in a scoop of sand. Jonah didn't have a license, so had spent the trip with his long legs wedged behind the glove compartment, face sandwiched between his silver Beats. As Polly exited the highway, he pried the headphones off and slung them around his neck, grabbing his backpack from the floor beneath his feet. "Hang on," she said, pulling into a spot by some scraggly trees and wrenching the gearshift into Park. She reached for her crossbody bag on the backseat, unzipped it, and dug out a crumpled twenty. "In case you see anything good."

The front seat was already a mess of snacks Polly had bought for the road, chips and trail mix and a one-pound bag of Twizzlers that Jonah had barely touched. But he pinched the twenty between a thumb and finger, his nails coated in gold polish. In Brooklyn, Jonah's friends all looked like him—pierced, inked, vaguely androgynous—but in certain parts of New England, like this one, he would stand out.

Sure enough, as he made his way across the lot, stainless steel gauges in his earlobes, Polly saw a customer standing at a gas pump outright frown—a guy in jeans and suspenders, a car with an American flag plastered across the back window—and felt the same furious protectiveness she had when Jonah was shoved on the playground as a kid. He ducked into the store, emerged with a key attached to a block of wood, then slipped behind the bathroom door, orange backpack hooked to one shoulder. The pack was all he'd brought for the weekend. *That's it?* Polly had said as they were leaving, but when he just shrugged, she didn't push it. With her students, Polly had a reputation for directness; over the past year, teaching remotely, this had been even more true. If a student was absent, or even unusually quiet, she always followed up to make sure they were okay. Students having panic attacks, students holed up alone in studio apartments with weak Wi-Fi signals. A student without adequate food. A student with a parent on a ventilator, emailing her from outside the hospital. *This isn't teaching, it's triage,* summed up Janelle, one of the seventeen adjunct comp instructors with whom, in normal times, Polly shared a single part-time faculty office, during a Zoom meeting to discuss student mental health.

With her own teenager, that directness was not so easy. Jonah had always talked to her, yet crammed together in their small apartment, he'd become closed off. He'd quit his photography classes. For online school, he'd done the bare minimum, disabling his camera and drifting around his computer or just lying on his bed with eyes closed.

At night, instead of joining her to watch Netflix while she graded papers, he stayed in his bedroom, inhaling the Internet. Message boards, TikToks, and Reddit threads about government corruption, environmental collapse, social justice—all the systemic problems that in the absence of life's usual distractions had risen so blatantly to the surface. Polly had been tempted to get on Instagram just to follow his accounts, but she decided to afford him that privacy. Give him what space she could. He was angry, but Polly understood it—how could you be a thinking person and not be angry? Jonah had become an ardent Bernie supporter. He'd declared himself a socialist. He and his best friends, Xavier and Nicholas, marched in a Black Lives Matter protest. They attended Brooklyn Pride online. On Election Day he stood in line with Polly for over an hour, eating free slices from Bella Luca, and waited while she cast her vote.

After the restrictions eased up in the city and he'd managed to pass his senior year—an act of mercy on the part of his exhausted teachers—Polly saw him even less. He was always out with his friends; after a year spent trapped inside the apartment, she understood this, too. But she only felt more disconnected from him. She missed him. When he wanted to drive to Maine together, she couldn't say no.

So far, though, the trip had not been the bonding experience she'd hoped for. For long stretches, Jonah had been submerged in his phone, surfacing only to describe the latest outrage—the record heat in the Pacific Northwest, the rocket set to launch a billionaire into space—or to comment on the smog, the traffic, the gas-guzzling SUVs. From her parking spot by the trash cans, Polly kept an eye on the bathroom, where he was probably getting stoned. She wanted this weekend to be a break for her son: a chance to reset, reconnect with an old friend. Jonah had spent three summers at Elmwood, an overnight camp in the Catskills that one of his art teachers had recommended. At first, Polly had dismissed the suggestion; it was wildly expensive, and based on the price tag, she doubted these were kids Jonah would relate to. Plus, selfishly, she couldn't imagine a full month without him. But there was financial assistance, and this teacher was friends with the director, and who was Polly to stand in the way of someone trying to help? She'd had teachers like this— *was* a teacher like this. And Jonah had loved Elmwood, not for the top-of-the-line facilities, but the lakes and mountains, the darkroom in the arts and crafts studio, the camaraderie with the other campers. Polly could still picture the scene on the last day, the pile of trunks by the mess hall, the boys sobbing without inhibition as they hugged goodbye.

Since aging out of Elmwood four years before, Jonah had been focused on his friends in Brooklyn. He hadn't seen any fellow campers but said he talked to them online. Still, four years was not insignificant—even if it was nothing compared to how long it had been since Polly had set foot in Sewall, Maine. The very thought of being back on campus made her queasy.

She turned on the car, lowering all four windows. The air was warm and smelled like diesel and cigarettes—God, she'd kill for a cigarette. She settled for tearing open the Twizzlers, as she did the math. The last and only reunion she'd attended was the five-year. She'd been twenty-six years old, living in Astoria with two strangers she'd found on Craigslist and teaching freshman comp at the community college. Friday night, she'd marked her return to campus by gorging herself on free beer and seafood; Saturday, she'd caught up with McFadden, then gotten drunk with her classmates, smoked cigarettes with Adam. She and Hope crashed in their old dorm, recapping the party as they fell asleep. It had felt, in some ways, like nothing had changed.

By the ten-year, her life had changed completely. She hadn't even considered going to the reunion and hadn't been back since.

As Polly watched a seagull circle above the Quick Mart, a knot formed in her stomach. Twenty-one years: exactly one college-aged self. She was no longer in touch with anyone from Walthrop except Hope and Adam, and outside their flurry of contact during lockdown, even that was rare. When the reunion was rescheduled, Hope had started firing off texts—*We're emerging from quarantine! And the 25th is a milestone! This is the one you show up for!!!*—punctuated by emojis and showers of confetti. Polly had recalled the way Hope typed papers on the computer she'd brought from home freshman year, a boxy beige Macintosh that was then cutting-edge; she'd sit cross-legged on her desk chair, mug of tea at her side, wearing her Walthrop sweatshirt—gray with blue letters, neck painstakingly removed with scissors—fingers clicking quickly, decisively, on the chunky keys.

The last time she'd seen Hope was Christmastime, a year and a half ago. Hope's husband had a conference in Manhattan—

Polly pictured a hotel ballroom filled with shiny ties, stuffed suits—and so Polly and Jonah had met her and the kids. Polly was glad not to deal with Ethan. She found him boring, and it bugged her how Hope catered to him. It didn't help that his job and Polly's existed in the same universe, even if at opposite poles, Polly an exploited adjunct and Ethan an administrator who probably made ten times what she did. Still, even without him there, the outing felt strained. Hope's son cried the entire time, and her daughter looked uncomfortable in her thick makeup, her necklace made of—were they teeth? Hope had gone on and on about college, updating Polly on old classmates and retelling old stories, between attempts to distract her son with YouTube videos. Polly had regretted bringing Jonah, though he tolerated Hope's many questions, even smiled for a picture with her kids in front of the giant, glittery tree.

The gull was now cawing loudly, perched on the gutter of the Quick Mart roof. The last time she'd seen Adam was four years before that. He and his wife had spent a weekend in the city; the four of them went to MoMA, then the grown-ups had dinner in the East Village while Jonah slept over at a friend's. Andrea, six months pregnant, had sipped mocktails and patiently listened to Polly and Adam reminisce about college. Polly's blue-streaked hair. Adam's carpenter jeans. The mixtape called Moody Music that Polly played on a seemingly endless loop. Then, after one too many, Polly had found herself telling them about McFadden, breaking her long-ago promise to herself. She blamed the drinks. The ease of being with her old friend. The kindness of his wife. The headline in the recent alumni bulletin: "Campus Reacts to Tragic Loss."

The gull's beady eyes seemed to be boring right inside her. Even now, touching the memory of his death triggered a well-spring of feeling—shock, embarrassment, regret. The pain in her stomach was intensifying. She visualized folding it up, again and again, until it was a small, precise square. This had been her strategy for years, and would be her strategy this weekend: take the past, pack it in a box, and stash it away.

The bird let out a final, indignant shriek, and Polly watched it sail off toward the highway, turning her attention to the bathroom door. Jonah had been in there a long time—too long, she thought. For her classmates, this weekend was about the reunion, but for her it was about the well-being of her son, who was definitely getting high in the Quick Mart off I-495.

As if on cue, Jonah stepped out, headphones still draped around his neck, hoodie drawn tightly around his ears. With just his face exposed, his features were even more striking, the sharply defined eyebrows and square, stubbled chin. Polly had always been told he looked like her, and she could see it, though maybe this was what people said when there was no other point of reference. He ducked inside the store to return the key, then loped back to the car empty-handed.

"All set?" she asked as he closed the door.

"Yep."

"No good snacks?"

"Nah."

He shoved the backpack beneath his feet, as Polly registered the musty smell, his reddened eyes. Check and check. But she wouldn't mention it. Because it wouldn't make a difference, and she didn't want to corrupt the rest of the drive. She trusted her son knew how to behave around his hosts that weekend, to curb the smoking and watch the swearing, which over the past year had risen to the level of casual punctuation. Fleetingly, she thought of Charlie's mother, who, when Polly called to confirm they were comfortable with him coming, had been gracious but perceptibly confused. *I'm Jonah's mom*, Polly said, and Charlie's mother paused and asked: *I'm sorry, who?*

"Then we're off," Polly said, starting the engine. She put on her cheap sunglasses, the ones Jonah had once said made her look like a hungover B-list celebrity.

"How much longer?"

"Not too long."

"In actual hours, Polly."

"Two?" she said, which was a slight exaggeration. "But we're almost in Maine." In a few miles, they'd be in coastal New Hampshire, and from there it was only a handful of exits. But Maine itself was deceptively enormous. All those woods.

As Polly merged back onto the highway, warm air rushed in through the open windows. Jonah shrugged off his hood and pushed up his sleeves. His latest tattoo, on the inside of his forearm, still looked tender around the edges. He'd come home with his first one last summer—Xavier's cousin, a tattoo artist, had given him a discount—and already had three more. Polly never stood in the way of Jonah's decisions, and the designs were admittedly beautiful, but it made her feel sad each time, the permanence of it.

"So, what do you actually do there?" Jonah asked.

The question caught Polly off guard, but this was what her son was like lately: distant, except in the moments when he suddenly felt like talking.

"On the island?" she asked. "Not much. I think that's the whole point."

"I meant the reunion," he said. "Do people, like, trade business cards? Compare net worth?"

"God, let's hope not." Polly laughed, though she feared he

wasn't far off base. It was one of the most unappealing aspects of a college reunion, the compulsion to measure one's success against everybody else's. It didn't help that many of Polly's classmates were, by conventional standards, highly successful—tech investors and CEOs and hedge fund managers—and some were doing genuinely amazing things. A federal judge. A director at the Smithsonian. Three Fulbright scholars—one of them, an anthropologist, won a freaking MacArthur Genius Grant. Among Walthrop alums, Polly's career was singularly unimpressive, and since her last appearance, not much had changed: still adjunct faculty, still criminally underpaid. That fall, when enrollment took a hit, she'd lost half her classes and filed for unemployment. She'd spent her stimulus checks on groceries and heat.

"You just hang out, I think," she told Jonah. "Awkwardly socialize. Drink. Eat."

"Sounds depressing."

Polly was tempted to remind him that he was the reason she was going, but didn't want to put him on the defensive. "Well," she said, "don't underestimate the eating. The food's good. They're kind of famous for it."

He frowned. "This is college food?"

"I know," she said. "It's an oxymoron. But it was an expensive school. I guess we got what we paid for."

Jonah started poking through the snacks in the center console. "So the people who go there are all rich."

"Not all," she said. "I mean, some are, of course." She didn't want to stray too far in this direction. Jonah could get quickly heated about the 1 percent, and she didn't want to lose him. The truth was that Polly had often felt like an outlier at Walthrop, raised by a single mother in a small fifth-floor walk-up. Last spring, when students objected to having their cameras on for

Zoom classes, some faculty called it an excuse to slack off, but Polly defended the students. It was a matter of privacy. Of equity. Had she been forced onto a screen during college, there would have been no concealing the water-stained ceilings, the grimy windows, the mother who, in any state of sobriety, might wander into the frame.

Jonah tore open the barbecue chips, the bag exhaling a puff of salty air. "You never talk about it."

"What?" she said. "College food?"

"College," he said, stuffing in a handful. "In general."

"Well, it was a million years ago," Polly said, deflecting. She held the steering wheel with both hands, knuckles straining against her skin. "But I'm told that the twenty-fifth is the one you show up for."

"Why's that?"

"I guess because people are still young enough to be reasonably healthy. But old enough to not care about stupid bullshit."

Crunching, he said, "You might be underestimating people's capacity to care about stupid bullshit."

"I might be," Polly admitted. She had a horrifying vision of being trapped in a weekend-long loop of conversations about investment portfolios and kitchen renovations. She thought again about her colleague Janelle, a twenty-nine-year-old PhD in comp lit who supplemented her teaching income by delivering for DoorDash. When Polly had private-messaged her during a Zoom meeting to say that she was going to her reunion, Janelle replied: *Went to my five and it made me question all my life choices. Demoralizing. Do not recommend.*

"Regardless, this one will be different, right?" Polly said. "After the past year, it has to be. Unless these people are deeply in denial. And if it's truly unbearable, Hope and Adam will be there."

Her son didn't reply. Maybe he was recalling that awkward afternoon at Rockefeller Center. Maybe he was stoned and it was making him hungry. Or he was thinking about the fall, and starting college. His GPA had dropped at the end of senior year; he would need to refocus, keep his grades up to maintain the scholarship that covered his tuition. And Xavier and Nicholas were both going to college outside the city, while Jonah would be living at home. Polly had always been touched by the closeness among the boys, unlike her half-baked high school friendships, girls with whom she'd blown off classes and gotten detentions and lost touch long ago.

"Adam's the environmental lawyer," she reminded him. "You met him that time at the museum. He and his wife." Jonah had liked them, Polly remembered. They'd asked questions about his photography, and he'd been uncharacteristically chatty, showing them pictures on his phone. "They don't live too far from here, actually. Somewhere in the woods."

Jonah glanced out his window. "Really?"

"They moved from Boston a few years ago. Just packed up and bought a house in the middle of nowhere. And Hope lives outside Philadelphia," she continued. "But we were all in the same dorm."

"And just think," Jonah said, sucking salt off his thumb, "if you were in a different dorm, your best friends might be two other people."

"It's possible," Polly allowed. Certainly the connection between her and Hope hadn't been apparent right away. When they first met, Polly had formed a quick, ultimately unfair impression of her roommate, a knee-jerk reaction to her monogrammed luggage, the curtains she'd brought to brighten the windows. She found her stuff excessive, her friendliness overbearing, and held her at arm's length. But Hope wasn't easily dissuaded, and persisted in inviting Polly to brunches and dinners. Polly mostly declined. Fittingly, it was the night Adam stumbled into their room, mistaking it for his, that they finally started to become friends; after he passed out in Hope's papasan chair, the two of them stayed up all night, laughing into the dark.

Polly squinted up at the bleached blue sky, the sign for the Maine–New Hampshire bridge, and pressed down the sun visor. She felt another craving for a cigarette—was it edging closer to campus that was awakening all her old bad habits?

"But that's how life works, isn't it?" she said. "Accidents of time and place. It's like you and Xavier and Nicholas ending up in that judo class together in second grade."

"It's not like that at all," Jonah said. He crumpled up the bag, wiping his fingers on his jeans, then turned back to the window. She should have known better than to draw comparisons between his friends and hers.

"Well," Polly said. Just ahead, the green exoskeleton of the bridge was rising into the clouds. "I'm glad we're doing this. It's going to be a good weekend."

It was an attempt at manifestation—set a goal, will it into existence—though if anything, this conversation had Polly second-guessing the trip even more.

"College is such an important experience," she said. "It's an amazing time in your life."

But her son had retreated into silence, and could she blame him? It sounded like the beginning of a generic five-paragraph essay, the sort of hollow sentiment she'd flag in student work. Shallow, unrevealing, an evasion of the truth.

"I can just picture how happy you'll be there," she continued. "Studying something you truly care about. Being with people who value the same things you do. I know you're going to love it," she concluded, and this part she believed: despite all the setbacks and stress of the past year, her son would thrive in art school.

Again, Jonah didn't reply. He'd rolled up his window, leaned his forehead against the glass.

"This weekend will be good for us," Polly assured him, as she drove onto the bridge. The ridged asphalt thrummed beneath their wheels. "A change of scenery. A new perspective," she said, and as if in a show of support, the world opened up in all directions, the river unfurling below the bridge and thick green pines swelling on the other side. But when she glanced at Jonah, she realized he'd put his headphones back on and was reading intently on his phone, and she was talking to herself.

FOUR

HOPE

Driving into downtown Sewall, Hope took care to note, as she always did, the small things that had changed. In the nineties, Sewall had been a little rough around the edges, the lovely old campus buildings situated a half mile down the road from the local bars, beauty shops, and Laundromats. A sizable chunk of downtown real estate had been occupied by a cavernous department store that sold seemingly everything—clothes, toys, furniture, even hot dogs and ice-cream cones. Polly had a talent for picking through the discount racks and unearthing slightly pilled cardigans and functional flannel shirts she managed to make look edgy. When the store closed, a few years after they'd graduated, the space was diced up into several smaller shops selling jewelry, kitchenware, artisan pizza. It was a shame to see the old spots go, Hope thought, although the town *did* look pretty. And their favorites remained—the Coffee Barn, which had opened junior year, introducing Hope to mochas and cappuccinos, and Szechuan Star, the all-you-can-eat Chinese buffet where Adam would consume a half-dozen plates of greasy noodles while she and Polly drank mai tais the size of fishbowls without being asked for ID.

Hope was relieved, as she continued down College Avenue, to find the town looked more or less the same. Szechuan Star appeared to have reopened; there was a "Help Wanted" sign in the window. Outside the Coffee Barn, customers were sitting at small tables on the sidewalk, holding to-go mugs and disposable cups. Hope smiled. Twenty-five years ago, she'd been addicted to their maple cinnamon lattes, and made a point of getting one every time she came back.

Twenty-five years, she thought: a quarter of a century. It literally did not seem possible. Hope could still summon that time in her life at will, like turning on a tap and letting it flow through her.

Yet when Hope stopped to picture it, really thought about the details, she marveled at how different it had been. A world before cell phones or even in-room lines, in which Laura Rhodes carried on weepy conversations with her long-distance boyfriend on the shared phone in the hallway while the other girls sidestepped her flip-flopped feet. A world before social media, when instead of checking Facebook, all incoming freshmen received a copy of the facebook, a poorly Xeroxed booklet containing fuzzy photos of every student in their class. It wasn't until senior year that email found its way to campus. She remembered camping out in the computer lab, waiting for her allotted thirty minutes, then watching messages from her high school friends load with miraculous, excruciating slowness. They didn't have Internet in the dorms—some students didn't even have computers! To Izzy, this would sound prehistoric. But Hope maintained there was something delicious about it all: the sense of possibility in that pulsing red dot on the answering machine, the scribbled message on a dry-erase board, the phone conversation that meandered for hours, tethered to the wall by a warm receiver. As Hope drove under the blue-and-white banner—WELCOME BACK, ALUMNI—she was faintly humming with nostalgia. *You're obsessed*, Izzy had said, to which Hope should have countered: What's wrong with loving where you went to school? She felt sorry for people who didn't.

She pulled into the parking lot of the Driftway Inn. Once upon a time, the first floor had been a hole-in-the-wall Mexican restaurant, with studio apartments upstairs, but now you'd never know it. The renovation was impeccable, the original building with its ragged awning and sweaty windows transformed into a dignified white Colonial with a barn-red door and black trim. Hope shut off the engine and just sat for a minute to gaze at the campus across the street. Incredibly, it was all still there. A marble archway marked the main entrance—the superstition was that if you walked directly beneath it, you'd never get married—and the quad on the other side looked like a page out of her calendar, lush with green. In the center of the lawn, a crisp white canopy had been assembled, hung with blue paper lanterns; around its perimeter, round tables were topped with linens and fresh flowers. Within a few hours, Hope thought, people would be arriving. Classmates gathering after an interminable fifteen months, Polly returning after twenty years. She sensed an opening in her chest and recalled something her friend Nicole had said on a Moms' Night last summer after returning from a week at the beach with her sister: *I was so happy that I realized just how unhappy I've been*.

Then, feeling guilty, Hope thought about her own family. When she checked her phone at the rest stop in Kennebunk, Ethan had sent a few harried-sounding texts. Rowan was *melting down*. He was hungry. Disney Plus wouldn't load. Surely Ethan's impatience wasn't helping. That morning, Rowan had been upset when she told him about the weekend, but by the time she left, he was contentedly watching *Paw Patrol* while Izzy made pancakes. Hope had reasoned it would be like dropping him off at preschool: he cried every time, but the teachers reassured her he was always fine two minutes after she'd gone.

But today, according to Ethan, that wasn't the case. Around two, he'd texted Hope to say he was heading to campus, handing Ro off to Izzy for a while. She reminded him about Izzy's four o'clock therapy appointment, now starting in less than thirty minutes; once Hope was checked in, she'd make sure that he remembered. For now, she fished her lipstick from her purse and reapplied it—because who knew who she might run into in the lobby? When she opened the car door and got out, her knees were stiff, but she inhaled and instantly felt better. There was something magical about Maine weather. In Philadelphia, the humidity was already unbearable, but here the air felt like a tonic, weightless and cool.

Hope wheeled her suitcase to the front door and stepped inside, setting off a friendly knot of bells. "Hello!"

The young woman at reception had a thick ponytail, pink-rimmed glasses, and a name tag that said Ashley. She wore a mask that looked handcrafted, made of flowered fabric. "Masks for Guests Optional," said the sign taped to the front of the desk, so Hope fished one from her purse; around people required to wear them, it seemed the polite thing to do.

"Hello!" Ashley greeted her. "Welcome to the Driftway."

"I cannot tell you how good it feels to be here."

"Reunion?"

"Unbelievably, yes. Last year's. I'm still pinching myself, honestly," Hope said. "It was our twenty-fifth, which was disappointing, but then it got rescheduled! Not all of them were—only the biggest milestones. They say the twenty-fifth is the one you show up for. The ten and the fifty are later this summer, but other years were canceled."

"Well," Ashley said. "I guess that was lucky."

"In the end, I guess it was," Hope agreed. "And didn't we get perfect weather?"

Ashley smiled, a crinkling of the eyes behind her glasses, but said nothing, as if she had information Hope didn't. She seemed to be waiting for something. "Your name?"

"Oh! Of course. Hope Richardson."

Ashley turned to the computer, nudging the keyboard, and the screen appeared as two pools in her round lenses.

"I don't know about you, but I feel like I'm still remembering how to behave in public," Hope said. "I mean, basic social conventions. How to *be* in the world. Like giving your name when you check into a hotel. Or tipping a delivery person. My husband says I've forgotten how to drive." She laughed, though when Ethan had said it, he wasn't being funny. It was November, the week of the election and the second week back to school on a hybrid schedule, and Hope had been sitting at a red light on her way to pick up Rowan when she drove into the BMW in front of her. In her defense, she wasn't *not* paying attention; she saw the light turn green, so she went.

"I think it's understandable, though, don't you?" Hope said. "I mean, we're all just out of practice."

Ashley's eyes were on the screen, fingers poised above the home row and clicking nimbly. Hope was impressed: it was the way she'd been taught in middle school, touch typing, which seemed to have become obsolete in the era of the cell phone. She reminded herself not to interrupt and glanced around the lobby: a fireplace, quaint seascape, antique sideboard, and three overstuffed flowered chairs. Propped on the reception desk was a little card in a gilt frame—LIKE US ON FACEBOOK—beside a dish of Hershey's Kisses. Hope slipped one into her pocket. She usually resisted chocolate, but felt as if all of her senses were on high alert.

"Richardson," Ashley said. "A single. Queen-sized."

Hope smiled inside her mask. "That's me."

Ashley nodded, then slid open a drawer. "Room 103."

"Oh—" Hope grimaced, touching the edge of the desk. "I hate to be this person. But is there any way I could get a room on the second floor?"

Ashley paused, pushing up her glasses, which had gotten slightly foggy. Her fingernail was pink with a rhinestone glued to the middle. "I probably shouldn't, but you're the first alum to check in . . ."

"Oh, if you could, I'd appreciate it," Hope said. "So much."

Ashley consulted the screen once more. Hope was tempted to ask what other alums had booked a room there but didn't want to push it.

"207?"

"Like the area code," Hope said. "Perfect."

Ashley executed a few purposeful taps. "One key or two?"

"Oh, just one," Hope said and felt another pinch of guilt.

Ashley returned to the drawer, contents rattling, and handed her not a plastic card but an actual key. Hope tucked the warm metal into her palm.

"Checkout is on Sunday at eleven," Ashley told her.

Three days—it was unimaginable.

"And continental breakfast is seven to ten."

"Wonderful," Hope said, but she was already picturing the brunch on Saturday morning. It was one of her favorite parts of reunion: they ate in stages over several hours, mimosas and blueberry pancakes and made-to-order omelets, catching up with old classmates as they filtered in, wincing at the stories of the night before.

"The elevator's across the lobby." Ashley looked at her suitcase. "Need help with that?"

"Oh no," Hope said. "You've been such a help already."

"If you need anything, you know where to find me," Ashley said, and though she probably said this to every guest, the offer made a lump rise into Hope's throat.

"Thank you," she said, then wheeled the case across the lobby. As she waited for the elevator, she opened Facebook, found the Driftway Inn, and pressed Like.

Growing up, Hope never truly enjoyed family vacations, too aware of the fact that they would soon be ending. On their annual trip to Barnegat Light on the Jersey shore, she always woke early, itching to get to the beach. Her parents would smile affectionately, trying to keep her occupied—a bike ride, a doughnut run—while she waited for her big sister. Around eleven, Linsey would peel herself from her bedroom in shorts and a skimpy bikini, telling Hope to chill. But as much as Hope loved vacation—*because* Hope loved vacation—she could not chill. *Remain present in the moment:* so went the advice of Dominique, the twentysomething online yoga instructor whose classes she'd attempted a handful of times last fall. But remaining present in the moment was not something Hope was good at under normal circumstances—lying in corpse pose at the end of class, all she could do was think about everything else she could and should be doing—and last year it felt particularly intolerable. To sit in silence with your thoughts—who could do it? Who would *want* to? *There's nowhere else you need to be right now*, Dominique repeatedly assured them, but these were women confined to their houses! Wasn't this the very thing they were trying to forget? During Hope's final class, she'd coaxed Rowan in front of the screen and snapped a photo of him in mountain pose—*My little yogi!*—then posted it on Facebook, where it got over two hundred likes.

This weekend, though, Hope would be following Dominique's advice. She wanted to experience every moment. She was determined not to waste it. She unlatched the French doors and stepped onto the balcony: the change had been worth it. From the second floor, she had a bird's-eye view of the entire quad, the classic redbrick buildings and jewel-green lawn. Academic buildings sat on one side, dorms on the other. At two o'clock, the gorgeous old English building with its stained glass windows; at eight, their freshman dorm, Fiske Hall. At twelve, the student union that had been built her junior year but that their class would always call new. The grass was so green it looked almost fluorescent, laced with curving brick paths and quaint lampposts that by sundown would be glowing. A forgotten memory returned to Hope whole: walking home from the library on winter evenings in the cozy light of those lampposts. Crunch of duck boots, cloud of breath, taste of snow. It felt immediate, visceral, not a still image but a scene in three dimensions that she might step right inside.

Hope held up her phone and snapped a picture, gave it a quick crop and retouch, then uploaded it to her Facebook page. *Reunion weekend! Better late than never!!*

Then she texted Polly and Adam: Here!!!!

They were both staying in Fiske: Polly because she was Polly, and Adam because he was bringing his boys. Hope thought this was silly—there were plenty of nearby motels—but at least their dorm was only a stone's throw from the inn. And Adam's boys might have fun there. Hope would never have predicted she and Adam would end up with kids so close in age—the result of Adam not settling down until his late thirties and Hope trusting that getting pregnant would be just as easy the second time around—but his twins were only a year younger than Rowan. Hope felt another guilty pinch; it would have been nice for the boys to get to know each other. They'd met just that one time and were too young to remember. She'd meant to get back to New Hampshire sooner, but as Rowan got older, he had a harder time with long car rides. And then, of course, the past year had disappeared.

Her phone chirped.

Running a little late, Adam wrote.

Hope typed right back: Hurry pls!

No response from Polly, unsurprisingly. She was erratic on text (she might respond pointlessly, days later, or not at all), but at least she was coming. When Polly bailed on the fifteenth and twentieth reunions, she'd had lame excuses: she was busy with Jonah, burned out from teaching. Her skipping the ten-year was different; she'd had Jonah two years before—an accidental pregnancy, some random guy she'd met in a bar. *Oops!* she'd told Hope, like she'd gotten on the wrong bus. She hadn't wanted to spend the weekend sober, chasing a toddler, even though Hope had promised to help. The five-year she'd shown up for, though she arrived late on Friday, making a dramatic entrance with her new hairstyle, a choppy bob with one shaved side. Then she'd disappeared for most of Saturday, hanging out with Professor McFadden, with whom she'd spent bewildering amounts of time in college. Hope had never liked him; he was always writing cranky letters to the student paper, and he clearly played favorites, giving her the lowest grade of her life. But a few years ago, when she read in the alumni bulletin that he'd died—a heart attack, only sixty-one years old—she'd left a message on the online tribute page. She'd texted Polly, but Polly being Polly, she hadn't texted back.

Hope accepted that it might be some time before either of her friends appeared. But this was fine. It meant she could be leisurely. Duck out for a maple cinnamon latte, take her time deciding what to wear. Cocktails began at six, leaving her nearly two hours. She refreshed her Facebook post: twenty-three likes already, people she would soon be seeing in person, people whose pictures had populated the original facebook freshman year. If in high school, social rank had been a vertical ladder—Hope, an honors student with plenty of friends, had fallen somewhere in the middle—college friendships felt more lateral, more flexible, clustered around sports, fraternities, dorms. By senior year, everyone knew everyone, or at least Hope did. She'd pored over the washed-out facebook photos so many times the pages were soft and furry. *Polly Dawn Gesauldi, Brooklyn, NY.* Straight mouth, face half in shadow, single feather earring. *Adam Lawrence Dalton, Fairfield, CT.* T-shirt, mussed hair, wide grin. In the row below Polly's was *Michael Patrick Grady, Andover, MA.* In her mind's eye, Hope paused on his neat tie and jacket, his crew cut and rakish smile. As a freshman, he'd been so popular with girls that during pledging, his fraternity brothers dubbed him Foxy. Hope had gone out with him for most of senior year—well, *gone out* might be pushing it. They regularly sought each other out after parties, but wasn't that the extent of most relationships in college?

Her heartbeat was tripping lightly as she glanced once more

at the Facebook page. Grady hadn't RSVPed, which probably meant he wasn't coming. They weren't friends on Facebook, but occasionally he tagged mutual friends in photos. She closed the app and checked again for a text from Polly—still no word— then returned to her last exchange with Ethan. It was 3:56 and he hadn't replied to her reminder about Izzy's therapy.

Now she texted Izzy: How's it going?

Instantly, the little dots appeared. Her daughter's phone was stuck permanently to her person.

Fine

I mean basically?

Ro misses you

Tell him I miss him too, **Hope** replied. And don't forget the taco casserole!

K, Izzy wrote.

Is Dad back?

Not yet

He said by 4 tho

Did Ethan need to cut it so close? He would argue it was a small thing. But life was made of small things. If he didn't appear in the next ninety seconds, Izzy would need to set up Rowan to occupy himself during her appointment. Turn on *Paw Patrol*, give him fruit snacks and Gray Rabbit, and hope he stayed content until Ethan got home.

Izzy, though, didn't sound bothered. She always let her father off the hook. Hope had once laughingly mentioned this to the other moms during one of their Zoom calls, and they shook their heads in commiseration. *Daughters and their dads!*

To express her frustration would, Hope knew, accomplish nothing.

Well give Ro a big hug for me!! she wrote. And have a good
appt!

A thumbs-up, then Izzy disappeared. She never shared details
of her conversations with Sandra, but last year, when teenagers
were struggling all over and therapists had waiting lists, Hope
was grateful her daughter had someone to talk to (even if it was
a bit unsettling to hear the easy, confiding murmur of her voice
through her bedroom door).

At least, Hope thought, by the time the appointment was
over, it would be nearly time for dinner. Izzy would heat up the
casserole. They would eat, and then she'd read to Rowan, help
him with his pj's, get him started on his nighttime routines—
sparkle toothpaste, shoulder squeezes, weighted blankets—and
by the time she left for the dance, the evening would be sliding
into night.

It was then, picturing her parallel life at home, that it truly
sank in: Hope was here. She closed her eyes and just listened to
the quiet, letting it drift around her ears. The beautiful summer
evening stretched before her. Cool air wafted through the French
doors. In her belly, she detected a low, pleasant simmer. She remembered the Hershey's Kiss in her pocket and unwrapped the
silver foil—the sugary chocolate was cheap and delicious. The
breeze felt like fingertips on her skin.

Hope walked over to the bed, a four-poster topped with an
avalanche of shiny bedding, and set her phone facedown on
the nightstand. She lay next to the pile of pillows, looking up
at the coffered ceiling, and closed her eyes. Loosening her zipper, she slid a hand down the front of her jeans. Her face was
warm, blood quickly filling her cheeks. The French doors were
still open, which felt a little brazen, but who would possibly see?

Then her phone started chirping again, and she sat up, grabbing it. *Izzy would like FaceTime.* When she answered, Rowan's face filled the screen.

"Mom?"

He must have been holding the phone just inches from his nose. Hope could see only one damp brown eye and the shaggy hair at his temple, in desperate need of a trim.

"Mommy," he said. "It's an emergency."

Hope didn't panic. This could mean many things.

"What's wrong, Ro?"

"When are you coming home?"

His voice sounded shaky and uncertain, even though they'd gone over the schedule several times that morning. He often just needed repetition. Reassurance.

"Sunday, remember?" Hope told him, keeping her own voice light and level. "Today's Friday. So Friday, Saturday, Sunday."

"But I need you."

A flare of guilt. She should have done a better job preparing him. It was a mistake, she thought, not to tell him sooner. Maybe she should have brought him—brought all of them.

"It's okay, Ro," she said calmly. "It's just three days." Downstairs with Ashley, the prospect had sounded luxurious; already it felt shorter, more fraught. "Is Dad home yet?"

"Uh-uh," he said, rubbing Gray Rabbit's worn ear against his cheek.

Hope felt a tick of anger burrow beneath her skin. Why couldn't Ethan get back on time? Did he not understand that Izzy couldn't watch her little brother? Was he *trying* to make this harder for her? *He's six,* Ethan would say. *He can be left alone for fifteen minutes.* But actually, he couldn't, because a noise on *Paw Patrol* might be too loud, or an apple slice too mushy, and without Ethan there she had to worry, and for a few days she just wanted not to worry, and couldn't he give her this?

But she swallowed her annoyance, saying, "I'm sure he'll be there any second."

Rowan gazed at her, his eyelashes sharp, wet points. "Where are you?"

"At my old school, silly!" Hope said. "Remember I told you? The place I went to school when I was a big kid." She carried the phone to the balcony and scrolled slowly around the quad, hoping that a visual would make her being away less confusing. "Isn't that pretty?" she said and smiled at the screen, but her son's face had crumpled.

"Mom," he said, looking upward and sucking in his cheeks. "I have hard feelings."

Hope kept her composure. He had been working on this with Ellen—naming his feelings, identifying the four zones of emotion—though this phrase was his own, and it broke her heart.

"What kinds of hard feelings, Ro?"

"Yellow zone, I think," he said.

"Okay." Hope nodded into the phone. "Good job, Ro. The yellow zone. So, now, how can we get *out* of the yellow zone?"

"I don't know." He mashed Gray Rabbit against his teeth and shook his head, hair whipping around his ears.

"How about a candle breath?"

"Uh-uh."

"Just one. We'll do it together."

"I don't want to."

"Please," Hope said. She held her index finger to her lips. "For me?"

No doubt this was the exact opposite of what she should

be doing, using guilt to manipulate her six-year-old into self-soothing, but Rowan lowered Gray Rabbit and gazed at the screen. Reluctantly, he copied her, raising one dimpled finger, and they each unleashed a long exhale. With their last ounces of breath, they extinguished their candles, and he seemed a little calmer. They repeated this five more times, once for every candle on his pretend birthday cake.

FIVE

POLLY

Ledgemere Island was just thirty minutes from the college, a narrow, two-mile strip of woods and water on the other side of a short stone bridge. A quiet two-lane road ambled down the middle of the island, dotted with humble cottages and pockets of evergreens, splashed with sunlight. Behind them, serene coves and wooden docks slipped in and out of view, the water salted with boats and buoys. Polly was an avowed indoor person, but the few times she'd come out there with Adam in college, she'd been stunned by its beauty. It had seemed incongruous that this place should exist so close to campus, and still did; it nearly allowed her to forget where she was going next.

Jonah was sitting forward, newly energized, peering out the window. "I didn't know people actually lived in places like this," he said. "I mean, I guess I knew. But I didn't."

"Pretty gorgeous, huh?" Polly pushed her sunglasses on top of her head so she could absorb the view in full color. The ocean was a shimmering blue, smooth as a pane of glass.

"It's so pure," he said. "So fucking *simple*."

"Only in the summertime," she reminded him, recalling her endless college winters—the constant stuffy noses and clanging radiators and lumps of dirty snow that squatted in parking lots well after spring break.

"No way," Jonah said, raising his phone to take a photo. "Winter would be the best part."

Unlike Polly, who felt most herself in the city, Jonah had always been drawn to the outdoors. It came through even in his photographs: the crack on a brick wall that at first glance looked like a jagged mountain range. The yawning shadow that doubled as the mouth of a cave.

"Imagine what lockdown must have been like up here," he said, snapping a picture of a weathered cottage, a soft pyramid of chopped wood sagging against one side. "An island on an island. An island you'd actually *want* to be trapped on."

Polly smiled—her son's happiness was infectious. She was glad to see him taking pictures. No matter how hard this weekend proved to be for her, it would be worth it. He peered into the camera phone as they passed a general store advertising coffee and cheeseburgers, a fire station, a cluster of homemade signs standing among the cattails on the side of the road. COMMUNITY ART SHOW. SHRIMP DINNER. VACATION RENTALS. A few posters showed cell phones stamped with emphatic red X's. Polly wondered if the entire island operated like a public library, where using a phone was considered rude.

"It's like life stripped back to the essentials," Jonah said. "Life outside the materialistic, capitalistic system. I have total respect for it. Like—this is what the world could be like if humans hadn't fucked it all up."

Polly could have pointed out that the island sat less than twenty miles from a moneyed college town and wasn't at all outside the system, but she didn't want to dampen his enthusiasm.

"They have all these new initiatives up here," he continued.

"Reducing the carbon footprint. Committing to clean energy. Charlie's really into it."

"Is he?" Polly said. "But he lives in Massachusetts, right?"

"Technically. But I think he considers this his real home. He's always posting about it. And remember him at Elmwood? The guy was a fucking ninja. He could pitch tents and tie knots and shit."

Polly remembered Charlie differently—as a shy, awkward preteen in tie-dyed shirts and basketball shorts. On Visiting Day, he'd gotten stage fright and hid in the wings at the all-camp talent show.

"He's really into ocean conservancy," Jonah went on. "It's all over his feed—"

"Don't forget to direct me," Polly interrupted lightly.

Jonah lowered his phone to consult the text Charlie had sent with directions. "Left after the post office," he said, then looked up and pointed. "Post office. Boom."

So it was: a building the size of a corner bodega in a small clearing. Just beyond it stood a green sign—PRIVATE ROAD— and a short row of mailboxes on wooden posts. The boxes were stuffed with newspapers, metal tongues wagging. As Polly turned, she pictured the map of the island: the long, thickly forested fingers branching off its spine. This road was a single lane, the houses hidden from view, their driveways identified by ornamental signs nailed to tree trunks. SAFE HAVEN. REST NEST. ISLAND REPOSE. This place could go in one of two directions, Polly decided: a cabin or a mansion.

"Does Charlie's house have a name?" she asked.

"Yeah," Jonah said. "It's that one there."

He was pointing to the last sign on the right, a shiny wooden placard shaped like an oar. TRANQUILITY. Polly maneuvered the car down a dirt driveway crowded with pine trees, gold-tipped and bushy, then found herself in a huge circular driveway paved with pink-gray stones.

"What the fuck," Jonah said under his breath.

It was nothing like the modest homes up by the main road. This was a New England–style Colonial, but outsized and modernized, with fieldstone pillars and geometric windows under a sharply pitched roof. A pile of colorful kayaks, a brightly chlorinated pool. In the driveway sat a Mercedes SUV, a Jeep, and two gleaming sports cars. Polly pulled up beside them and shut off her tired Toyota. It was silent, except for the tick of the engine beneath the hood.

"You've got to be kidding me," Jonah said. The buzz from moments ago had vaporized. He must not have known Charlie's family was so wealthy. As a camper at Elmwood, he wouldn't have registered the distinctions of family money; Polly had felt this way even as a college student. It wasn't until senior year, going for her exit interview with financial services, that she realized she was the only one of her friends with student loans.

"It's still beautiful," Polly reminded him. "Remember how much you've been looking—"

"Four. Cars." Jonah swiped his backpack off the floor. "How do you live surrounded by all this natural beauty and own *four* fucking cars?"

"Open mind," she said, but he was already pushing open the door. She watched him cross the driveway, the pebbles crunching beneath his Chuck Taylors. Despite the metal in his ears, the new tattoo peeking from beneath his sleeve, he looked young, and vulnerable, and Polly felt an old, bone-deep impulse to protect him.

Her phone buzzed, and she lifted it from the grimy cup holder—Hope. She'd been texting them for the past hour; naturally, she was already on campus. She was probably all checked in. Polly was reminded of move-in day freshman year; by the time Polly rolled up with her mother, Hope was more or less unpacked. She was waiting to consult Polly on the bunk bed, cheerfully insisting this was a joint decision, though with Hope's massive pile of bedding Polly didn't see how her roommate could possibly fit on the top.

Then Polly heard a faint slam and looked up to see a woman stepping onto the front porch. She quickly undid her seat belt, sliding her sunglasses back on and shoving her phone in her pocket.

"Caroline! Hi!" she said, waving as she opened the car door.

Charlie's mother was fair-skinned, surprisingly plain-looking, dressed in linen shorts, a crisp white blouse, and matching leather belt and sandals. It was the kind of unfussy yet immaculate ensemble that probably cost a thousand dollars. Polly had no memory of her from the throng of parents in the bunk at Elmwood four years before.

"Sorry we're late," Polly said. "Traffic."

"Oh, no worries," Caroline said, placing one hand like a visor above her brow. "Hi there, Jonah."

Polly wondered how her son looked through this other mother's eyes. At camp that final summer, Jonah had been six inches shorter, still wearing cargo shorts and retro tees. But if Caroline was surprised to find he now had ear gauges and tattoos, she didn't let it show.

"This is an amazing spot," Polly said. "We had no idea. Did we, Jonah?"

"We didn't," he said—not quite rudely, but on the edge.

Then Charlie stepped onto the porch. At thirteen, he'd been round-cheeked, his skin showered with freckles. Now he was broad and tanned, wearing lime-green shorts and a gray long-sleeved shirt that said LACROSSE. His hair swung across his brow, a glossy blond swoop that nearly reached his eyelashes.

"Charlie, I hardly recognized you!" Polly said.

It was just the sort of comment she'd once sworn never to make. As a kid, on the rare occasion her father dropped in from whatever corner of the Earth he'd been hiding, claiming to miss her but usually needing money, he'd say it over and over, only reinforcing how little he knew her.

But Charlie smiled, nudging the hair from his eyes. His wrists were entwined in multi-colored threaded bracelets, like something the boys might have made in the Elmwood arts and crafts studio. "Thanks," he said. Caroline put her arm around his shoulders, as if the weight were a reminder of a talk they'd had. "Hey, man," he greeted Jonah.

"Hey," Jonah said, pausing at the bottom of the stairs.

Charlie reached down, and they lightly tapped fists. His smile was friendly but restrained. Four years, Polly thought. She recalled the last day of camp, the sadness among the kids building to a fever pitch; at the moment, it was hard to even picture, though she understood how living in such close quarters could be an incubator for that kind of emotion. Jonah had said he and Charlie were friends on social media, but was it even possible to know a person on social media?

Her phone buzzed again, and she ignored it, as Charlie's father walked up from behind the house—a scoop of deep green grass, bordering deeper green woods. His sleeves were rolled up, tanned forearms furred with blond. He extended a hand to Polly. "Tom Wheeler."

"Polly," she said. "Gesauldi. And this is Jonah."

"Welcome to Maine," he said.

He was a golden person, Polly thought, brawny arms and wide shoulders and sun-burnished hair. Not a single person looked this healthy in all of New York.

Jonah took his hand and shook it stiffly. "Hello."

"Glad you could come visit us," he said. "How was the drive?"

"Depressing," Jonah said, and Polly quickly jumped in, adding, "It was kind of surreal. This is our first time leaving the city in what—fifteen months?" She looked to Jonah for corroboration, but he didn't seem to be listening. He was looking at the pool. "Honestly," she said, with an apologetic laugh. "This feels a little like stepping onto a different planet. And you're up here for the whole summer?"

"Actually, we've been up here most of the past year," Tom said. "When everything went remote, we figured, why not?"

"Sure," Polly said, nodding. *An island you'd actually* want *to be trapped on*—Jonah wasn't wrong. It wouldn't be so bad to be stuck up here. It might even be pleasant. Polly remembered those early weeks in the apartment, the laptop on the sticky kitchen table next to the toast crumbs and coffee rings, the empty streets outside and stale air inside, their only contact with the natural world the struggling herb garden on the kitchen windowsill, the treetops in the park just visible above the dark Bella Luca pizza sign across the street. It was an insane social experiment, how wildly the experience could vary depending on your circumstances. Whether you lived in a city or on an island, had kids or no kids, a partner you liked or despised, were an essential worker or could do your job on a screen. Whether you were bored and inconvenienced or grieving, sick, and terrified. It might have been interesting if it hadn't been so enraging.

"It seemed like a good idea," Caroline said, sounding a little sheepish. "Can we offer you something? A drink?"

For a moment Polly toyed with the idea of hiding out on the island for the weekend, calling the number on the sign for vacation rentals and ditching the reunion altogether. The thought of driving her actual car onto the actual campus caused a dip of dread behind her knees. But if she didn't show up, Hope might never forgive her. "Thanks," she said. "I would, but I'm already behind schedule."

There was a confused beat, and Polly realized they were waiting for further explanation. "I guess Jonah didn't tell you?" she said. "This weekend is my college reunion. That's what brought us up here."

"Aha," Caroline said, probably relieved to know this stranger hadn't driven her child six hours on a whim.

"The college is so close by," Polly added.

Tom smiled. "A Walthrop grad, then."

"Class of ninety-five," Polly said.

He nodded appreciatively, which Polly had come to expect. Over time she'd put less and less stock in alma maters—she'd taught enough brilliant community college students to know that where you went to school was largely about what opportunities were available to you—but in her undistinguished adult life, her Walthrop degree was one of the few cards she had to play.

"So it must be your—" Caroline looked at her palm, as if about to count fingers, then paused, probably not wanting to offend her.

"Twenty-fifth," Polly supplied. "It was supposed to be last year and got rescheduled. But I haven't been back in ages. I wasn't actually intending to go this year, but Jonah convinced me. He's been so excited about this visit."

She stopped, not wanting to embarrass him, but Jonah wasn't even pretending to pay attention. He was focused somewhere beyond Polly's shoulder, his face closed over, all traces of his earlier happiness gone. Polly suddenly wished she didn't have to leave him. Because staying here might make her son feel uncomfortable, or inferior. She tried to catch his eye, to communicate a look of understanding, but he was gazing past her, in the direction of the woods.

SIX

ADAM

Adam hadn't planned on stopping, but as if by muscle memory, he found himself turning into the parking lot at Happy's Beer and Sub Shop. The place looked exactly as it used to. Same burst of tall, hairy weeds by the door. Same grinning beer mug on the same dull, blinking sign. A fringe of trees stood along the back of the parking lot, pale trunks and patchy leaves, possibly the ugliest trees in the state of Maine. Inside, the store even smelled the same, like cardboard and mothballs and kibble for the sinewy cat slinking its way around the cramped aisles—he could have sworn it was the same cat. As Adam faced the fridge, he debated: a crappy college beer or respectable adult one? One of each.

He grabbed a six-pack of Allagash and twelve-pack of Natural Light and approached the counter, which was crowded with dusty boxes of lighters and fishing tackle and Slim Jims. The white-haired guy behind the register cast him a wary look, and Adam had a flash of the driver's license he'd carried in his wallet until he turned twenty-one—Mike Cahill, fellow runner, three years older, zero resemblance beyond their heads of brown hair—then reminded himself he was almost fifty and now bought beer with his own ID. Adam gave the guy an assured smile and told him to keep the change, and as he walked out, screen door clipping his heels, a feeling rose in him—a dash of vigor, a sprint of energy in his veins. It was a feeling he remembered from when he was young. After the past year, all the stillness and the vigilance, it felt good.

He tossed the beer on the floor of the front seat and shut the door just as his phone buzzed.

Where are u two??

Hope was clearly itching for them to join her. Adam had intended to be on campus by five, and it was almost five thirty. Turned out there *was* weekend traffic heading into Maine—after his late start, he'd ended up in rush hour outside Portland.

Here, he wrote. At Happy's.

She replied:

Some things never change!!!

Polly? she continued. U there???

It all felt comfortingly familiar. It was typical Hope to arrive early, and typical Polly to be MIA. Adam had been surprised to hear Polly was even coming, especially after what she'd told him and Andrea in New York. Looking at his phone, Adam tried to recall how much he'd confided in his two friends last spring, but he couldn't reread those old texts even if he wanted to. They were deleted after a year.

Instead, he texted Andrea: Just pulled into town. How are they?

While he waited, he tore open the twelve-pack and cracked a beer, savoring the first sour, satisfying mouthful.

Full recovery, Andrea replied, followed by a photo of the boys. They were sitting in the kitchen nook, stabbing forks at plates of pancakes that Andrea had decorated with blueberry eyes, banana mouths, and whipped cream hair.

Breakfast for dinner!

The boys were clearly brimming with joy. Zachary was doing an impression of the pancake, rounding his chubby fingers into eyeballs, while Sam looked on with a delighted grin.

Tell them I miss them, Adam wrote.

Behind them, on the orange-and-lemon wallpaper, he could see the imprint of the sky, a ladder of golden light. A perfect evening for a walk.

What's the plan for tonight? he added hopefully, but she replied: Movie marathon :)

Then she said they'd call him later, and he set the phone on the passenger seat, squinting into the hard sunlight above the Happy's sign. It felt bizarre not being with them. He would have loved to hear they were venturing outside. But the boys were having fun, he thought. And he was here. And Andrea had encouraged him to be here. He popped open the glove compartment and rooted around for the sunglasses Andrea used to keep in there for driving, rubbed the dust off on his sleeve, and put them on.

When he started the car, the radio blared a country song, and he jabbed at the dial—religion, country, religion—until he found the old college radio station, playing Pearl Jam's "Better Man." Somewhere, an undergrad was sitting in front of a laptop, charged with cuing up hits of the midnineties. The thought made Adam smile. He took one more swallow and stuck the can in the cup holder, then hesitated; at eighteen, it wouldn't have crossed his mind not to drive with a beer at his elbow, but the world was different now. He was different. He reasoned that it was less than a mile, and he'd drive below the speed limit, and as he headed out of the parking lot and down the main drag, window down, a lukewarm Natty Light in the console and Eddie Vedder on the radio, it might have been 1994 again—if not for his wife and kids at home, his thinning hair, his thickening gut, the stress of the past year lodged like a softball in his chest.

Slowly, he proceeded through downtown Sewall. Like him, the town had aged. But instead of more decrepit, it looked newer and shinier. Gentrification had sunk its teeth deep into the coast of Maine. Rusty's, once a hole-in-the-wall serving six-dollar pitchers and shots of Goldschläger, was now a two-story microbrewery. Video Village, staple of the early nineties, had rebranded itself as retro: LAST VIDEO STORE ON EARTH! The inn where Hope was staying looked like it belonged in one of those fake tabletop colonial villages—his mother had had one she set up every Christmas, a collection of sedate little buildings with wreathes and ribbons—but it had once been home to a far superior establishment, a Mexican joint called Tony's that sold enchiladas for fifty cents.

Then the marble archway came into view, the same one Adam had ridden past with his parents freshman year. He'd watched them sitting stiffly in the front seat—his father's silver hair, his meaty hand and fat watch, his mother's damp neck, thin pearls with the gold clasp—while he waited in the back, duffel bag under his feet, coiled like a spring.

He stole a quick sip as he drove around the outer perimeter of campus, past the side streets where the frat houses had once been. They were now long gone, phased out in the early aughts. Adam had never pledged a fraternity—during rush week, spring of freshman year, a couple of houses had recruited him, but he'd just been scared shitless by the dean and was too preoccupied with not getting kicked out of school. In the end, not joining hadn't mattered. He'd had friends all over campus. The track team. Polly and Hope.

Adam carefully signaled as he turned onto the upper campus,

following the narrow road that threaded its way around the quad, past the library he hadn't set foot in until near the end of freshman year. Past the science building that had once housed environmental studies. In the early nineties, ES had been a relatively small major, the death of the planet not yet at the front of people's minds. Now it had its own building, outfitted with solar panels and windows made from recycled glass. He cruised past the dining hall, glimpsed the grassy hill behind it that led down to the lower campus and the running trails.

He was feeling loose now, faintly buzzing. The radio was playing Blues Traveler. He snuck another sip. But his mood plummeted when campus security appeared behind him. An asshole in aviators, riding on his bumper. Adam slid to a stop in front of the student union and turned off his engine as the guy pulled up alongside him. "Sir? Is that an open container?"

Adam's reflexes were rustier than he realized because it took him a full fifteen seconds to register that it wasn't campus security but Troy Abernathy behind the wheel of a golf cart. When he did, a hard laugh escaped his chest.

"Jesus. Give me a heart attack, why don't you?" Adam said. "What the hell are you driving?"

"Found it parked outside the gym." Troy reached out to clasp Adam's hand. "It's good to see you, man," he said, holding on an extra beat.

"You, too, man," Adam said.

The pandemic had not been kind to Troy Abernathy. In college, he'd been nicknamed the Gladiator for his barrel chest and appetite for picking fights at Rusty's. At the last reunion he'd been broad-shouldered, ruddy-cheeked, with a full head of hair.

Now his nose looked red and swollen. His hair on top was thinning. The banter felt the same, though, like they were teenagers in adult clothes.

Adam offered him a beer, and Troy snapped open the can. "Cheers," he said. He took a drink and lapped a drip of foam from his wrist. "So we got through it."

"So we did."

"Everybody okay? Everybody good?"

"Everybody's fine," Adam said. Even if he'd been inclined to talk about what was going on at home, he'd never been particularly close to Troy Abernathy. Still, he felt surprisingly happy to see him. "How about you?"

"Me?" Troy propped one foot on the dashboard. "My wife, now ex-wife, is dating a chiropractor. I see my kids on weekends. I work from home. I'm bored. My bones hurt. In a cruel twist, I need a chiropractor."

Adam laughed again, recalling Troy's rambling conversation with Andrea six years before. Troy had been wasted at every one of their reunions; over the years, this kind of thing became increasingly apparent. At the five-year, people could still keep pace with their younger selves—it was nostalgic, worth the hurt they'd inflict on themselves the next morning—but as time went by, most people slowed down. Some stopped. Others kept going, and it became hard to watch.

"Hey," Troy said. "Where's your wife? I didn't scare her off with my bullshit at the last reunion, did I?"

Adam was impressed he even remembered. "Nah, she can take it," he said. "She had a trip planned this weekend. A yoga retreat," he added, lying for no particular reason, except that he liked what this suggested: a wife who was earthy, vaguely spiritual, weathering this crisis with a Zen-like calm.

"Too bad," Troy said. "Let her know that I've matured, will you?"

Adam chuckled. "Will do."

"You mock me, which I deserve, but I'm actually serious. I've been doing a lot of work on myself."

"Yeah?"

"Cognitive behavioral therapy," Troy said. "I see my guy twice a week. We're doing the whole nine. Masculinity issues. Father issues. I actually feel like I've grown and shit."

"No kidding," Adam said. He wouldn't have thought Troy had it in him. He couldn't imagine spending two hours a week talking about his own father, what old resentments might get coughed up. "Good for you, man."

"Thanks," Troy said, then took off his aviators and hooked them onto his collar. His face took on a pensive look. "Hey. You been in touch with Herman?"

"No. Why?"

Greg Herman had been Adam's roommate freshman year, a fellow runner. Teammates usually weren't assigned rooms together, but maybe someone in Res Life had made an exception because they were otherwise so different. Greg was orderly and disciplined, a distance runner. He was now an orthopedic surgeon. Married with three kids, living in DC. They'd exchanged a few messages last spring, but Adam hadn't kept up with him. Suddenly he wished he had.

"His parents," Troy said. "They died."

"What?" Adam said. "Wait—both of them?"

"Yeah."

"From . . ."

"Yeah."

"Holy shit," Adam said.

Troy drained his can and tossed the empty on the floor of the golf cart. "It's our duty to lift his spirits," he said, nodding toward Adam's beer. "And you're falling behind already. We got lost time to make up for. Go drop your shit off. Grab a name tag." He gestured toward the long table in front of the student union. "So that we can recognize each other now that we're all fat fucking fossils." He reached over and squeezed Adam's shoulder. "Really glad you're here, man."

"Yeah," Adam said, caught off guard by his sincerity. "Same here."

Troy pushed his glasses back on then revved the engine and drove away. For a minute, Adam just sat still, pulse blinking like a cursor in his neck. His excitement of ten minutes ago had dipped, tempered with sadness. He took in the student union—the "new union," they'd called it, now a square of mossy brick—then finished off his can and grabbed another. He left the keys hanging in the ignition as he approached the table, draped with a banner—WELCOME BACK, CLASS OF 1995 (WE MADE IT!!!)—and topped with gift bags. Any other year, the table would be staffed with undergrads, but the students who had been living on campus had all gone home, leaving check-in unmanned and a little eerie. With its marked jars for used/clean markers, industrial-sized hand sanitizers, and signs about safety protocols, the table looked like something out of a dystopian thriller. Adam grabbed a marker, scribbled his name on a sticker, and smacked it onto his chest.

"Adam Dalton?"

He turned to find himself looking at slightly older, softer versions of Eve Erickson and Miranda Cohen. Again, a laugh escaped him—it felt abrupt and giddy, like a contact high, the appearance of these faces from the past triggering a burst of joy.

"Oh my God," Eve said. "Is that really you?"

"I think so," he said, glancing at his name tag.

"It's so good to see you," Eve said.

"It's good to be seen."

Eve and Miranda had lived on the same floor of Fiske as Hope and Polly. The joke then was they'd looked practically identical. Both of them were tall and athletic, with long blond hair and lift tickets dangling from the zippers of their multi-colored ski jackets. Eve had been loud and funny; Miranda was more reserved, except for her impassioned performances of "Total Eclipse of the Heart" in the Fiske lounge. Now they looked less alike: Eve's blond hair was chopped at the shoulders, in what Andrea would call a "mom cut," while Miranda's was dark brown.

"This feels surreal," Miranda said. "It feels like we're getting away with something."

Eve pointed at the beer in Adam's hand. "You do know we can afford better now, right?"

"Hold that thought," Adam said. He loped back to his car, reaching through the front window, and returning with what remained of the twelve-pack.

Miranda eyed it apprehensively. "Adam. We're middle-aged."

"And legitimate cocktails are in fifteen minutes," Eve said.

"No excuses," he said, distributing two cans. "It's tradition. On three."

They rolled their eyes, but cracked the beers, flinching at the taste.

"If my sixteen-year-old could see this," Eve said, "he'd have me up on YouTube."

"Jesus, Eve," Adam said. "You have a kid who's sixteen?"

"We *both* do, if you can believe it," she said, and they took turns filling him in on their teenagers, who had survived the past year thanks largely to Xbox and lowered expectations, and were currently at home unsupervised because their fathers had been dragged along for the weekend. "Speak of the devil," Eve said, as the husbands meandered over, absorbed in conversation, outfitted in jeans, baseball caps, Apple Watches. Adam recalled meeting and liking them six years before. "Now if we could just get them to talk to anyone besides each other," Miranda said. By way of greeting, Adam doled out two more cans, like the Pied Piper of cheap beer. They nodded thanks and cracked them without missing a beat.

"And where's your wonderful wife?" Eve asked.

"We love Adam's wife," Miranda reminded the husbands. "She's the sweetest person."

"She is," Adam said. "But she's home. With our boys." As he said it, it occurred to him he'd told Troy a different story; he'd become a habitual liar, if not a particularly smart one.

"Pardon?" Eve said. "Your *who*?"

"God, that's right." Adam rubbed a thumb between his eyebrows. The last reunion would have taken place about a month before Andrea found out she was pregnant. "Zachary and Sam," he said. "They're five."

"*Five*," Eve said, and her face melted as she turned to her husband. "I miss five. Don't you miss five?"

"Enjoy it," he said. "They'll be assholes before you know it."

She punched him in the shoulder and said, "Ignore this man. Over the past year, he's lost all social graces. Not that he had many to begin with."

Miranda was shaking her head slowly. "That must have been so hard. I mean, every age was hard. But *five*."

"It was tough," Adam said. "But Andrea was great with them. She was a preschool teacher, remember." Again, he'd conjured an edited version of the truth, but they nodded along.

"Well, please tell her we wish she was here," Eve said. "And where's Hope? Did she make it?"

"Are you kidding? She wouldn't miss it. She's at the inn."

"Oh, good, same as us," Eve said. "You too?"

"The *inn*? No freaking way," Adam said with a grin. "Dorms, baby."

Eve's eyes widened theatrically. "You're in *Fiske*?"

"Adam, no," Miranda said, but she was smiling.

"We should all be in Fiske!" he said. "You two aren't fully committed. Polly's staying there, too."

"Wait—Polly's *coming*?" Eve asked. "I assumed she was too cool for reunions." She told the husbands, "I'm not being sarcastic. She was literally cooler than the rest of us. Has she ever come back?"

"Not since the five," Adam said. "I didn't think she was coming to this one either. She changed her mind at the last minute."

"Oh, this makes me so happy," Eve said, clasping her hands together.

But Miranda looked wistful. "I get it," she said. "After last year, it feels like we can't take events like this for granted. Who knows when it could all come crashing down again. Nobody wants to miss anything else."

For a beat, no one spoke, the mood turning briefly sober, but this felt right. This, Adam thought, would be the rhythm of this weekend, the highs of being together interrupted by these moments of gravity, acknowledgment of the loss and the strangeness, of what they'd all been through. What they were still going through.

"Sorry," Miranda said, tracing a finger beneath each eye. "I don't mean to be a downer. I keep getting emotional. It just feels so good to be here, you know? To be back in the world," she said, and Adam felt a tightness in his chest, like a held breath, but raised his beer.

"To not missing anything else," he said, and they all solemnly clinked. He drained his can, tucking the carton under one elbow and a gift bag under the other. "I better get over to the dorm," he said. "I hear the best rooms go fast."

"I recommend the second floor," Eve said. "Very quiet radiators."

"And comfortable mattresses," Miranda added.

"More comfortable than the roof?" Eve teased, and as Adam jogged back to his car, she and Miranda were still talking animatedly to the husbands, probably telling them about the time he went missing. He'd disappeared for four days, ultimately passing out on the roof of Fiske and waking up near midnight, in a snowstorm, then clambering down the fire escape to the second floor and finding his way to Polly and Hope. It was the night that sealed his friendship with them. The night that sealed his reputation as fearless, possibly a little nuts, when the rest of the dorm heard the story. This, he thought, was who he'd been in college. That he'd survived four years with no permanent damage to his brain or body was just dumb luck. His old classmates would be surprised by who he was now, the quiet, settled life he lived. Yet being here, Adam felt that younger version of himself awaking, the way the scar across his eyebrow tingled in the cold. Being around these people made him remember the person he had been when he was with them, which was maybe simple logic, but surprised him nonetheless.

Rooms in Fiske were first come, first serve. Adam headed for 114, the room he'd shared with Greg Herman, and found it unclaimed. Not that there was much competition. The building felt deserted. No doubt most members of the class of 1995 were staying in hotels or renting houses out on the water, whether because they were cautious or because they were reasonable middle-aged people who were done sleeping in dorms.

Adam deposited the beer on a desk and the gift bag on the bed and slung his thirty-plus-year-old duffel onto the floor. The room had been seriously upgraded since he and Greg lived there, the nicked wooden furniture and peeling radiators replaced with subtle ceiling ducts, metallic mini-fridges, and ergonomic chairs. Still, he thought, camping wasn't all that far off the mark. A dorm was a dorm was a dorm.

He fished his keychain from his pocket and grabbed an Allagash, then walked over to the open window. That first day, Adam's parents had stood in this very spot, while Greg's parents hopped around the room. Greg's dad had hung up his son's posters—the neon Einstein and the twisting Escher staircases that would mess with Adam's head when he was stoned—while his mom stocked their kitchenette with sodas and homemade cookies. Later that night, he and Greg would roam the campus, getting drunk, and return to polish off every last cookie. But in the room with their parents, they'd both seemed slightly embarrassed, Greg because his were so enthusiastic, and Adam because around other families his lack of closeness with his own felt so exposed. The Hermans attempted to make friendly conversation while Adam's father stood by the window, giving short answers, rattling change in his pocket. His mother barely said a word. They'd left after only twenty minutes. When he watched them drive away, Adam had caught his father's eye in the rearview mirror and given him the finger, not knowing he'd never see him again.

Now all four of those parents were gone. As Adam stood by the window, his heart pounded firmly. He took a long pull of his beer. Outside, a big white tent sprawled in the middle of the quad. In the corner by the chapel, a bouncy castle in primary colors bulged cartoonishly. His boys would have loved it, he thought. Then a happy cry went up under the canopy— the crowd was starting to assemble. Only 6:15, but at this age no one cared about being fashionably late. Hearing the gleeful shrieks and shouts of laughter, Adam felt that old spike of adrenaline again, like the high he used to get from running. Andrea had been right to make him come. He'd needed this. Then he heard a car drive up, the engine accompanied by a blast of music and a raspy muffler. This could only be Polly. Adam peered out the window and, sure enough, saw his old friend parking her beat-up Toyota in one of the spots behind the dorm. She turned the car off, and the music stopped abruptly. But she just sat there, hands frozen on the steering wheel and face hidden behind dark sunglasses, until he opened the window and stuck his head out. "Ma'am, are you lost?"

Polly jumped, looking up, then her shoulders dropped. Adam saw her shake her head: an emphatic and all-purpose no. He grabbed a can and headed for the hallway. By the time he stepped outside, she was leaning against the car's scratched and dented fender. Her arms were folded, a crossbody bag strapped on her chest. "I seriously can't deal with seeing anyone else," she said as Adam wrapped her in a hug.

"It's great to see you, Pol."

"We're hugging," she said. "I remember hugging."

He felt the stiffness in her shoulders, and her face looked tense even behind the glasses. He knew that, for Polly, being here must feel beyond strange. Even for him, the experience was a little surreal—so much had changed for him in the past six years—but for her it had been much longer and was, he knew, more fraught.

"How are you holding up?" Adam said.

"I'm freaking out," she said.

"Fortunately, I have just the thing."

He handed her a Natty Light, which elicited a small smile. "Classy."

"I was going for nostalgic."

She took a wincing sip. "God, that's undrinkable."

"Isn't it?" he said, retrieving her suitcase from the backseat. As he led the way inside, she kept talking in a spiky, anxious staccato. "This is very weird. Isn't it? This was our actual dorm. Our hallway. That was your actual room. I mean—" She paused in the doorway of 114, and let out a short laugh. "Was that your actual *duffel bag*?"

"If it ain't broke, don't fix it," Adam said, tapping his knuckles on the door to 116 and depositing her suitcase inside.

Polly wandered into Adam's room and sat on the edge of the bottom bunk, her bag mashed on her lap and arms wrapped around her knees. "Maybe I'll just hide out in here this weekend," she said.

"That would be sort of anticlimactic."

"I'm alone in a small space." She shrugged. "I'm used to it."

Adam was glad to hear her joke, even if she still seemed on edge. "Hope would kill you," he pointed out.

"Hope would be fine," Polly said. This was far from true, and Polly knew it—Hope would be heartbroken if she didn't show—though Hope was in her element at reunions. She knew everyone, remembered everything about their time there in precise and glowing detail.

"Well, Miranda and Eve would be disappointed," he said. "They were just telling their husbands how cool you were in college."

"Jesus. They were mistaken."

"What?" he said. "You were."

Polly rolled her eyes. "I was attempting to mask the fact that I was deeply ill at ease."

"Well, regardless," he said, "they're psyched you're here," and the fact was, their classmates would be genuinely excited to see Polly. She'd always been hung up on the fact that she wasn't like the average Walthrop student, but that had been part of her appeal.

"Troy was asking for you, too," Adam told her.

"The Gladiator?" she said, with a shudder. "That confirms it. I'm not leaving this room." She picked up the gift bag from the bed beside her and rooted around inside, surfacing with a Walthrop-branded bottle of hand sanitizer, then said, "Hey— weren't you bringing your kids?"

Just like that, regret tugged hard at Adam's lungs, like a cord on a life vest ready to inflate and yank him back home. "They got sick. Nothing serious. Just a stomach bug, but . . ."

"Shit. Sorry." Polly looked at him an extra beat. "So who are they with?"

"Andrea," he said.

"I thought she had a yoga thing."

"Oh—yeah. It got canceled." Another lie, this one entirely pointless.

"I guess she must be doing better, huh?" Polly said.

"She is," he said. "Much better." He wanted to tell Polly the truth, but for now, this was all that he could manage. The rest was too complicated, and he was feeling too good. He took another drink to water down his guilt, and pulled out his phone. "The three of them are having a blast. Breakfast for dinner."

Polly stood and pushed her sunglasses onto her head, to look at the screen. "Which is which again?"

Though the boys were identical, it always amazed Adam when people couldn't tell them apart. Sam, with his freckled nose, like Andrea's. Zachary, with his unruly cowlick, the exact same spot and temperament as Adam's own.

"That's Sam," he said, pointing. "He's the artist. Zachary's a science kid."

"They're so little," she said. "They look so happy."

They did, Adam thought, looking at their smiling faces. He wasn't sure why hearing her say it should make him feel so sad. "I think so, yeah," he said. "And how's Jonah? He's what— eighteen, right?"

She nodded. "Eighteen this past January."

"Same age we were when we met."

"I know. It's insane." Polly rummaged in her bag, dredging up her phone and thumbing through a few photos until she found one: Jonah sitting cross-legged on the floor next to a small Christmas tree, a knotty afghan drawn like a cape around his shoulders. He looked strikingly different than he had when Adam saw him in New York. Older, but thinner. More angular. He'd always resembled Polly, but at twelve, his brown hair had been thick and curly, so dark it looked almost purple. Now it was cut short, with ice pick sideburns. He wore black ear gauges, a guarded smile.

"How is he?" Adam said. "You said he's out on Ledgemere?"

"With a friend, yeah."

"I'm jealous."

"He was really psyched," Polly said, dropping the phone back in her bag. "But this house—Adam, you should have seen it. It was like a Maine McMansion. He hated it. I think he'd been picturing a cabin in the woods or something."

Adam smiled, reminded of himself when he was young. The house he'd grown up in had been formal, uncomfortable, full of quietly carpeted rooms with drawn shades, as if in a perpetual state of bracing for something terrible to happen. Then it had, and after the funeral, his mother was swallowed by her darkened room, and he'd returned home less and less often.

"He looked totally disappointed," Polly said. "And it killed me because he was so looking forward to this trip."

"He'll come around," Adam said. "The island has healing powers."

"That'd be nice," she said.

"Is he still into photography?"

"I think so. I mean—yes. But he quit his classes once they went online."

"Too bad." He remembered how animated Jonah had been when showing him and Andrea his photos, wandering through the museum with his mother, his skinny arm around her shoulders. In her texts last spring, Polly had described the two of them alone in their small apartment, the stress of it, the wailing sirens and frightening statistics. It had been hard everywhere, but in New York City, people had lived through something different.

"He'll get back into it," she said. "He was taking pictures on the drive up. Last year was just too much. He bailed on school, too—I think he technically should have failed some classes. But who can blame him? He was sad. Distracted. Overwhelmed."

"I get it." Adam smiled. "It sounds vaguely familiar, actually."

"Yeah." She smiled back. "Except for the sadness. You were

one of the happiest people I'd ever met," she said, and again, the line hit Adam sideways. Was that who he'd been? Once, Andrea had run a finger along the scar on his eyebrow, the one he got tearing away from his house on his bike at thirteen, and said: *You're not as carefree as people think.*

"Anyway," Polly said. "He came out of it. And fortunately, in art school, admission is based mostly on the art. Now he's mostly angry. He's pissed off, pushing back—though against what exactly, I'm not sure. I'm not sure he's sure."

"Now he sounds like you at eighteen."

"Does he?" She sounded genuinely surprised. "Was I angry?"

"Maybe not angry," he said. "Nonconformist."

"Right. And now my son sees me as a boring middle-aged mom," she said, with a laugh, and Adam felt badly for his old friend. One day, he supposed his boys would pull away from him, too, even if this was impossible to imagine.

"Not that I have any experience parenting teenagers," he said, "but to me that all sounds pretty normal for eighteen. Eighteen and emerging from a global pandemic."

"I think so," she said. "I hope so. Art school will be good for him," she added, just as a gust of celebratory noise rose up on the quad. She wandered over to the window and paused, considering the scene. "Maybe I belonged at an art school."

"Nah," Adam said. "You belonged here."

"I'm not so sure," she said, raking her hand through her hair. "Anyway. He's a great kid. You'd like him."

"I already like him. I met him in New York, remember?"

As soon as the words came out, Polly visibly froze and Adam kicked himself for mentioning that weekend. He hadn't meant to say anything—if Polly wanted to talk about what she'd told him over dinner, he'd let her bring it up—but suddenly it was a presence in the room.

"Shit," he said. "I didn't mean—"

"No, it's okay."

"Sorry."

"Seriously. It's fine."

But she didn't turn from the window, pressing her thumb into the metal tab on her can. Adam wanted to ask if she'd told Jonah. Or ever talked to Hope. Five and a half years ago, in the restaurant, the most shocking part of the story was that Hope didn't know.

Then their phones buzzed in unison, Adam's on the desk and Polly's muffled inside her bag. Without turning, she asked, "What'd Hope say?"

Adam picked up his phone.

Where r u guys?!!!!??

You're missing it!!!!!

Seeing her exuberant punctuation, Adam felt bad for falling so far behind schedule. "She's wondering where we are."

"Tell her I'm still mentally preparing," Polly said.

On our way, he typed, and a red heart popped up beside his message.

Hurry!!! Please!!!!!

"It's almost seven," he said. "We should get out there."

Polly looked at her beer. "Fine. I'll go. Except I'm going to need at least one more of these first," she said, setting her can on the sill. When she turned around, though, her face looked pained. "I'm not sure I can do this, Adam."

"We'll get through it."

"You will," she said.

"If you need to bail, just say the word," Adam told her. "That's my specialty, remember?"

At this, she managed a faint smile. Adam reached for two more beers and pried off the caps. "To being back," he said, handing one to Polly. She looked unconvinced, but raised her bottle, and they clinked, as another wave of cheers swelled on the quad for someone who'd just arrived.

II

SEVEN

HOPE

Even as a child, Hope had prided herself on being skilled at socializing. *Good at small talk*, she'd been told. Her parents, frequent party throwers as well as guests, had stressed the art of conversation—asking questions, filling gaps, taking a strained moment and sanding off its rough edges—but as she approached the tent, Hope stopped at the edge of the quad, overwhelmed.

In the past year, the majority of her social interactions had been with four other mothers, all stay-at-home moms. They volunteered for the same PTO committees, served as block captains and homeroom helpers. When the school district announced a two-week closure, they texted one another, praying it was temporary, and when two weeks turned into three months, they made a standing date, Wednesdays on Zoom.

They convened at nine p.m., when their younger kids were (hopefully) sleeping. At first, they talked almost exclusively about their children, the shock of being cut off from friends and classmates, grandparents and teachers, asthma doctors and dance classes and soccer teams. They worried about the siblings who were constantly fighting, the only children who were alone constantly, the dangers of regression and isolation. They traded concerns about screen time (they used to limit it, but now there was no avoiding it) and the trials of muting and unmuting. They told themselves that, hard as it was, having kids forced you to stay positive. Stay afloat.

They talked about the numbers, which were rising. They worried about their parents, especially those who lived on their own.

They exchanged instructions for disinfecting groceries and making homemade hand sanitizers. Hope described her daily schedule—it helped, they all agreed, to maintain a daily schedule—written on a whiteboard with different colors for schoolwork, snacks, screens. They forwarded think pieces about how these kids would grow up to be adults with greater compassion, who valued things like nature and home cooking and spending time with family. They shared information on where to find the best content for kids—virtual story time with Michelle Obama, those videos of penguins waddling around deserted zoos.

In mid-April, Beth's grandmother got it. Ninety-one, in a nursing home in Delaware. She died three days later. They sent Beth flowers and care packages and attended the live-streamed memorial service.

They told each other: *You can only do what you can do.*

As April seeped into May, they began talking about their hair. About the grays that were overtaking their roots—whether to dye with the cheap drugstore stuff, or attempt one of those professional kits, or take the plunge and just let them grow in. They compared the inexpert haircuts they'd given their sons and husbands and acknowledged the mental health benefits of showering every morning and putting on jeans instead of leggings at least once a week. They commented on the ease of wearing less makeup (maybe they'd always worn too much—really, what was the point?).

They talked about their husbands' jobs. Jen's husband, a dermatologist, was holding telemed appointments. Nicole's advised his clients about their finances by phone. Hope offered that Ethan was under a lot of pressure at the university, transferring an entire history department online, and they responded with sympathetic nods.

When Melissa's daughter turned ten, they all drove by her house, waving and honking. They pinned flags in lawns for their graduating seniors. Beth was the first to break down and order takeout, in celebration of her son Porter's acceptance to Cornell, and described their dinner from Sushi Town like it was a meal in a five-star restaurant.

By then, Hope had more or less abandoned her daily schedule, the color-coded goals making way for simply getting through the day without Rowan melting down, though she didn't talk about this. She didn't like complaining. She remembered the matter-of-fact way her great-grandmother would refer to having lived through the Depression; one day, they'd look back and this would be a thing they had been through.

They reminded themselves: *You can only do what you can do.*

In late May, they saw the video of the white policeman kneeling on the neck of a Black man. It was shocking, watching this man, George Floyd, die. Hope felt an acute awareness of her good fortune, though she wasn't sure what to do with it. They ordered books and made donations. Izzy made a BLM sign for their yard. They showed their little kids the *Sesame Street* Town Hall. They marched through the neighborhood, waving frantically at one another from behind their masks (until Rowan started crying so hard that Hope took him home).

Sometimes, nervously, they laughed about the ways their bodies had started to betray them. Nicole's lower-back pain.

Hope's cracked tooth. The funny high-pitched sound that came and went in Melissa's right ear. Jen reported reading that "hair loss" was the number one Google search.

At the end of the school year, they drove their kids through empty parking lots, waving to their masked teachers. Nicole emailed them a step-by-step guide to building a pandemic time capsule (something Hope could not conceive of doing). In July, they organized small, socially distanced gatherings on decks and in driveways. On sunny days, they went to the pool in timed intervals. On rainy days, they watched *Hamilton*. They discussed whether they were planning summer travel, treading carefully around the subject—*no judgment*! They offered leads on hard-to-find hand weights, Nintendo Switches, inflatable pools.

In general, they didn't talk much about the upcoming election, which Hope didn't mind. She'd been raised by parents who didn't discuss politics with anyone but each other. It wasn't worth damaging friendships over, they said, and Hope agreed. Especially now. All that outrage—where did it go? And she was fairly certain the other mothers were left-leaning (Jen's Mini Cooper still had an Obama sticker from 2008), though on the Main Line, people could surprise you. She wondered about Melissa, who grew quiet if the conversation turned in this direction (once in the lobby after the middle school production of *Little Shop of Horrors*, Hope had heard her husband refer to Hillary Clinton as a *frigid bitch* and quickly excused herself, relieved Izzy hadn't heard).

Then, like that, the new school year was approaching!

Online!

Again!

They debated the pros and cons of learning pods versus cohorts. They swapped recommendations for ergonomic desk chairs, headphones, and blue light glasses. Hope shared the printables she'd downloaded from the Internet and, ignoring Izzy's eye rolls, had clipped onto both kids' workstations: DO YOUR BEST! I'M PROUD OF YOU NO MATTER WHAT! They marveled at how well kids adapted to wearing masks—better than the adults had!

Ethan was still working remotely, putting in fourteen-hour days or longer, his absence increasingly apparent. After one memorably awful evening when Rowan was jumping on the couch, shrieking because he'd burned his tongue on a Pop-Tart, and Ethan just stood up and left the room, Hope googled "parent uninvolved potential impact on child," a fear too embarrassing to admit to the mothers, and almost to herself.

Rowan continued to see Ellen, on the computer, though it was a far cry from her playroom with its trampolines and rope ladders. Still, they practiced breathing. They identified feelings. At home, Hope tried to introduce strategies for regulation. Deep pressure. Kinetic sand. Sensory tubs filled with birdseed and dry macaroni. Izzy chased Rowan around the backyard to help him burn off excess energy. In many ways, she was better with him than her mother was; Hope's eagerness to placate him sometimes made things worse.

Again, Hope didn't discuss this with the other mothers, because it was complicated, and they'd want to know if he had a diagnosis, which was still vague, and anyway, Hope assumed there were plenty of things about their kids all mothers kept to themselves—with the possible exception of Jen, who admitted that her tenth-grade daughter had been caught communicating with a thirty-two-year-old man on Snapchat, and despaired over how to punish her when she couldn't leave the house.

They exchanged strategies for stress reduction. Meditation. Melatonin. Beth raved about Dominique, her instructor on the yoga app. Hope's mental health strategy, she told them, was online shopping (they laughed, though she wasn't actually kidding—often the only thing that settled her nerves was the pressure of her thumb on the lit screen, swiping through sweaters and jeans and outrageously expensive leggings, anticipating the soft thump a few days later when the package landed on her porch).

They talked, always, about their kids. Beth reported that Porter was doing well at Cornell (on-campus, hybrid courses). Izzy was doing well, too, Hope said—straight As! She didn't mention Izzy's weekly appointments with Sandra (that was her daughter's business) or her recently declared ban on Hope posting her photo online. About Rowan she said only that it was a challenge, and they nodded sympathetically, but she didn't feel the need to elaborate on what a hard time he was having (shutting down when called on, rolling on the floor in front of his workstation, chewing on Gray Rabbit while Hope begged him to focus—flash a thumbs-up at his teacher, count fingers, do dance breaks—and plied him with fruit snacks and fidget spinners) or about his intense attachment to Hope (which was understandable, she maintained, given the circumstances) and his refusal to wear a Halloween costume or let her cut his hair or his nails.

Some things were best not shared.

Then they were returning to school—in person!—but only on alternating days, and Izzy's and Rowan's days did not align. Hope drove the kids to and from school to avoid their riding potentially contaminated buses, dragging Rowan with her to drop off and pick up Izzy, and he grew so upset by the constant changes to his routine that he couldn't sleep.

But she didn't like unloading on other people. Compared to many—most—she had it easy.

They repeated: *You can only do what you can do.*

In October, they brainstormed how they'd handle trick-or-treating, finally deciding to set up tables on their yards and sidewalks. Melissa planned to poke Blow Pops into her front yard at six-foot intervals (she'd seen it on Pinterest). The nights were getting chilly, so they bought wood for fire pits, invested in restaurant-quality heat lamps and outdoor movie screens.

Then unbearably, inevitably, the cases were on the rise again. Melissa's husband. Dominique the yoga instructor. Half the JV soccer team. The third grade.

By now, they were talking about the election. Jen wanted to hash out whether to vote by mail or in person. Beth's nerves were so frayed she couldn't sleep. The night after the polls closed, they were still anxiously watching the returns, but a week later they (minus Melissa, who had a sinus headache) raised their glasses in a virtual toast.

Through it all, they didn't talk about their marriages. They talked about their husbands, in affectionately exasperated tones. Jen sighed about her husband's snoring getting louder. Nicole rolled her eyes at her husband's obsessive new fitness regime. Beth claimed hers was now hooked on the yoga app! One Wednesday, her eyes gleaming earnestly, Melissa reported that this time had made her marriage stronger. Hope smiled and sipped her wine. (What she couldn't say was that hearing them talk about their husbands set off an alarm somewhere inside her, a fear that her own marriage might be deeply lacking, because while their grievances were superficial, Ethan seemed not only unappreciative but resentful, in spite of all her efforts, and though they were constantly together she had never felt lonelier, and the sex that had been infrequent had dwindled to nothing, and every day was a tidal wave of small things, an exercise in just-getting-through-it, and Hope felt sometimes that she was skating on the surface of her life and if she looked down the cracks would spider beneath her feet.)

Much of this, maybe even *all* of this, Hope could chalk up to the unnatural way all of them were living. The extraordinary stress all of them were feeling. Besides, despite their worrying, Zoom Moms' Night Out was a generally affirming place: personal but not truly private, and the problems tended to be ones they all had in common. Or could at least understand.

Now, though, standing at the edge of the quad and watching her former classmates greeting one another, Hope missed the mothers, their predictable conversations. Missed being half hidden under a nest of blankets behind a screen. *We're all just out of practice,* she'd told Ashley, and maybe that was why she felt so off-kilter. Or maybe she felt guilty about Rowan, who was having a harder time than she'd expected, or possibly distracted by the furious text she'd shot off to Ethan, unedited, when at 4:42 he still wasn't home. Rowan is upset and Izzy has her appt and I'm in a different state where the hell are you????

She'd steadied herself by imagining Polly's vote of affirmation—*fuck yes, don't hold back, let him have it*—the rush of relief at being with someone who really knew her, hearing her say what her new friends never would.

Except Polly and Adam weren't there. Adam had stopped at the beer store around five fifteen, over an hour ago. He must have made it to the dorm by now. Maybe he'd run into someone on the way, or been delayed by his boys. Polly, God knew, could be anywhere between Maine and New York City. Not that Hope shouldn't be capable of socializing without them. She knew everyone. But she couldn't bring herself to step into the party alone.

"Hope!"

She turned, smiling automatically, focused on the breezy-looking, honey-haired woman waving and advancing in her direction. After all these years, some classmates might require an extra beat of recognition, but Hope knew her instantly: Olivia Haskell-Jones.

"Olivia!" Her smile widened, unsure if they were touching.

Olivia air-hugged her. "You look amazing."

"You too. Really. Exactly the same."

Hope would have said this to anyone, but in this case it was true. Olivia looked lovely, and always had. She was half of what, in their graduating class, constituted a celebrity couple: she'd married Jason Haskell, co-captain of the hockey team. If most college relationships had consisted of hooking up after parties, theirs was the exception. They were the first classmates to get married, a photo from their wedding consuming a full page in the alumni bulletin, a sea of crooked ties, flushed faces, and loosened collars surrounding Jason and Olivia and the Walthrop banner. They'd settled in midcoast Maine, as if in allegiance to the place they'd fallen in love, and had four kids, though looking at Olivia's waistline, you'd never know it. Was it because they'd met in college that neither of them seemed to age? Olivia's skin was smooth, almost dewy. Her shoulder-length hair fell in glossy, careless curls. She was wearing a Walthrop sweatshirt with a peel-and-stick name tag (Hope had completely spaced on getting one at check-in) and the wide-legged jeans that were back in fashion. Hope—who, after hanging up with Rowan and texting with Ethan, had only twenty minutes to get ready, hurriedly choosing a white blouse, gray cardigan, black pants, suede boots—now felt conspicuously dressy. She wondered if, after the past year, to make any sort of obvious effort was somehow unseemly, if despite her thorough packing, her outfit was all wrong.

"Can you believe it?" Olivia asked.

"Honestly, I can't," Hope said. She held her purse against her side, wishing she'd left it back in the room. "I was starting to think it would never happen."

Olivia raised her bottle of pale ale. "I'm so happy I might drink myself into a stupor."

Hope laughed, wishing she had a drink in her hand, too. "Is Jason here?"

"Oh God, yes. He's like a kid on Christmas morning." She pointed toward one of the bars—there were three, Hope noted—where Jason was standing with some old teammates. Drew Bollinger. Chris Constantine. They all looked the same to Hope, just thicker, like she was watching a movie on the wrong setting. "Middle-aged dads," Olivia said. "When exactly did this happen?"

"Beats me," Hope said and laughed again, but it felt odd, as if she were acting the part of herself.

"Well, we can all pretend we're kids again this weekend," Olivia said. "God knows we've earned it. And our actual kids are here somewhere." She gestured airily in the direction of the tent. "What about you?"

"Oh—mine stayed home."

"Very sensible of you," Olivia said. "I mean, things seem better, knock wood, but you can't be too cautious." Then she touched her elbow. "So how did you all get through it? You have two, right? Boy and a girl?"

Hope was impressed. At the last reunion, Rowan was just a

baby. He'd made a few brief appearances, sitting on Hope's hip and gnawing on Gray Rabbit, before he was whisked back to the inn by a former student of Ethan's whom they'd paid to come along and babysit. "Isabel and Rowan," she confirmed. "Eighth grade and kindergarten. Remote, then hybrid."

Olivia gave a commiserating nod.

"My husband works in academia. He was a professor, now a dean. Fully remote all year," she added, with a wince. "How about you?"

This would be the new script, Hope thought, all the routine catch-ups inflected with whatever lucky or unlucky combination of home/school/work/child care everyone had been dealt. She tried to pay attention as Olivia was explaining that both her job and Jason's had gone remote fairly easily (digital marketing, investment banking) and the parents at their kids' private school had pitched in to help fund open-air classrooms in heated huts, which had enabled the students to go back full-time.

Olivia lowered her voice. "Weirdly, it was the most time Jay and I have spent alone since college. Don't tell anyone, but honestly, at times it was kind of . . . great?"

"Oh, I get it," Hope fibbed, and was about to excuse herself to get a glass of wine when a beautiful little girl of ten or eleven, Olivia's youngest, marched over, glittery barrettes pinned haphazardly in her tousled hair. She wore a tutu, jeans, fisherman's sweater, and cowgirl boots, an ensemble that conveyed both her spirited personality and Olivia's laidback parenting style. She ignored Hope, tugging at her mother's sleeve, and Olivia bent to listen. "You'll have to excuse me," Olivia said. "She's spotted the desserts."

"Oh!" Hope smiled. "Perfectly understandable."

"Maybe it's the deprivation of this past year, but I feel like dining services has really outdone themselves. The desserts look even more delectable than usual. To be continued!"

"Yes! Please!" Hope called. She watched Olivia walk off, holding her daughter's hand, and let her eyes wander to the dessert table, which was especially lavish: tiered cupcake stands and chocolate shot glasses, Maine blueberry cobblers and whoopie pies. Beside it, an extravagant raw bar—clams, crab legs, oysters the size of small purses—perched in a rowboat filled with ice. She was starving, Hope realized, but wanted to wait to eat until her friends got there.

She pulled out her phone: 6:52. Where r u guys?!!!!?? You're missing it!!!!! she typed, then kept her eye on the screen. The text right below it was Ethan's response to her angry message, two hours before: home, kids are fine, ordered pizza. Reading it infuriated her all over again. No apology. No mention of his lateness—or her taco casserole. And if their kids were fine, it was because Hope had spent the past hour ensuring they were. Ethan probably thought she was micromanaging things from afar but when her son called her alone and crying, had he left her any choice?

Her phone chirped.

On our way, Adam wrote.

Hurry!!! Please!!!!! she replied, then drew a patient breath. Her friends were coming. They would be there any minute. In the meantime, she could at least attempt to be social—but first, she slipped her phone into her purse and made her way to the closest bar, the one with no line. "Pinot grigio, please," she said to the bartender, an older silver-haired gentleman, one of a handful of masked dining services staff pouring drinks and replenishing food. As he popped a cork out of a bottle, Hope looked for a tip jar—unless tipping would be an insult. Were they not meant to tip at an event like this? Or should they now be tipping more? Hope erred on the side of not offending, giving the man a gracious smile, then scanned the crowd under the tent. Everything about the scene looked slightly strange to her—familiar, yet off by a few degrees. Several of the men had lost more hair, or all of their hair, since the twentieth. One woman had let hers go completely gray. A few were wearing masks, or had them tucked beneath a chin, looped around an ear. Hope spotted Laura Rhodes and her husband—she'd ended up marrying the long-distance boyfriend—and surveyed a group of men on the far side of the tent, raising a phalanx of shot glasses in a toast. A semicircle of broad backs, fleece vests, khaki shorts—was that Mike Grady? At this distance, it was hard to tell. Hope was struck by their sameness. The clothes. The whiteness and affluence.

"Enjoy," said the bartender, and as he handed Hope a clear plastic cup wrapped in a thick Walthrop napkin, she realized she'd been twisting her rings. "Thank you so much," she said. She took a gulp that filled both cheeks. Closing her eyes, she traced the warmth sliding down her throat, the tingling sensation in the backs of her hands. It was on the quad, freshman year, that she'd tentatively sipped her first beer, offered in apology by a drunken upperclassman who had sloshed some of his on her shoe. The taste had shocked her—*this* was the stuff everyone was so desperate to get their hands on, that her sister had consumed so much of that she'd thrown up after prom? It was awful. But Hope smiled, forcing down the watery keg beer, and by Thanksgiving had learned to sort of like it.

A voice behind her said, "Hope Stokes."

This time it took a minute. The man was slight and fit, wearing chinos and an expensive-looking, plum-colored V-neck tee. "Hello!" she said, resisting a glance at his name tag.

He pointed to it. "Keith Hammond."

Hope stared at the tag, then back at his satisfied smile. "Keith? Oh my God!"

Keith Hammond from New Haven had lived in her dorm freshman year, but she hadn't seen him since graduation. He hadn't gone to any previous reunions. In college, he'd been studious and shy, dressed in argyle sweaters, chin tucked into his chest like a gosling.

"I'm so glad you came!" she exclaimed.

"The twenty-fifth." He shrugged. "It felt like a milestone."

Hope nodded vigorously. "I couldn't agree more!"

"This is my husband, Reginald," he said, linking arms with the man beside him. He was strikingly handsome—perfect bone structure and wavy copper-colored hair.

"Oh!" Hope said. She hadn't even realized Keith was gay. "So nice to meet you!"

"Pleasure," Reginald said, touching his elbow to hers.

"This is Hope Stokes." Keith paused. "Or?"

"Richardson."

"Hope Richardson. She lived in my dorm freshman year," Keith said. "At eighteen, she was more mature than the rest of us all put together."

Hope let out a short laugh. "Oh my God, I was plenty immature."

Keith looked pointedly at Reginald. "This woman kept a jar in her room filled with quarters. If anyone needed them to do laundry, which everyone did—because what eighteen-year-old had a bottomless supply of quarters?—they could bring cash to Hope's room and she would trade. Isn't that sweet?"

"I did *not* do that!" Hope protested.

"You *absolutely* did," Keith said, turning back to Reginald. "She was like our dorm mom."

"Oh no, I really wasn't," Hope said, trying to suggest she was deflecting a compliment, but in truth she didn't like this description. It was unflattering and, moreover, inaccurate. She had no memory of a jar of quarters, and it was something she'd remember.

"Refill?" Reginald asked, nodding at Hope's cup.

"Oh, fine for now," she said. "I'm trying to pace myself." As Reginald stepped up to the bar, she turned to Keith and changed the subject from herself. "So tell me about you two. How did you get through it?"

Keith told her that they lived in upstate New York. Keith did something with computers, and Reginald was a writer; they'd both acclimated easily to working from home. Smiling and sipping her wine and commenting at appropriate intervals, Hope started to feel her old self locking in. On weekends, Keith said, they'd taken an online sommelier course. They'd watched their way through all of Hitchcock and Fellini and Sidney Lumet. Frankly, they'd be content never to go back.

"And what about you?" Keith asked.

"Well, my husband's in academia," she said. "A dean. He was remote all year. And my kids were mostly hybrid. I have two. Fourteen and six."

"You must be an amazing mom."

"Oh, I don't know," she said and laughed. "I do my best."

"Well, your children must be stunning. Let me see," he said and held her drink as she dug her phone from her purse and produced the picture she'd teed up for just this purpose: Izzy and Rowan last summer at Barnegat Light. They were sitting on the dunes at sunset, Izzy with her arm around Rowan's shoulders, cheek pressed against his. Rowan had a gap-toothed smile, a nose splashed with freckles, and Izzy looked fresh-faced, pretty. Despite her efforts, her daughter couldn't not look pretty.

Keith shook his head admiringly. "Gorgeous. What did I tell you?"

Reginald returned with two cups, gushed briefly over the picture, then they bid Hope goodbye and drifted toward the crudités, heads bent together like nesting birds. Hope knew they were talking about her. Because that's what you did at a reunion: met people and talked about them. It was easier with a partner, Hope thought, and for an instant wished Ethan were there—but it quickly passed. Remembering his text, she was seized with a fresh wave of indignation.

"Stokes? Is that you?"

This time, Hope didn't wonder for a second who the voice belonged to. She turned toward Mike Grady, features arranged into what she hoped was an expression of bemused surprise. He looked older than he had six years ago, his face lightly weathered, like someone who went sailing on the weekends. Freshman year, he had quickly dropped his polished prep school look, stuffing his dark hair under a filthy Red Sox cap and swapping boat shoes and blazers for Tevas and Patagonia half zips. Now, he was dressed in the same shorts and vest as the scrum of men she'd spotted earlier, the grown-up version of what he'd worn thirty years ago. He had a beard—neatly groomed, glints of silver. Even in this relatively well-preserved group of almost-fifty-year-olds, he looked good.

"Drinking alone?" he asked.

"Just taking a minute," Hope replied.

He put his arms around her, catching her off guard, and for

a moment Hope let herself sink into his chest. He towered over her, as he always had—six two to her five three—and it made her feel small, and she liked this feeling, though in this day and age she probably wasn't supposed to admit it.

"It's good to see you, Stokes," Grady said. "How are you holding up?"

"Oh, you know," she said. "Good. Great."

"That wasn't too convincing."

She shrugged, a twitch of one shoulder. "I'm fine."

"Fine," he said, nodding thoughtfully. "Same here."

The wine she'd already consumed on an empty stomach had left Hope feeling looser. "Is your family here?" she asked.

He peeled one finger from his cup and pointed. "There's the fam right there," he said, and Hope pretended not to recognize them immediately; Grady popped up frequently enough in her suggested contacts on Facebook that she had his profile picture memorized, a shot of himself, his wife, and their two boys standing in the living room of their town house in Boston, dressed for a formal event. Grady and his sons were wearing tuxes, his wife a mermaid gown. Tonight, the boys were draped in baggy sports jerseys, and she wore a black jumpsuit. Hope had met Grady's wife at previous reunions. She'd gone to UVA and was several years younger.

"Beautiful family," Hope said.

"Where's yours?"

"Home," she told him. "I'm flying solo this weekend."

He raised an eyebrow. "Seriously?"

"I know." She shook her head. "Don't ask me how I pulled it off. I haven't had a moment to myself in over a year." She tipped back her cup, the soaked napkin plastered to one side, before realizing it was empty.

Without comment, Grady emptied the rest of his cup into hers. When she took a sip, the sharpness of gin made her eyes water.

He looked at her again, a look with weight behind it. "You sure you're hanging in there, Stokes?"

Hope shrugged again. "It hasn't been easy."

"Yeah," he said. "It's been rough. For sure." He sounded genuinely somber. Hope always tried to avoid complaining, yet standing there with Grady, she found herself wanting to commiserate about how hard the past year had been. To hear it had been hard for him, too. But now he was talking about his management consulting company, how at first business had been shaky but then rebounded. Hope found herself watching his mouth, thinking about the fact that this same mouth had once kissed hers.

Then she noticed he'd stopped talking. He was looking at her with an expression she knew well—a playful half smile, a hint of a dimple—and it sparked an old, familiar rush of pleasure. To be in a crowd, at a party, quietly singled out.

"You look good, Stokes," Grady said, leaning toward her. She could smell his breath, beer and mint. "We look good," he added, and Hope felt a sloppy somersault in her belly. Was he flirting with her? Maybe after all these months she was just reacting to the unexpectedness of another human being standing so close.

Then she heard: "Hope!"

And there they were, Polly and Adam, heading toward her arm in arm. Adam was wearing jeans, a T-shirt, and an untucked plaid button-down, an ensemble that might have been lifted from any decade. Polly's relatively subdued outfit—black jeans and a green sweater—was accessorized with oversized sunglasses and tall black boots. Despite the past year, despite all the years, they were so recognizably themselves that Hope felt sentimental, and a tiny bit jealous. She could tell from the way they leaned into each other that the drinks in their hands weren't their first. It needled her a little—she'd been waiting for them for hours—but she opened her arms as they walked toward her. "About time!"

"Hopey," Adam said, folding her into a giant hug.

"It's Adam's fault we're late," Polly said and pecked her cheek. "He insisted I start drinking this shitty beer the minute I pulled up."

Hope just smiled, letting this roll off her. "I'm so happy to see you."

Adam slung a flannel-covered arm around her shoulders. "Ditto."

"I can't believe it. I mean—can you believe it?"

"I truly can't," Polly said, with a dry laugh.

She might have been the one person whose appearance remained unaltered by the pandemic, looking to Hope exactly as she had eighteen months before in New York. Her face was unlined. She hadn't gained a pound. Her hair had a little more gray, but the gray looked somehow purposeful, in twin sunbursts at her temples. There was something permanently youthful about Polly, her attitude and energy. Maybe it was city living, or staying single all these years; as far as Hope knew, she hadn't dated anyone seriously since Jonah was born.

"This feels fucking weird," Polly said. She faced the quad, hidden behind the sunglasses, one forearm draped across her waist, fingers holding the opposite arm.

"It is," Hope agreed. "I was just talking about that at the inn. How weird it feels."

"Was that Foxy Grady?"

Hope glanced over to the buffet, where he was getting food

with his sons. "That's him," she said. "He looks disturbingly good, doesn't he?"

"Still a fox," Adam said.

"Still a Masshole," Polly said.

Hope chuckled and let this go. Polly had never been a big fan of Grady, knowing him mostly as the guy who rallied the crowd at home hockey games, banging a lobster pot in the stands. For Polly, the games had been an act of endurance. She could never follow what was going on, and was always griping that her toes were cold.

"What's he up to?" Adam said.

"Oh, you know," Hope said. "Beautiful kids. Successful business. Younger wife."

Polly said, "Can we just take a minute to acknowledge that we went to a college where people were called Foxy? And The Gladiator? And this practice was accepted as normal?"

Adam squeezed Hope's shoulder. "You'll have to excuse Polly. She's still adjusting."

"Oh, I know. I get it. I mean, aren't we all!" Hope said. "I was just saying, it's a shock to the system, being expected to socialize again. We're all so out of practice." Then she looked at the empty lawn behind them and said, "Wait! Where are your boys?"

Abruptly, the relaxed smile dropped from Adam's face. "They're sick."

"Oh no!"

"Nothing serious. Just a stomach bug. They're home with Andrea."

"What about her yoga weekend?"

"Canceled," Adam said.

"That's too bad," Hope said. "She must have been disappointed."

"She was," he said, and Hope thought he looked genuinely forlorn. Older, too, and softer around the middle—for Adam, who'd always had the metabolism of a teenager, this was new. His face, though, looked leaner, and a deep wrinkle seamed his brow. Then he smiled, his forehead smoothing over, and asked her, "So how long have you been braving this scene alone, Hopey?"

"Oh, not long." No need to mention the twenty minutes she'd stood immobile on the edge of the quad. "I've barely talked to anybody yet, except Olivia. And Keith Hammond—who looks amazing. And has a husband!"

"Good for Keith," Polly said.

Hope frowned. "He claims I was a *dorm mom*. I wasn't, was I?"

"You did have a first-aid kit," Adam said. Then he straightened up, cupping his mouth and shouting: "Herman!"

Adam's freshman-year roommate was sitting at one of the round café tables, wearing a red fleece and Walthrop baseball cap, looking so much like everybody else you'd have no idea what he'd been through. Last spring, Hope had seen online that both of Greg Herman's parents died in the same week; it was one of the first losses she'd heard about that involved someone she knew personally, and still one of the most tragic. She watched as Adam bounded over and gave him a bear hug, and said to Polly, "Did you hear? About Greg's parents?"

"Adam told me. That's fucking awful."

"Unimaginable," Hope said and paused for a moment to recognize her own good luck: unlike Greg and Adam—and Polly, and many of her classmates—both her parents were still alive and in her life. Then she turned to Polly, just as someone was tiptoeing up behind her friend's shoulder. It was the woman with the striking gray hair Hope had seen earlier. She widened her eyes, as if Polly were an exotic species that might or might not be standing there. "Polly Gesauldi?" she asked, then stepped in front of her and gasped. "You came!"

Up close, Hope realized it was Vicky Lahey, who had been a Spanish major like Polly. Hope recalled a few facts about Vicky from the last reunion: her job was related to immigration. She lived in Arizona. Divorced, no kids. But her primary reaction was to Vicky's hair. It was true gray, the color of steel wool. Though her skin was virtually poreless, and her neck didn't sag even a little, the overall impression she gave was of someone older. If there had been any doubt on Zoom Moms' Night Out that letting your hair go gray aged you ten years, here was the proof.

"I heard it but didn't believe it," Vicky marveled, then said to Hope, "Well done. You finally convinced her."

"It only took twenty-one years!" Hope said.

"God, has it been *that* long?"

Polly said wryly, "Exactly one college-aged self."

"Well, catch me up," Vicky said. "Where are you? Still in New York, I assume."

It was the thing people remembered most about Polly. She was a city person. Freshman year, when most students arrived on campus tanned or freckled, Polly was so pale she might have summered in a cave. She was a practiced smoker, a thrift store shopper. Other girls were dressed in J.Crew and Birkenstocks, but she wore ripped jeans and chunky black boots, and her hair had a single streak of bright blue. Her family sounded like something from a daytime talk show—a mother who had her at eighteen, a father who left when she was three—all of which Hope found fascinating. On move-in day, Hope had waited eagerly for her to get there, and Polly and her mother had shown up late, carrying Polly's belongings in liquor store cardboard boxes, bickering like siblings. When Polly's mother asked where Hope was from, Hope said Philadelphia, though she'd grown up in an exclusive suburb thirty minutes outside.

"Senior year," Polly was saying now. She was talking about Jonah. "Remote. He barely passed his last semester."

Vicky shook her head. "Who can blame him."

"Exactly. He did more or less the entire year in a fifth-floor walk-up."

Hope nodded, trying to be supportive, picturing Polly's apartment, the same one she'd shared with her mother grow-ing up. Hope had gone to visit several times after Jonah was born; she'd take the train up for the day, bringing adorable little outfits, baby-sized jeans and rollneck sweaters. But the reality wasn't that adorable. It was kind of shocking, this tiny purple being screaming from a crib in the corner of Polly's bedroom or strapped to her chest while they wandered the neighborhood inhaling iced coffees and slices of pizza. Sometimes Hope spent most of her visit holding the baby while Polly slept. Back home, she'd describe these trips to Ethan, feeling relieved that their life was not so complicated and slightly giddy because they were talking about babies, even if someone else's, which was a little like being guests at a wedding, imagining it might be them one day, but different.

"He's here, actually," Polly said. "Visiting a friend out on Ledgemere Island. I wasn't coming but he talked me into it."

Hope couldn't help feeling a little hurt by this, but Vicky said, "Hey, whatever it takes."

"He's going to art school in the fall," Polly continued. He was a photographer, she said. An environmentalist. A socialist, too, apparently.

"Good for him," Vicky said approvingly. "That's the kind of engagement we need from his generation. We're counting on them. We can't get complacent. I'm still recovering from the trauma of the past four years," she added, and then they veered into talking about the election deniers. The attack on the Capitol. The border wall. Hope glanced around the quad in search of a lighter conversation. It wasn't that these things weren't important, but it was their reunion. She didn't want to talk about politics. About trauma. She located Adam, still talking to Greg Herman; they'd been joined by Abby Archer, a fellow runner whom Adam had dated junior year. Olivia's daughter was skipping around the dessert table, holding a black-and-white cookie the size of a small Frisbee, nearly crashing into Eve and Miranda from Fiske. Their room had been down the hall from Hope and Polly's; they now lived in neighboring Boston suburbs where—according to Miranda's Instagram feed, a chronicle of joint barbecues and rainy movie nights—their families were best friends and constant companions. Once upon a time Hope had fantasized that she and Polly would live like this.

"And Hope!" Vicky said. "Tell me all about you."

She collected herself and smiled as she offered up her pandemic stats. Husband, virtual, professor and dean. Son and daughter, K and eighth, hybrid.

Vicky expelled a sigh. "Two kids. I can't imagine."

"It wasn't easy. But we got through it."

"And you could work remotely?"

Hope missed only a beat. At home, no one would make this assumption, but in this crowd, it was plausible that her not working wouldn't even occur to them. "I'm a full-time mom," she said. "For now, at least. My son is still so young."

"Of course," Vicky said. Hope didn't make eye contact with

Polly, who knew she'd put her career on hold when Izzy was born. Not that it had been Hope's original plan. She was going to take a six-month maternity leave, but when the time came to return to the PR firm, she didn't feel ready. Izzy was still a baby. And she liked her new lifestyle more than she'd expected—taking Izzy to the Mommy & Me music classes and swim lessons and getting to know the other mothers on the playground circuit—so when her parents offered to help financially, she accepted, throwing herself even more energetically into the role. She initiated group playdates and organized preschool fundraisers, resolving that if she wasn't working, she would do an extra-good job at everything else. A year later, she was ready to have another baby, but Ethan convinced her to wait a little. He was coming up for tenure; he needed to finish the book. By the time they started trying in earnest, Izzy was three; six months later, Hope started to worry. They saw a fertility specialist and moved right to intervention, ultimately doing six rounds of IVF (it never once occurring to Hope they wouldn't keep trying, because even if it wasn't working, according to the tests there was no reason it *couldn't* work, except she was now almost forty—still fertile, though clinically geriatric—and because her parents were paying for it and now that they'd come that far, how could they stop? And what if they had, and had never known Rowan?).

"I have no clue how working parents managed the past year," Hope said. "We got off easy. And my daughter is very self-sufficient. You know they say some kids actually thrived without all the pressures of going to in-person school every day?" she said, then hoped this hadn't sounded insensitive, given how Jonah struggled. "My son had a harder time," she added, glancing at Polly, but with her face half hidden by her sunglasses, Hope wasn't sure she'd even heard.

"Well," Vicky said. "My hat's off to both of you. I'm a childless single lady, and I am so damn drained—though *drained* doesn't begin to cover it." She appealed to Polly. "What's the word? You're the English teacher."

"Depleted?" Polly said. "Embattled? Haunted?"

Hope shook her head sympathetically. "You can only do what you can do," she said.

Then Vicky excused herself, and Hope readied herself for whatever Polly might say—something about Hope implying her not working was a temporary situation—but she seemed distracted by something across the quad. Hope finished the last drop in her cup and announced, "I need another drink. And something to eat. The food looks so amazing. But first, a refill. Let's go, shall we?"

"Give me just a minute," Polly said, pulling her phone from her back pocket. "I just want to check in with Jonah."

"Oh, sure," Hope said, nodding. Already her head was lightly swimming. "Just don't get sucked in. I was on the phone with Rowan for an hour."

"Really?" Polly looked up, eyebrows raised, and Hope realized this had sounded strange. "Is he okay?"

"Oh, he's fine," Hope said. "It's just, you know, an adjustment. I haven't been away from him for more than a few hours in . . . well, ever."

"I figured you would bring them," Polly said, returning to her phone.

"I thought about it," Hope said. "And who knows. Maybe I should have. But Ethan doesn't love reunions, and he wanted to work on his book this weekend—remember the book? He wasn't thrilled about me leaving. To be honest, though, I wanted to come alone." Admitting it, Hope felt another twinge of guilt, yet as she looked at Polly, she realized what she wanted was a response—for Polly to pick up on her frustration, get offended on her behalf.

But Polly said only, "Everybody needs a change of scenery. Jonah needed a break, too."

"Right," Hope said, disappointed. What she'd said had barely registered, like tapping one foot and imagining she was dancing.

"He really wanted to visit this camp friend."

"Yes," Hope said. "You mentioned that."

"They haven't seen each other in years," Polly went on. "But I think it will be good for him. To reconnect with an old friend."

"I'm sure," Hope said. If there was hurt in her voice, Polly didn't catch it. As she sank her gaze into her cup, Hope was overcome with sadness. Tears swelled behind her eyes, and she opened them as wide as she could, her old trick to keep from crying. For ten seconds, she didn't blink, and the tears subsided, and Hope smiled. There was no reason to feel sad. That was silly, wasted energy. They were all together; they were all, finally, here.

EIGHT

POLLY

If Adam hadn't spotted her from the window of Fiske, Polly might have turned the car around and left. From the minute she saw the sign welcoming her to Sewall, the knot had returned to her stomach. In the dorm with Adam and his jokes and his cheap beer, being on campus had felt tolerable, but out on the quad, Polly felt vulnerable. Thin-skinned. She sat on the steps of the library, trying to relax. She knew she was being prickly—Hope had been giving her funny looks, Adam making excuses for her—but couldn't help it. She was wishing she hadn't come. Wishing she'd told Jonah they weren't going, or found somewhere to stay out on the island. The thought of Jonah having a good time was the only thing keeping her grounded. She wanted to talk to him, but didn't want him to feel she was hovering over his shoulder.

Instead, she texted: Having fun?

Alone, clutching her phone, Polly looked up at the campus. The sky was a pinkish gray, with a pale wedge of moon. In the past twenty-one years, many of the buildings had been upgraded, and some were brand-new, more glass and curves than brick and corners. Thompson Hall, though, looked exactly the same. A monument to the past, a platonic ideal of a campus building: four stories of red brick with a web of ivy clinging to one side. On the facade were three stained glass windows, a detail featured on all the college literature. McFadden's office had sat behind the one in the middle. It materialized, unbidden, in her mind's eye: the sagging tan couch, two straight-backed wooden chairs, the dying plants with crispy leaves. The entire office had been shades of brown, except for the dusty sunbeams that spilled through the stained glass, an intricate puzzle of red and blue shapes that blurred into a puddle of rainbowed light on the floor.

The pain in her stomach was worsening. She knew Hope was waiting for her by the bar, but Polly couldn't move. She closed her eyes, attempting to recall her strategy for getting through the weekend. Laughable, to think she'd believed she could simply put the past out of her mind, shove it into a box and close the lid. At a reunion, there was no forgetting the past. The past was the point.

Her first visit to his office was fall of sophomore year. She was majoring in Romance languages but took one of his classes as an elective—Topics in Modern Literature: Daredevils and Dissidents. Only once it started did Polly realize the literature was from the early twentieth century. She hadn't read the course description carefully; she'd assumed it would be modern. But none of her peers seemed surprised, if their ease in the classroom was any indication. They raised their hands to offer confident opinions on the readings and their rejection of traditional forms. Polly never spoke in class, not because she had nothing to say (turned out she liked modernist literature, which was pretty weird and experimental) but because to hold her hand in the air felt too exposed. She was not shocked when her first essay came back with no grade, only a note in neat ink at the bottom: *Can we talk?*

In high school, a summons had never been a good thing; it meant Polly had screwed up. She was cutting class or getting drunk on the loading dock behind the art room or scoring so well on the standardized tests that it was clear she was falling short of her potential (for that one, Diane had been there, playing the part of the concerned parent, clutching her house key so tightly Polly could see the point digging into her palm). The one exception had been the meeting with her Spanish teacher, Senora Silva. Silva wore jeans and blazers and oversized beaded earrings, and Polly couldn't help liking her. Still, when Silva claimed she saw promise in her, Polly was instantly distrustful. *I was late for your midterm. I'm not that promising*, she replied. It was a tactic she'd employed with moderate success throughout high school: announce herself as a fuckup, so by owning it she could prevent feeling embarrassed when it proved true. A year later, she'd adopt a similar approach when showing up to college in her combat boots, leather jacket, blue-streaked hair—she was so worried she wouldn't fit in that she made sure she didn't.

Silva was unmoved. She asked about Polly's plans for the future (Polly had avoided giving it much thought) and said she pictured her at a college outside the city. Smaller classes, fewer distractions, strong programs in the liberal arts. She mentioned schools Polly was sure were reaches, but Silva felt a smart admissions team would *see the bigger picture*. As Polly listened, she tried to figure out why this teacher cared—she'd heard about her mother and felt sorry for her? She was trying to fill her annual quota for helping girls who secretly liked to read and reminded her of her own young, troubled self? In the end, it didn't matter; it was the first time Polly had considered going away to school, and the hope this awoke in her was almost too much to bear. Eight months later, when she was accepted to a small, competitive college in New England, she chalked it up to Silva's letter of recommendation (and her surprisingly high SATs).

But when she arrived at Walthrop, Polly felt like the imposter she'd known she would be. Most freshmen seemed to have already taken a seminar in college living. Many of them had gone to elite high schools, and come equipped with mental rolodexes of upperclassmen—friends' older siblings, fellow private school alums—who would help facilitate their entry into campus culture. Polly, meanwhile, tried to cultivate an air of ironic detachment. She resisted her roommate's efforts to befriend her (fearing they were based in charity, or pity) and wore her leather jacket even when the temperatures dipped below freezing. But to her own surprise, by second semester Polly had found a tentative life forming around her, thanks to Hope's refusal to take no for an answer and Adam's crashing into their room one night and mistaking it for his. Still, when a professor asked to see her, she assumed the gig was up.

"Am I flunking?" she asked after exchanging pleasantries.

Professor McFadden leaned back in his desk chair, arms across his chest and hands tucked into his armpits. "Why would you think that?"

Polly occupied one of the hard wooden chairs, backpack strapped to both shoulders. Her hands, freighted with cheap silver rings, remained knotted in her lap. "I guess, for one thing, I don't participate in class," she said.

"I've noticed that," he said. "Have you done the reading?"

"Yes," she said. "All of it."

"Just not a talker?"

"Actually, I am." She licked her lips, which were constantly dry from the drugstore lipstick she wore. "I'm just not that interested, I guess."

It was like a solo game of chicken: dare herself to say a thing, then follow through with it, even if what she said was obnoxious or untrue. But Polly was no longer in high school, where rudeness was viewed with a modicum more compassion, or at least consideration of what might be behind it, the absence of role models or lack of parental support. This was college. For a moment, Polly let herself imagine Hope's horror. She'd never speak this way to a professor; Polly felt certain no Walthrop student would. Walthrop students tended to be polite and polished (though those same students could be disgusting on a Saturday night).

McFadden, though, looked more amused than offended. "I see," he said. "Anything else?"

"I know my essay's bad."

"Is it?"

"I assume so. I didn't even get a grade on it," she said, before adding, "Not that I care about grades."

She didn't, in theory, though she had to care a little, because she needed to maintain a minimum 2.0 GPA to receive financial aid.

"To not care about grades," McFadden said. "That's refreshing. Not many students here feel that way." He ran a palm over his head, a shiny bald spot surrounded by unkempt curls. "But your essay isn't ungraded because it's bad. It's just inconclusive. It has no thesis," he said, then paused, maybe sensing that Polly didn't know exactly what a thesis was, which she didn't. "It needs to pose an argument. Take a position."

"Right," Polly said. "Well. I wrote it in like an hour." She said this to save face, then worried it only made her look careless. And it was far from true.

"Here's the thing," McFadden said and leaned forward, propping his elbows on the desk. He picked up a paper clip from the blotter and began untwisting it. "The ideas are all over the place. But they're interesting. Between you and me, they're some of the more interesting ideas I've seen in this class. And I'd rather an essay be messy and interesting than polished and boring, wouldn't you?"

Polly laughed, to drown out her heart's nervous ticking. She wondered if this was a trick question. She thought of Hope's B-minus on McFadden's twentieth-century lit midterm, fall of freshman year; it was the only grade below an A she'd gotten since middle school.

"Tell you what," he said, peering at the clip, which was now unwound completely, straight as a dart. "Take another week. Rewrite it and bring it back," he said, then pitched the clip onto his cluttered desk and sat back in his chair. He turned to gaze at the stained glass window, face folding into a contemplative expression. It was a look Polly recognized from class, when he'd sometimes stop midlecture and squint into the middle distance, as if searching for the perfect sentence. It would have struck her as performative if he hadn't looked so silly doing it, eyes scrunched and mouth slightly agape. Finally, he turned back to her and said, "You can teach a student to write a better sentence. You can't teach them to be a more interesting person." Then he smiled, and she smiled back, as if touched by some current of secret understanding. "I think you're an interesting person," he said.

* * *

Physically, he was awkward, tall and ungainly. He was a comically bad dresser, his signature look being ill-fitting wool sweaters and corduroys that stopped an inch above his ankles. His age was indeterminate—pre-Internet, this kind of information was not readily available. Polly thought he could be anywhere between twenty-eight and forty-two. He wore a plain silver wedding band above a hairy knuckle. The single decoration in his office was a drawing of a stick-figure mom, dad, and little girl in a field of flowers. His shoulders were prematurely round, probably from hunching over books. The combined effect, she thought, was that of a person unconcerned with the meaningless bullshit of the material world.

During office hours, McFadden read her revised essay, dinging her overstuffed paragraphs but praising her thoughts on first-person narration. Mostly, though, he wanted to talk about literature. He was dismayed by how little Polly had read in high school (even though she'd read all the time in high school) and loaned her copies of titles by authors he deemed important. Orwell. Dostoyevsky. Books that asked questions, he said, that challenged the status quo. Polly devoured each one, trying not to wrinkle or to spill coffee on the pages, and returned it the following week. If she was quiet in class, she was brimming with opinions in McFadden's office. Polly grew to love that office. She loved the lumpy couch and the stupidly uncomfortable chairs. Loved the disordered mess of papers and the drafty window and the smells of coffee and sweet, moldering book pages. Sometimes McFadden made them tea with an electric kettle. Other times, they walked laps around the quad. They made an unlikely duo, Polly with her blue-streaked hair and fingerless gloves and clipped city stride, McFadden in his hiking boots and knit caps and baggy sweaters. He said the cold helped him think.

"What do you even talk about?" Hope asked. Second semester, sophomore year: another freezing February afternoon. Polly had again underestimated just how cold Maine winters could be. Their radiator clanged like it was being hammered from inside with pickaxes, and their windows were webbed with frost. She had a paper due the next day for McFadden, but it was too cold to walk to the library. Fortunately, Hope had her own computer and was generous about letting Polly use it; she'd traded in her old square Mac for a sleek new PowerBook. It looked vaguely futuristic, like a compact suitcase.

Adam was in Hope's papasan chair, munching on the Smartfood she kept in constant supply. He had an off-campus apartment with some other runners but was constantly in the girls' room, snacking, ostensibly studying.

"What do you mean," Polly replied, "what do we *even* talk about?"

Hope was applying her makeup in the round mirror on her dresser, the kind that enlarged your pores to look like moon craters. She was getting ready to brave the snow for the dining hall; she didn't like missing meals, either the socializing or the food. "I'm just curious," she said.

"But I mean, why *even*? It's like you find it hard to believe we have things to talk about."

"Obviously that isn't what I meant," Hope said. She was sweeping mascara onto her lashes, blotting half off with a tissue after each coat. The overall effect of Hope's makeup was extremely subtle, but the process of achieving this took ten times as long as Polly's: two slashes of lipstick, bright red or bold red, depending on her mood. "I'm literally just wondering. I know you can hold your own with Professor McFadden. Of *course*."

It was one of Hope's best and worst qualities: she was always so affirming. If Polly made a self-deprecating remark, Hope would enumerate her strengths until it grew so torturous that Polly begged her to stop.

"I don't know," Polly said, blowing her nose. She always had a cold. "I mean—books. Ideas."

"Ideas?" Hope said, sounding skeptical. "Like?"

"Death, life, art," Polly tossed off. "Literature that challenges the status quo."

Hope frowned. She had little patience for abstractions, and little interest in challenging the status quo. "I just don't really get it," she said with an apologetic wince. "Honestly, he sounds a teeny tiny bit like Marcus."

Adam let out a low whistle. "Ouch."

"Oh my God, Hope, that was completely different," Polly said. In her three semesters of college, Polly had hooked up with numerous guys and felt no shame around this. There were only two encounters that she truly regretted, and the first of those was with Marcus. He was a music major who made her dark, creepy mixtapes. He showed up at their room one night, tripping on mushrooms and rambling about his art. For Polly, this kind of thing was not so unusual. She tended to attract drama— on some level, even liked it. Plus, in the nineties, angst was fashionable: grunge music, ripped jeans, and long, moody conversations over cigarettes and burnt coffee. True disaster hadn't yet touched their generation; the world still felt hopeful, trusting, naively invulnerable. Later on, that would all change permanently, but in the meantime, they had the luxury of manufacturing angst themselves.

But Hope was too upbeat, and too practical, to sit around marinating in her own juices. She rejected the very premise of ripped jeans. She'd come to college with an ironing board and half a dozen blouses sheathed in plastic. She was an achiever, an English and econ double major, and made no attempt to hide her hard work. Polly attributed Hope's confidence to her parents, who were relentlessly positive. They thought Hope could do anything, and Hope moved through life with the expectation that it would all work out the way she wanted; Polly, on the other hand, never let herself expect too much. She preferred not caring: it made life easier, and in the nineties, it was a valid way of being. It also attracted guys like Marcus, whom Hope had correctly called out for being pretentious, making the comparison to McFadden all the more unflattering.

"Marcus was a poseur," Polly acknowledged. "But McFadden is a serious intellectual." She appealed to Adam, whom she'd convinced to take his Politics and Literature course that semester. "You like him, don't you?"

"Sure," he said. "I like him."

"Does that mean a whole lot, though?" Hope said, leaning into the mirror and tracing her top lids with eyeliner. "Adam likes everyone."

He lobbed a piece of popcorn at her from across the room, then said, "Wait. I do?"

"It's a good thing," Hope assured him. She widened her eyes, erasing a speck from the corner with a Q-tip. "And I'm not trying to be critical—"

Polly let out a laugh. "You kind of are, actually."

"It's just that you spend a lot of time with him," Hope said, then added more gently, "and you might not have the best judgment in this department." Polly knew this was a reference to her father, who'd shown up at the dorm the previous semester, unannounced, wanting to have dinner. Polly hadn't heard from him in three years; she assumed he needed money. Hope, upon seeing the expression on Polly's face, had smoothly invited herself along. They'd gone to Szechuan Star, where Hope grilled him with friendly questions about where he was living and whether it was his first time in Maine and what Polly had been like as a kid, which had apparently so disarmed him that he took off without asking for a cent.

Since then, Hope had repeatedly invoked Polly's father as the root of her ill-advised relationship choices. She'd latched on to this logic almost excitedly, as if she'd never before considered the ways in which parents can fuck up their children. "McFadden isn't some kind of pseudo-father figure," Polly said, defensive. "We have intense conversations. He respects my opinions. He thinks I'm an interesting person," she added, then wished she hadn't. It had felt special when McFadden said it, but now sounded embarrassing. She blurted, "You're just bitter about the B-minus."

It came out more harshly than she'd intended. She saw Hope's smile falter. The day of the B-minus, Polly had found her collapsed on her desk, sobbing, her disappointment in herself so palpable it felt radioactive. If Hope wanted Polly to live more carefully, Polly had declared it her mission to make Hope care less.

But Hope shrugged, quickly recovering her composure, and returned to the mirror. "Maybe I am," she said. "I was just looking out for you." Then she went quiet, which only made Polly feel worse; Hope never stopped talking. And it wasn't like she hadn't given Hope reason to think she needed looking out for. Polly's second regret had been a guy she met in Rusty's, in whose studio apartment she'd woken up with no memory of how she got there—a man with thin muscled arms, a bearded neck, a cup of brown dip spit beside the bed. Polly had thrown on her clothes and crept out of his apartment then run through town to call Hope from the phone booth in front of the 7-Eleven. Two weeks later, Hope had walked her to the campus health center to get tested, sat beside her in the waiting room, and squeezed her hand.

It was Adam who broke the tension. "Hope can't help being protective," he said. "Don't forget, she's forty-five."

At this, both young women smiled. The previous semester, when Adam was majoring in psychology—after declaring biology and before finding his way to environmental studies—he'd had them take a questionnaire about their subjective age. *Name the age at which your inner and outer selves will be perfectly aligned.* Hope's age was easy. *Forty-five*, Polly said. They all agreed. Hope was undeniably a middle-aged woman in the body of a college sophomore. Adam's age was relatively simple too: late teens. *That means I'm perfectly aligned right now*, he said, and Polly thought that tracked. Despite his miserable childhood, his father dying freshman year, Adam was one of the most happy-go-lucky people she'd ever met.

Polly's age had not been so obvious. Adam guessed thirty-five, which was a non-guess: not young, not old. Hope thought thirteen, which felt insulting. But Polly had no idea either, which bothered her, suggested something about her that was unfinished.

"Correct," Hope said, capped her mascara, and smiled into the mirror. "I'm older and wiser than both of you. Now let's go eat."

She didn't recall having a crush on McFadden. Maybe she'd had a crush on the idea of McFadden: a brilliant professor, a respected mentor who took an interest in what she had to say. Yes, they spent a lot of time together, but was that so different from Senora Silva staying after school to help Polly with her college applications? Besides, in the nineties, professors' lives were far more enmeshed with students'. Though political correctness had arrived on Walthrop's campus, and language was under scrutiny— a trend McFadden was deeply and vocally against, arguing in a letter to the school paper that this stifled free expression—in other ways there were few boundaries. Professors hosted dinners at their houses, got drunk at campus happy hours. There were no harassment trainings, Title IX coordinators, open-door policies; the sensitive scaffolding universities would have in place three decades later had not yet been built.

At the end of sophomore year, McFadden tipped off Polly to a work-study job opening up in Thompson. She applied for and got it, no doubt because he'd put in a good word. Starting that fall, for fifteen hours a week, she would sort professors' mail and make and staple copies—a vast improvement over her original, far-too-public-facing work study at the campus store. The only person she had to chat with here was Linda, the department secretary, who kept a jar of hard candies on her desk, the ones with the wrappers that looked like strawberries. When her shifts were over, Polly would stop by McFadden's office, fingers inky from wrestling with the Xerox machine, and they would talk—about books he loaned her, and her other classes (mostly in the Spanish Department, though she'd picked up an English minor), and his other students (he usually refrained from using names, but in general found them diligent yet dull). For Polly, these visits were an escape, a validation, a refuge from the hockey games and frat parties that she tolerated but most everyone else seemed to love.

And if Hope still had objections, she didn't voice them; possibly she was too preoccupied with Mike Grady, a frat guy she frequently hooked up with on Saturday nights. Polly didn't like him—not, as Hope assumed, because he was a frat guy nicknamed "Foxy," but because around him Hope became jarringly insecure. She worried constantly about whether he liked her, convinced herself there was something more between them than drunken hookups on weekends. Later, Polly would think that if they'd been able to combine her own confidence around the opposite sex, and Hope's confidence around everything else, they might have created one fully confident young woman.

Spring of senior year, McFadden proposed an independent study: essentially, a DIY semester of reading, talking, and taking walks. It wasn't unlike what Polly did already, but this time for academic credit. One afternoon in March, they were circling the quad when McFadden raised the subject of her plans after graduation. "No clue," she said, pushing her hands into the pockets of her jacket. "I guess I should figure that out."

It was a topic Polly had been deliberately ignoring. Though after three-plus years at Walthrop she still never quite felt she belonged, the prospect of leaving had her feeling unmoored. Other people's next steps seemed to be materializing before them.

Hope had been offered an entry-level position at a PR firm back in Philadelphia; she would be doing content marketing, a job Polly didn't understand (a trend that would continue into her adult life). Even Adam, in no rush to figure out a career, had found a container for his planlessness: he was going to spend the year on a trail crew at Acadia National Park. Polly felt disorganized, directionless, except for the results of her required mock interview with Career Services, which revealed she said "like" too often and moved her hands too much.

"You should go to grad school," McFadden said from inside his big hairy-hooded parka. "You belong among smart people engaging with books."

She laughed. "Right."

"I'm serious. Some of the deadlines have passed, but not all. There's still time to apply."

"I'm not going to grad school," Polly said, balling her fists in her pockets, which were filled with damp, linty tissues.

McFadden stopped in front of the student union; it had opened that fall, a brand-new building with pool tables and a coffee bar. His breaths were coming in short white puffs. "Why not?"

Because she didn't believe she'd get in, Polly thought. Because she didn't think she'd fit there if she did get in. It wasn't rational, not anymore, but still felt true.

But McFadden misread the reason for her silence. "There's tuition assistance, if that's your concern," he said.

"No," Polly said. "It isn't." She felt her face flush despite the cold. They had never discussed her financial situation, but she realized then it had been obvious all along.

So she applied, and McFadden wrote her a recommendation letter. As a thank-you gift, she bought him a bright blue throw pillow for his dull brown office. He made her promise to keep in touch.

Five years later, when Hope informed her their reunion was coming up, Polly balked at going. She recalled when her mother turned forty and called it a *take-stock event*: a chance to step back, look honestly at your life, and see how you were doing. It was a dangerous premise that, for Diane, had spiraled into an ugly evening. A reunion was a *take-stock event*, too, Polly thought. Five years after college, she was still living in Queens with her Craigslist roommates. She'd finished grad school (she'd gotten into two programs and chosen the one that offered a better financial package) and was teaching freshman comp at a community college, three or four or sometimes five sections of ESL classes a semester, but still struggling to make ends meet. She had no health insurance, not to mention dental or vision. She got good student evaluations, and this had led to more classes, and it was in this way that she'd found herself as a college instructor: not so much a plan as a series of happenings that became her life.

Then, two weeks before the reunion, she got an email from McFadden, her first ever. When Polly graduated, the Internet had only started infiltrating campus. He wrote that it'd crossed his mind her reunion was approaching, and would she be attending? He'd love to catch up. She replied that she was, and proposed Saturday morning.

He emailed back almost immediately: *Coffee shop at 10?*

Hope was annoyed that Polly was bailing on the Saturday brunch, since she'd gotten to campus late on Friday, and missed half the opening-night party. Polly didn't point out that she hadn't arrived late on purpose; it didn't occur to Hope that she'd had to take the cheapest bus from New York, or that the fee to attend the reunion was in itself more than she could afford. It was just one more way her life felt out of sync with those of her classmates—not a new feeling, but five years into adult life, the disconnect was confirmed. Even the people who in college had been dedicated slackers now seemed to have their shit together. They had MBAs and law degrees, high-paying jobs in finance and tech. Polly recognized this as a decision (for graduates of a school like Walthrop, you could choose to become a rich person), but it didn't make her feel any less different.

It was a relief to step away from the festivities and see Mc-Fadden. She arrived early to the Coffee Barn, dressed in the Doc Martens and baggy low-rise jeans she still wore almost every day. She rubbed her knuckles back and forth above her ear; the week before, she'd shaved one side of her head and had grown addicted to the feeling of shorn hair against her skin.

She saw McFadden before he saw her. He was wearing one of his slouchy sweaters and looking around the shop, neck swiveling, eyebrows perched high on his forehead. They'd never met off-campus; was that why he looked different? Or was it that he seemed older, more eager and more disheveled? She felt a little embarrassed for him. When he spotted her, his brows sank back down.

"Polly," he said, walking over and leaning in for a quick hug. "It's really good to see you."

"Same."

He tilted his head to one side. "I like the hair."

"Thanks. It's new." She touched her fuzzy head, suddenly self-conscious. "I'm still getting used to it."

"It suits you," he said and smiled. "It's a beautiful day. Should we walk?"

The day was truly perfect, the kind of fall day that was probably the reason people moved to Maine. The leaves were vivid reds and yellows, the air crisp, the sky a saturated blue. As they wandered through town, sipping their coffees, Polly told him about the first night of the reunion. *Unlike me, these people are like legitimate adults*, she said. Two of them were married. One had patented some kind of computer software. When McFadden said he'd rather hear about her, she described her life in New York, teasing out the good parts. Her favorite local bookstore. Her reputation in the English Department for being able to fix the copier—that work-study gig had paid off! The books she'd been loving, her obsession with Zadie Smith's *White Teeth*. Her students, who were genuinely amazing, most of them "nontrads" with jobs and kids and actual lives.

When they stopped by the marble archway, she realized they'd been walking for close to two hours. "I've been doing all the talking," she said.

"As it should be," he said. "Your life is far more interesting than mine."

"You like that word," Polly said. "*Interesting*."

McFadden frowned. "That can't be true."

"The first time I met you in your office, that's what you called me," she said.

"Well." He paused. "Was I wrong?"

Polly felt a sharp sadness then, something like longing, and looked toward the quad. Under the changing leaves, her classmates were drinking craft beers and tossing Frisbees, in what could have been a scene from a movie about college. When she turned back to McFadden, prepared to say goodbye, she found him watching her with a cryptic smile.

"What?" she said.

"I envy you," he said.

"No, you don't." She laughed. "I'm teaching five classes and can barely pay my rent."

"But your life is exciting and full of possibility."

She rolled her eyes. "Believe me, it's not that exciting."

"Polly. You're young and living in the greatest city in the world. That's exciting, even though it may not seem it." He ran a hand over the top of his head, now mostly bald, and smiled faintly. "I always meant to live in New York."

"So live in New York," Polly said. She was testing a new tone with him—blunt, slightly irreverent—but he didn't seem fazed.

"As you get older, life gets more complicated," he said.

"Okay," she dared. "Just how old *are* you?"

"That's a terrible thing to ask a person." He grimaced. "How old do you think I am?"

"*That's* a terrible thing to ask a person," she said, but took an honest guess. "Forty-three."

"Forty-six."

"That's not old," she said, though it did seem kind of old. Mc-Fadden was older than her mother. Older than Hope's subjective self. "Who cares? Age is irrelevant."

He smiled wistfully. "If only that were true."

The next email, in late summer, came from an AOL address, with the subject line: *hi*. When Polly clicked on it, she felt a smile spread over her face. McFadden said he'd enjoyed their conversation, as always, and been inspired to check out the Zadie Smith book she'd recommended, and had she read *The Human Stain*? A campus novel, too, a brilliant skewering of political correctness. It was new, but Polly splurged on the hardcover and tore through it, then sent him her thoughts. So began the online version of their conversations in his office. She shared dial-up Internet with her roommates so had to do her emailing in the middle of the night to avoid tying up the line.

First, it was one or two exchanges a week. Books, authors. Anecdotes about their students. Sometimes the emails had a playful edge, as when he chided her for her apathy about the election (she hadn't voted) and she teased him for his cluelessness about contemporary music. The emails were casual but, for Polly, took time to compose; they had to be well written, make her sound smart and literate and funny. Sometimes she spent hours crafting a reply. Sometimes she just read through past emails, as if they were a favorite story, following the plot arcs as they unfolded—this was when they started writing every day, this was when he mentioned his unhappy marriage, this was when he started signing them *Paul*, then *P*.

Polly didn't mention the email correspondence to Hope and Adam. In Adam's case, this was mostly circumstantial; after his year in the woods, he'd surprised them by announcing he wanted to study environmental law. He was now a lawyer, and technically a grown-up, even if he seemed to be partying more than ever. If he called her, it was often when hungover, not an ideal time to tell him. Later, though, Polly would wonder what might have happened if she had. Maybe, being a guy, he'd have picked up on something that felt off. Or maybe not. Adam's relationships, even his breakups, always seemed enviably straightforward; he often remained friends with his exes. And Adam liked McFadden, but as Hope was fond of saying, Adam liked everyone.

Hope, though, Polly talked to all the time. They had a standing phone date on Sunday evenings. It felt strange not telling her, but the more time that passed—months, whole seasons—the harder it was to imagine. Besides, Hope had never understood Polly's connection with McFadden. Never liked him, not since that B-minus. She thought he was weird, and would find their emailing weird, but that was Hope: opponent of weirdness. Defender of the status quo. At the PR firm, she'd been promoted to in-house blogger, tasked with coming up with catchy narratives to sell high-end shoes and dream vacations. In college, their differences had been muted because they'd been living the same life—same dorms, same meals, same classes—but in the real world, they were becoming more stark.

After 9/11, the emails grew even more personal. They dispensed with cleverness. Polly wrote about the nightmares she was having. The phone call from her mother, incoherent with panic. The unreality of walking past signs with names and faces of people who were missing. McFadden told her that his marriage was ending. He and his wife were barely talking. His daughter had left for college, and his house felt empty. He was deeply lonely. *Your emails are the brightest moments of my day*, he wrote, adding, *I hope that isn't too much*, and it wasn't, because it was McFadden, and because it was email, which felt real and not real at the same time.

Then, sometime after the new year, he wrote that he was coming to Manhattan over spring break, for an important meeting, and would she be free for dinner?

All these years later, Polly could still remember what she ordered (fried calamari, steak, chocolate mousse), because her dinners

usually consisted of Special K and Diet Coke. She would remember what she wore (plaid skirt, cropped sweater, fake pearl
choker) because she'd spent so long picking it out. She remembered her old cotton underwear, because when she was getting
ready and it crossed her mind to put on nice underwear, the
thought so unnerved her—who did she think would see it?—
that when he actually did see it, back in his hotel room, she felt
compelled to explain why she'd chosen it in the first place.

But when she first spotted McFadden in the restaurant, she
was gripped with such nerves that her vision briefly clouded
over. They'd spent so much time online that she'd grown accustomed to the person he was on the Internet, which felt both like
and unlike the person at the table, rising to hug her.

"Look at you," he said.

"Hey," she replied, and sat down, pushing her hair flat. She
folded her hands on the table, moved them to her lap. Her
palms were sweaty. She wished she'd taken a shot of something
at home. Being with him in person, in his hiking boots and
shapeless sweater, reminded her of sitting in his office. Except
now they were sitting in a restaurant, in New York. She noticed
he wasn't wearing his wedding band. When she looked closely at
his face, she saw a fresh shaving cut on his chin.

Then he ordered them a bottle of wine, and Polly asked about
his meeting, as if they were a couple catching up on their days.
He started to answer, then stopped. "This is dull," he said. "Tell
me about you." So Polly started talking, mostly about her students. Albert, who had written an incredible essay about his
parents, refugees from Angola. Meg, a natural poet, the first person in her family to go to college. As she talked, and drank, she
felt looser. Soon she was rambling, not because she felt nervous
but because it felt easy. By the time dessert arrived, she tucked

into it, stabbing raspberries with her tiny fork. At one point McFadden set down his spoon, his face softening into a look of undisguised affection, and said, "Do you have any idea how charming you are?"

Her first reaction was to want to kiss him, which caught her off guard. She'd never thought about it so explicitly. But when his knee pressed against hers, she felt an undeniable thrum of attraction. Was it because of him, or how he made her feel, or were they the same thing?

Back in his hotel room, he knelt in front of her and slid off her shoes, cheap black flats. He cupped her heels in his hands and kissed the arch of each foot. As he peeled off her sweater, he looked up at her with a kind of wonder. "It's been a long time," he murmured, and she felt benevolent. Empowered. They had sex twice, once with the lights on and once with them off. Afterward, lying in bed, he whispered, "I have a confession. The important meeting? This was it." Then he fell asleep, leaving Polly staring at his body, the warm freckled slope of his shoulder, the curve of his ear, parts she'd never seen up close, while her emotions veered from flattered to panicked to grief-stricken, because in the shift from the possibility of this happening to the reality of it having happened, she knew something irretrievable had been lost.

The next morning, McFadden went out to pick up coffee and breakfast while she showered, making the water as hot as she could stand. She stayed inside the steamy glass stall until her skin turned pink. When she stepped out, she wrapped herself in a fluffy towel and smoothed the fog from the mirror and stared at her face beneath the lights.

This was real, she thought. This had actually happened. There were her arms, speckled with droplets. Her dark eyebrows, the silver hoops climbing her left ear. There were McFadden's things on the edge of the sink. The leather bag. The plastic contact lenses holder. The disposable razor. Ordinary things, but they felt wildly intimate. She picked them up, pretending this was the sink in their New York apartment, furnished with books and plants and that lumpy brown couch. Then she heard him fumbling in the hallway and stepped out, towel knotted loosely around herself. He glanced at her, then turned quickly to the TV stand. "I wasn't sure what you liked," he said.

He set down several bulging white bags. Bagels. Muffins. Twenty-ounce coffees. The excess made her nervous.

"Coffee?"

"Sure," she said, and he handed her a cup. It burned her through the cardboard sleeve. She set it aside and sat on the edge of the bed, which at some point he had made. "You're not having any?"

"I better stick with water. I don't usually drink that much," he said. "You must be a bad influence on me."

Polly felt warm, sick to her stomach. He kept his eyes averted—was this modesty? Regret? Finally, he sat beside her, his eyes on the floor and his hands on his knees. "You know I have to leave soon."

"Of course," she said, but her voice came out sounding thin. She knew they needed to have sex again. Sober sex, morning sex. Sex that was unambiguously meaningful. She put a hand on his thigh. "You could change your return ticket," she said, trying to sound casual or seductive or something, but he patted her wrist.

"I better go pack." He stood up. "But take your time. Stay as long as you want," he added, and Polly assumed he didn't want them to be seen leaving together. She couldn't move. She registered the flat drone of the bathroom fan, the clinks of his razor and contacts case returning to the leather bag. She stared at the painting on the wall above the bed, a purple flower that looked half melted. Not five minutes later his suitcase was by the door. "I wish I didn't have to leave so abruptly."

Bullshit, she thought, but her ability to summon a teasing tone had abandoned her.

"I'll be thinking about you," he said.

"Oh really?"

He winced a little. Guilt, or pity? He kissed her forehead. "I'll write soon," he told her, then he was gone.

Inside the damp towel, Polly's heart crashed in her chest. She stared at her bare knees as she listened to the squeaky wheels of his suitcase, the ping of the elevator, the rattle of a housekeeping cart ambling down the hall. The coffee smell was sour and nauseating. She poured the contents of the cups down the drain and dropped the grease-spotted bags in the trash. She put on the clothes from the night before, minus the choker, which she stuffed in her purse, along with the little soaps and shampoos from the bathroom. Then she changed her mind and left them there.

Two days later, she hadn't heard from him. She'd waited exactly twenty-four hours after his departure to send him an email— eight sentences she spent two hours writing and rewriting, trying to strike the right balance between seriousness and flirtatiousness, with a touch of remorse—and since then had been compulsively checking her inbox. Her only new email, from Hope, was all about Ethan, her new boyfriend, who had two interviews for tenure-track positions, one of them in Philadelphia—*fingers and toes crossed!!!*

Polly couldn't tell her, even if she wanted to. Because she knew Hope would be distressed by what had happened, and because as long as the story remained hers, she didn't need to explain it or justify it. Because if she *did* tell her what happened, Hope would ask if she'd heard from him, and Polly couldn't bear to say no.

Besides, Polly genuinely believed McFadden would write back to her any minute. The awkwardness in the morning was probably because he was worried she was upset with him. He was just busy, catching up on grading. Figuring out what to say.

Or maybe his wife had gotten suspicious. Maybe she'd noticed he seemed preoccupied when he got home and was now monitoring his inbox. He'd told Polly some months ago that his marriage was essentially over—maybe this was the thing that would make it official.

Thursday evening, after Polly had muddled her way through teaching her six p.m. class—at one point so distracted she confused the names of two students, something she never did—she logged on to her email in the shared part-time faculty office, feeling hopeful again because it had been three hours since she'd checked. At the sight of her empty inbox, she felt like throwing up. One of the other part-time instructors was looking at her funny, a man who had been teaching comp there since the seventies, and Polly looked away, despising the fact that she'd become this pathetic person. She grabbed her backpack and left the building and stood paralyzed on the teeming sidewalk, unsure where to go. She couldn't face the silent computer in her apartment, didn't want to go drinking with the other instructors. She thought about hopping the Chinatown bus to Philadelphia to see Hope (but inevitably Ethan, too) or showing up in Boston to get drunk with Adam and his fellow lawyers. She even briefly considered taking the subway to Brooklyn, to see Diane, maybe stay the night in her old room. Then she pictured the college at night: the quiet of the quad in midwinter, the glow of the sleeping buildings under the star-filled sky. She began walking to Port Authority, where she bought a ticket and three candy bars and, two hours later, boarded a Greyhound bus to Maine. The ride would take all night, but her backpack contained everything she needed: wallet, Discman, a sheaf of papers that needed grading. She found an empty seat and watched out the window as the bus rolled slowly up the interstate, wheezing into rest stops, rain speckling the darkened windows, her destination a sweaty secret in her heart.

NINE

ADAM

Adam felt the soft wall of the bouncy castle yield gently beneath his head. On the other side, his classmates mingling on the quad reminded him of creatures in an aquarium, shadowy figures tinged an aqua green. He had no idea what time it was—eight thirty? Nine? Inside, whenever someone shifted even a little, the whole structure jostled back and forth. The castle felt almost like a room, but not quite, for the windows were made of mesh and the door was a makeshift drawbridge, a flap of red plastic that let the night air seep in.

They were all parents, and therefore bouncy house veterans, so they'd left their shoes outside in a pile, the way they'd once dumped their coats in a slippery heap at all-campus parties. To Adam's left, Eve had claimed a corner, leaning against the wall with bare feet crossed, wrapped in an oversized sweater. On his right were the Haskell-Joneses, Olivia resting against Jason's chest. Greg Herman reclined in the middle of the floor, hands folded neatly on his abdomen. It was a funny group, one that probably had never assembled around a table in the dining hall, but that was the beauty of a reunion. Being in their company, Adam felt the same expansiveness that filled him when he'd first arrived.

"I'm embarrassed to admit it," Eve was saying, "but I watched. And I loved it as much as I did then."

"Oh, same," Olivia said. "Anyone who says they didn't is lying."

They were talking about—what else? Age. Time. The past year, and how they'd coped. A TV show from the nineties. It had first aired when they were sophomores, ushering in the era of reality television; that spring, the original cast had reunited in the original apartment, except the one who got Covid and was beamed in on a screen.

"Even Jay watched it," Olivia said. "Didn't you, Jay?" His chin was perched on her shoulder, cap swiveled backward.

"I might have watched," Haskell confessed.

She traced a finger across his brow, moving a lock of hair. "I swear, the secret of growing older is no one actually stops liking the kind of stupid TV shows they watched when they were twenty."

Eve stirred her drink with her pinky finger. "I bet you Maddie Davis doesn't watch these TV shows. But she probably never watched them in the first place."

Olivia frowned. "Remind me who she is again?"

"Only the recipient of a MacArthur Genius Grant," Eve said.

"And how do we have a classmate who got a Genius Grant?"

"Because we're getting *old*!" Eve wailed. "Because we're the age of the people who win awards for being geniuses."

"Screw the genius," Greg said flatly. "She's making the rest of us look bad."

Adam smiled. They were funny, these people. He missed being around funny.

"I swear I don't remember her. And she isn't here this weekend, apparently." Olivia shifted to look at her husband. "Honey, why don't I remember her?"

"Because she was in the library while you were playing quarters," he said, not unkindly.

"Oh, right." Olivia expelled a sigh. "Well, that's okay. I was young. I'd rather be playing quarters. Can I get that on a T-shirt?"

"If it's any consolation," Eve said, "you look one hundred percent the same."

"See?" Haskell said and kissed her shoulder, a small moment Adam found endearing. It must be nice, he thought, being with someone you met in college, who knew that version of you.

"That's sweet," Olivia said. "But you all see me like I was then. Let's face it, we all look like middle-aged moms and dads."

Eve sat up, tugging her sweater more securely around her shoulders. "What about you?" she asked, nudging Adam's socked foot.

"Do I look like a middle-aged dad? Definitely not."

"Did you watch it, too, or are you above that sort of thing?"

"I'm above nothing," he assured them. "But we don't have a TV."

"My God." Olivia groaned. "You're one of those people. When did you become one of those people?"

"He's evolved," Greg intoned from behind closed eyes.

"I always assumed I would evolve," Eve said, sinking back into the wall. "Basically, I can't drink as much or stay up as late, but otherwise I think I feel the same. Or at least I don't feel that different. I assumed by now I'd feel more different. I thought I'd understand more, but I actually think I understand less."

"Speak for yourself," Greg said.

"Oh, Greggy," Olivia said, with real feeling, and the group let a respectful beat lapse. Adam thought of Greg's parents helping set up their room freshman year, embarrassing him with hugs and cookies. Greg did seem changed by their loss. He'd always been funny, but his humor had come out in quiet asides. Now it was sharper, delivered with a wry matter-of-factness, as if he had less at stake.

"Give us some of your hard-won wisdom, Greg," Adam said.

His old roommate raised one hand in the air. "If I learned anything this year," he said, "it's that there are only three things that are important." He ticked off his fingers. "Your health. The people you love." He let his hand flop back down, the floor swelling like a water bed. "That's two. But I guess that's fucking it."

"That's fucking it," Adam said supportively, because it was Greg, and because Greg was right. Your loved ones were all that mattered. Life was short. The clichés were true. When Adam thought about Andrea and the boys, the word *blessing* came to mind, even though, except for his parents' funerals, he hadn't been to church since he was fourteen.

Gazing up at the roof of the castle, the smudged arms of the trees, Adam wondered if his own father just never felt that kind of love for him. Once as a young kid, he'd climbed the maple tree in his backyard. He'd been following his brothers, who'd scrambled right up into the upper branches—the tree was huge. Or seemed huge. When eventually it was cut down, he'd studied the stump, which was no bigger than an inner tube. But at seven, Adam reached the top and was too scared to move. His brothers returned to the ground while Adam clung there like a koala, enduring their teasing, until they started getting nervous and ran to get their dad, who stared at him in disgust. *You got up, you get back down*, he said.

"Adam?"

"Jesus," Haskell said. "Is he sleeping?"

"He can sleep literally anywhere."

"Remember that time on the roof?"

Adam kept his eyes shut, letting a tide of laughter roll over him. It felt a little like he was eavesdropping on his funeral.

"He'd been gone for—what? Three, four days?"

"How long was it, Greggy?"

"Four days," Greg said.

"Poor Herman was so freaked out."

He had been, asking friends if they'd seen him and alerting their RA. Later, after he'd found his way back, Adam had been surprised to find anyone cared so much that he was gone.

"Four days," Haskell said. "Where the fuck did he go for four days?"

"Fuck if I can remember," Adam spoke up, and they all laughed. But he did remember. Parts of it, at least. The phone call from his mother telling him about his father's heart attack. *Don't come home*, she'd said. *They don't know if it's serious.* Wandering around campus, getting shitfaced, and waking up on a random porch at one of the senior apartments. The numb walk along the trails behind the gym and into downtown Sewall. Small clapboard houses. A muscled dog, a rusty fence. Lousy pot from some guy behind 7-Eleven. A jog along the darkened shoulder of the highway. A nap in the Laundromat, in a church. On the roof. The freshness of the snow, the closeness of the stars.

Then Olivia threw her arms open wide. "Hope!" she called out, and Adam saw his old friend peeking through the curtain on the door.

"What's this?" she asked. "Are we camping?"

He thumped the space beside him. "Hopey. Come sit."

She unzipped her shoes and dropped them into the pile and knee-walked across the floor, purse in one hand and red Solo cup in the other, before plopping down beside him and looking around. Her cheeks were rosy. "Everybody having fun?"

"I was just killing the mood," Greg said. "But the fun can now resume."

"Greggy," Olivia said, with a warning sigh.

"Actually, Hope, you're right on time," Eve said. "We were just reminiscing about the time Adam disappeared. Do you remember?"

"Remember!" Hope said, brightening. "How could I forget?"

Adam rested an arm around her shoulders. "You all may not know this, but Hope remembers everything."

"This is true," she said proudly. "Ask me any obscure bit of college trivia."

"Who was Madeline Davis?" Olivia said.

"Our most illustrious alum!" Hope exclaimed. "She lived in Reynolds freshman year. We had art history together. I was hoping she would be here."

"Olivia doesn't remember her," Jason explained.

"Oh well, she was quiet. But brilliant—I mean, obviously she was brilliant," Hope said. "But I especially remember when Adam disappeared. Because it's how Adam and Polly and I all became friends."

"Tell us," Olivia said, snuggling against her husband, as if they were gathered around a campfire.

Hope sat up straighter, tucking her hair behind her ears. "It was a Tuesday, around eleven," she said, earning a laugh for her specificity. "Polly and I were studying when suddenly this person walked in. He didn't even knock, which was weird, because we didn't know him. I mean, of course we knew *of* him—the wild guy who lived downstairs."

"Tell me about it," Greg put in.

"He'd come in from outside. There was snow in his hair. Right away, he started insisting that he lived there, and we realized he was wasted. I mean, totally disoriented. But not belligerent." She paused. "Adam was never a belligerent drunk. Just sweet. And needy."

"And hungry," said Greg.

"God, yes," Hope agreed. She was smiling, warming to her audience. "We tried telling him he was in the wrong room—his room was actually directly below ours—but it wasn't computing. So we let Jamie know he was okay—"

Nods, remembering. Jamie, the RA. A junior in the all-male a cappella group.

"—then we took him in and fed him. He was *starving*. I made him mac and cheese," she said. "Oh, and he had this nasty cut on his leg."

"I still have the scar," Adam said. He remembered the dog at his heels, the scab of rust on the fence.

"So I got my first-aid kit—"

Adam cut in again. "Yes, Hope had a first-aid kit."

"What's wrong with being prepared for emergencies?" Hope protested, but she was only pretending to take offense. This was Hope at the height of her powers. If they had to form a new civilization, he thought, she would be the historian, the keeper of the past.

"So we bandaged up the leg," she concluded, "and he crawled under a blanket and passed out in my favorite chair."

"And they didn't get rid of me for the next four years," Adam said.

They laughed again, drowsy, wistful. It felt good. Felt easy. Hope looked relaxed and happy. Adam couldn't help thinking about what had happened the next day, when he woke up hungover, apologizing to the two girls in whose room he'd crashed. Instead of punting him back downstairs, they'd kept him. Hope insisted that he hydrate. Polly gave him cigarettes. Bit by bit he started talking, describing the past few days as if he'd been on some grand adventure—making it sound fun and zany, maybe even briefly believing his own story—but eventually telling them about the phone call from his mother and admitting he was too much of a wimp to find out if she'd called again. Because this was the age before cell phones, when it was still possible to get lost.

What came next was hazy to him now. Hope and Polly convinced him to check his messages, and an hour later he was at their door. As he talked, Polly rubbed his back. Hope kept offering him food. Eventually, they decided they should eat a real meal, but going to the dining hall felt too weird, so they headed to the Chinese place downtown. Then they stopped at the discount store across the street, where Hope helped him pick out a shirt and tie for the funeral. Polly endorsed his wearing his Chucks. Next came the trip home—a silent ride with an uncle who'd been dispatched to retrieve him, a house full of strangers, his brothers with their subdued suits and weeping girlfriends, his mother who barely left her bedroom, the crushing weight on his chest. When he returned to campus, he didn't stop moving. The last few weeks of the semester were a fog of wasted nights, skipped classes, half-assed track practices. Compassionate professors granting him extensions, increasingly concerned professors issuing him warnings. He got four Ds, which landed him on academic probation. But he didn't fully grasp the gravity of his situation until that spring when he was summoned for a meeting with the dean, who explained that, much as she sympathized with his recent loss, if his grades didn't improve, probation would turn into suspension. When he told Hope and Polly, Hope said briskly, *Well, that's not an option.* Polly agreed, reminding him that he was one of her only friends. That was the night he'd kissed Polly on the quad, cloudy with sadness and panic; fortunately, she had the sense to stop it, kindly informing him he was spiraling. *Thank God,* Hope had said later. *If you two had made this awkward, I would have killed you both.*

Adam felt grateful now, looking at his old friend Hope, who he knew remembered all of this and more. The room she shared with Polly had been his second home for the next three years. Its location kept changing, migrating from the dorms to the junior and senior apartments—Hope unwilling to live off-campus, too afraid she'd miss something—but the contents stayed reassuringly the same.

Suddenly two bright beams saturated the castle, making them all shield their eyes. Improbably, Troy was still in possession of the golf cart. He left the headlights on, motor running, as he hopped off and trampled the moat, jamming his head through the door. "So this is where the cool kids are hiding?"

Eve cupped her face with both hands, peering through the netting. "Is that my husband? What have you done with him?"

"We're on a mission."

"That inspires confidence," Olivia said.

"I'm collecting recruits," Troy said, then unleashed a dramatic burp and stumbled backward out the door.

"He sure seems like a guy who's benefited from life-changing therapy," Greg deadpanned.

Eve sat on her knees, scrunching her face as she squinted into the glare. "Oh no. There he is. A sitting duck." She picked up her sandals. "I better get out there."

"Come on," Haskell said to Olivia, peeling himself from

the wall and clamping his cup between his teeth. "All of you. Let's go."

"I'm not getting near that golf cart," Olivia advised, but she was making her way toward the door.

"Right behind you guys," Adam said, though he was far too content where he was to join them. Greg didn't budge either, asleep or unfazed.

"Good luck," Hope called as they slid out of the castle, one by one, then turned to Adam. "So," she said. "Are you having fun?"

"I really am, actually," he said. "You?"

"Oh, definitely."

Hope was smiling, her default expression, but Adam thought the smile seemed strained. It was full and friendly but didn't reach the corners of her eyes. If he didn't know her better, he might have thought she looked sad.

"I'm sorry about your boys," she said.

"Yeah. You and me both."

"And Andrea—her restorative yoga weekend!"

"I know. She was bummed." He winced at his lie, and the fact that he'd embellished it by adding the word *restorative*. He didn't like lying to Hope any more than lying to Polly, but fact and fiction were so tangled at this point he didn't have the energy to sort them out. "I feel a little guilty, to be honest. Being here."

"Me, too," Hope said. "It feels strange, especially after last year. I think that's understandable, though, don't you? I'm never not with my kids. Rowan especially."

"How's he doing?"

"Oh. You know." She shrugged, looking into her cup. "Struggling. But that's to be expected."

"Sure."

"I thought about bringing them. But Izzy had a dance tonight. And Ethan—he wanted to come, but he's just been super-busy. His job—" she said, then stopped, as if she'd lost the storyline, and Adam realized she was lying, too.

Hope finished her drink, then peered up at the green walls. "You know what I was thinking? We need to get our boys together. How have they only met each other once?"

"We should," Adam said. He remembered that visit, Hope arriving with Rowan and a carful of gifts. She'd talked nonstop—about sleep training and babyproofing and tummy time—like a gust of wind blowing open a barn door. When she left, Andrea had observed that for all Hope's friendly energy, she'd seemed kind of unhappy. *It must be exhausting*, she said. Adam had been surprised; then again, his impressions were all based on who Hope had been years ago.

"It's silly we don't do it more often," she continued. "They're so close in age. They should get to know each other better. Especially now that they're older."

"Come to New Hampshire," Adam offered. "We have the space."

Hope touched her chin, looking at him, as if visualizing the scene. "A fall weekend, maybe? Foliage season? I would love that."

"Sold," he said, picturing his roomy house filled with people, guests occupying the extra bedrooms and the kids in tents in the backyard. He liked this prospect—and knew Hope would actually follow through with it—choosing for the moment not to think about what Andrea might say.

"Good." Hope nodded, satisfied. "It's a plan. It helps having things to look forward to, doesn't it?"

"We'll have to get Polly there, too," Adam said.

She let out a short laugh. "Don't hold your breath."

"Why not? You wrangled her for this weekend."

"I'm not sure I had anything to do with it," Hope said, balancing her empty cup on her thigh. She sounded a little hurt, but of course she didn't know the full story. Because Polly had never told her about McFadden, which Adam didn't understand. He'd always taken it for granted that Hope and Polly told each other everything. A roommate thing. A girl thing. Even the light tension he sometimes sensed between them felt like proof of the depths of their friendship, but now he suspected that it, like many things, was more complicated than he'd thought.

"Honestly," Hope was saying, "I've barely spoken to her. She never cared about coming back, and now she's like a celebrity. She's either preoccupied talking to somebody else or she's preoccupied with Jonah."

"I know she's worried about him," Adam said. "And it must be weird for her to be here," he added, remembering her misgivings in the dorm.

"I know. I mean—I get it. Twenty-one years. But then again, whose fault is that?" Hope said, with another unconvincing laugh.

Adam wished, for both of their sakes, that they could talk about McFadden. He wanted to reassure her that Polly had reason to be preoccupied; he also wanted to know if Hope had had any idea what was going on back then.

"I just wish she could *pretend* to be happy about being here," Hope said. Then the castle swayed from side to side, and Troy's red face squeezed through the door.

"You three," he pronounced. Adam had forgotten Greg was still right there. "Your presence is required."

Outside, the golf cart was idling. Adam could make out several figures piled on the rear seat. As if hypnotized, Greg rose from the wobbly floor.

"Greg!" Hope stopped him. "You don't even know where you're going."

"She's right," Greg said, blinking. "Where am I going?"

"Study Sprints," Troy said, then leaped back onto the ground, making the whole castle shake. Adam felt a grin growing on his face. Study Sprints had been a finals week tradition, pointless and foolish. It fit the bill exactly. If he'd questioned Troy's personal growth, he stood corrected: this was brilliant.

"I'm in," Adam said, prying himself up. "Let's go, Hopey."

"I'm going to pass," she said. "And in the absence of your wife—*both* of your wives—let me go on record as saying I think this is a bad idea."

"Can't you see I have no choice?" Adam said. He crawled toward the door, following the soles of Greg's striped socks. "Greg's doing it. And his parents died. That means I have to do it."

"He's right," Greg said. "He has to do it."

"Fine," Hope said. "Just—it's our reunion, Adam. I'm serious. We have three days. If you disappear for the rest of the weekend, I swear I'll never forgive you," she said emphatically, and though Adam assumed she was kidding, when he glanced over his shoulder, her face was flushed again. The drinks, he thought. The strangeness of it all.

"No one's disappearing," he reassured her. "What do you think I am, eighteen?"

TEN

POLLY

Polly hadn't heard back from Jonah—a good sign, she thought. At least he wasn't glued to his phone, texting his friends from home. No doubt he and Charlie had found their groove by now. It could take a while to settle in with an old friend, especially one you hadn't seen in so long.

After two hours, Polly had managed to relax a little, too. Her nerves had quieted to some extent, dulled by several drinks and a plate of food and the two cigarettes she'd bummed from Troy Abernathy, of all people. He'd just motored away on a golf cart, after telling Polly about the breakup of his marriage in unexpectedly insightful detail. So far tonight, to Polly's surprise, this had proven the most effective distraction: conversations with her old classmates, people she hadn't seen or thought about in years. It felt good to connect with them. Vicky, her old Spanish study partner, who talked about the immigration reform work she was doing. Greg Herman, who told Polly about saying goodbye to his father on a phone held by an ER nurse.

If Jonah had predicted that people would revert to shallow topics, Polly could report that the opposite was true. This was a reunion not only of people who once knew each other in college but of people staggering back into the world.

The exception was Hope, whose conversations never seemed

to dip a toe beneath the surface. Several times, Polly had heard her reel off the exact same script. There was something to be admired about it—Hope didn't catastrophize, Hope held it together—but this felt different than it had in college. As if her positive attitude had become more dug in, one-dimensional, a more concentrated version of who she used to be. In another year, another setting, Polly might have had more patience, but tonight she was finding it hard to take.

Polly finished her cigarette, ground the butt under the toe of her boot, and finished her beer. She wasn't accustomed to so much drinking, and needed more food. She took one last look at her phone, then slipped it in her pocket and made her way back to the buffet. The spread was just as opulent as she'd promised Jonah. She piled a plate with fat shrimp, bacon-wrapped scallops, crab cakes the size of hockey pucks. The pricetag on this one table was probably more than her salary for a semester's worth of classes.

"There you are!" Hope said, appearing by her side. "Back for seconds?"

"Apparently I am."

"Me, too. I'm starving."

"I'm primarily bitter," Polly said. "I was just thinking this spread probably costs more than I make in a semester."

Hope laughed, clearly not realizing it wasn't a joke. "Honestly, maybe it's because we've been so deprived, but the food this year seems especially delicious."

"Here, help me with this," Polly said, and she carried her plate across the lawn toward Fiske. "I was trying to explain the Walthrop food thing to Jonah on the drive up," she added. "But as I heard myself say it, it sounded really strange."

"Why strange?" Hope said, as they lowered themselves to the

steps in front of their old dorm. She tucked her bag by her feet, and Polly set the plate between them.

"It's just a strange thing for a college to have a reputation for," Polly said. "It's not like it's a five-star hotel." She dunked a shrimp in cocktail sauce. "Actually, it's kind of like it's a five-star hotel."

"Please." Hope peered at the plate, as if appraising her options before buying an item from a store. "You loved the dining hall food as much as anyone," she said, selecting a miniature toast smothered in Brie and blueberries. "Remember those bagels?"

"Those weren't bagels," Polly said, which made Hope roll her eyes. In college, Polly had routinely complained about New England—the cold, the absence of good bagels (it was truly shocking what passed for an everything with cream cheese)—though at its heart, her attitude wasn't so much a critique of New England as pride in New York.

"Oh my God," Hope said, mouth full. "I was just remembering how we would sneak in that suitcase."

"Suitcase?"

"My little rolling suitcase we used to steal cereal from the dining hall."

"Did we?"

Hope looked at her and swallowed. "Please tell me you remember."

"It kind of rings a bell," Polly said, though it didn't. She wondered where they'd gone, the details of her day-to-day life in college, if what happened with McFadden had occupied so much mental space it blotted out everything else.

Hope continued, undaunted. "Honestly," she said. "When I think about it now, it seems almost surreal. Living with your best friends, sitting in the dining hall for hours. Having all the freedom in the world but no real responsibilities. They say it's the happiest time in your life and you don't even know it. But I think I actually *did* know it. And when I think about these kids who missed a year on campus—" She shuddered. "If that had happened to us, I think I would have died."

She was a little drunk, Polly thought, but also entirely sincere. Hope's memories of college were all saturated in this perfect light. It was frustrating, and enviable, that Hope loved the place so unabashedly. That she could.

"Adam took off on a golf cart, by the way," Hope said, returning her attention to the food.

"Troy's?" Polly gave a half-hearted chuckle. "That sounds promising."

"Study Sprints." Hope picked up a miniature crab cake. "Some things never change." She leaned forward to bite into it, one palm cupped beneath her chin, then popped the rest in her mouth. As she neatly brushed her hands together, Polly was struck by how intimately she knew Hope's hands. Despite all she'd forgotten about college, she could picture Hope typing on her computer or picking toppings off a slice of pizza or carefully lacquering her nails with pale pink polish. Thirty years later, her hands were anchored with rings, but they were the same blunt palms, freckled and square.

"So how are your kids?" Polly asked her, but Hope interrupted, gripping her arm. "Guess who that is? In the purple shirt."

Polly scanned the crowd, locating the unfamiliar face above the V-neck, standing next to a man who looked like he'd stepped out of *GQ*. "I give up."

Hope gave her a knowing smile. "Keith *Hammond*."

Polly looked again, and she could see it, Keith's receding chin materializing above his open collar. "God. Yeah, it is."

"Doesn't he look amazing? And that's his husband."

"Jesus. Good for Keith."

Hope shook her head. "I had no idea he was gay," she said. "Did you?"

"I think I had some idea."

"But he wasn't out, was he? I definitely don't remember him being out."

"I mean, most people weren't out in college. It was the early nineties. And it wasn't the most open and accepting environment," Polly said.

Hope either didn't hear her last comment or chose to ignore it. She picked up her drink and peered at the crowd as if commentating from the booth at a sporting event. "Oh—look," she said. "There's Laura."

"Who?"

"Laura Rhodes. In the stripes."

Polly located the woman in the blue-and-white dress, holding hands with a guy in blue pants and a white shirt, and wondered if they'd coordinated on purpose.

"I still can't believe she ended up marrying that boyfriend," Hope said.

"What boyfriend?"

"The one she was always talking to on the phone?" She gave Polly a weary look. "This is not some obscure piece of trivia, Polly. He used to drive up every weekend. We talked about him constantly. Please tell me you remember."

"I might," Polly said, but she had no clue.

"Well," Hope went on, "that's him. They met the summer before freshman year, and they've been together ever since. Honestly, I always thought they were kind of melodramatic, but now it seems romantic."

"Really? I can't begin to imagine marrying someone I met when I was that age."

"That's because you only ever went out with those depressed artists," Hope said.

A joke, Polly knew, only a joke. Still, it hit a nerve. "It's also because I was a completely different person."

"You think so?" Hope asked, pivoting toward her. She seemed genuinely caught off guard. "Well, I find that sad."

"I actually find it reassuring. But I guess it depends on who you were in college."

"Exactly!" Hope said. "And you were pretty great in college."

This, Polly thought, was the paradox of Hope. If she was stubbornly upbeat, she was also steadfast and loyal. But Hope saw her in an incomplete light. Polly had a flash of herself, half her life ago—thin jacket, cold wrists, numb cheeks—rushing across the quad in the frozen rain.

"Some people just get lucky and meet the right person early on," Hope continued, picking a crumb off her sleeve. "I mean, look at Jason and Olivia. They're perfect for each other."

"Says who?"

"Have you talked to them? They're so in love it's sickening."

"You have no idea what's really going on in someone's marriage," Polly said. "If it looks perfect, it probably isn't."

"Well." Hope paused. "I guess that's true."

But Polly was getting annoyed, and though she knew her annoyance was outsized, she couldn't help it. Hope's insistence on the positive was so unexamined. "This place wasn't so perfect either," she said. "Lots of things about campus culture in the nineties actually look pretty fucked-up in retrospect."

She expected Hope to push back, but she gave a light laugh, saying, "Oh God. Believe me, Izzy gives me an earful."

"Does she?" Polly was surprised. Then she remembered Hope's daughter at Rockefeller Center, the hints of some future rebellion—the quiet eye rolls, the necklace with the teeth.

"I keep pointing out that it's all relative," Hope said. "I mean, at the time we actually *were* progressive. We had a women's studies major!"

"Yes, and how many students of color in our graduating class?"

"But that was the time."

"That didn't make it right," Polly snapped. No doubt she was making Hope uncomfortable, but she was getting drunk, her filter dissolving, and after the year they'd had, she couldn't tolerate anything less than looking at the world as it truly was. This was something she appreciated about Jonah and his friends, and their entire generation: their willingness to call things out.

"That may be true," Hope said. "I mean, it *is* true. But I like to remind Izzy that in some ways things then were actually better."

"Like?"

"Like"—she waved one arm toward the quad—"Laura Rhodes! All those phone calls and letters and drives up and down the interstate. It required actual effort! Now teenagers just talk online. Or they go to dances, except they don't call them dances, and no one even makes an attempt to look nice—they're deliberately trying to *not* look nice! But Laura did it the old-fashioned way, and she seems so happy." Hope smiled stiffly. "All these happy people," she added, and the smile seemed to hang there for a moment, unsure of itself, then she turned to Polly. "What about you?"

Polly raised her eyebrows. "Are you asking me if I'm happy?"

"I was asking if you're dating."

"Dating?" Polly laughed, a single, humorless note. "No. And no, thanks."

"Why?" Hope said. "You should! You never age. We should all be so lucky."

It was a benign comment, intended to be a compliment, but Polly rejected the premise that being single was a problem in need of fixing. She had an online profile she reactivated every so often, scanning for a man who sounded smart and fun to have a drink with; during Elmwood summers, she'd had a couple of one-night stands that extended into longer flings. But they never turned into anything more. She never wanted them to. She'd decided long ago that her first responsibility was to her son.

"I've been a little busy lately," she said. "With Jonah."

"Well, sure," Hope said. "But now he's going to college. You'll have more time than you know what to—"

"And I have a job," Polly reminded her.

"You can find the time," Hope said. "You're teaching two classes a semester, right?"

"In a normal semester, four," Polly said. "Last semester, it was two only because enrollment was down, and I'm an adjunct, which means my classes are dependent on enrollment. If they don't fill, they don't run, and I don't get paid."

"Oh," Hope said. "Well, that isn't fair."

"No," Polly clipped. "It isn't." Was it possible Hope didn't know university jobs so shitty existed? "But plenty of people are in the same situation. That's the reality of higher education. It's not all tents and crab cakes."

"Right."

"It isn't just me."

"I didn't think it was," Hope said. She sat up straighter, twisting her ring around her knuckle. "And I sympathize completely. Ethan was fully remote, too—"

"That's different, Hope. He's a dean. At an elite college."

"Oh, I know," Hope said. "I wasn't trying to compare."

But sometimes comparing things was good, Polly thought. Sometimes it was revelatory. Hadn't the past year proven that, again and again?

Hope was still swiveling her ring. "I'm just hoping now everything can go back to normal," she concluded, and Polly knew she should let it go, but the notion of just turning around and returning to the world as it once was—the world before the pandemic, the world of college two-plus decades ago—felt unbearably naive.

"I hate to tell you, but I don't see that happening," Polly said. "Normal is over. And in some ways, it should be."

Hope didn't reply, just gazed straight ahead.

"I mean, for kids, this was a nightmare. There is virtually no upside. But if there's some good to come out of this fucked-up year, it's that it exposed these inequalities, all the systemic problems in our country, and forced us to actually look at things we'd rather—"

Her friend's head shook, seemingly involuntarily. "Can we not talk about politics?"

"This isn't *politics*, Hope. This is life! Actual life! If we just go back to how things were before, then what was the point?"

"There doesn't have to be a *point*," Hope said. "It already stole a year of our lives. I just don't see why we have to keep talking about it."

"And I don't see how we can't! You're acting like it's over, when there are plenty of people still dealing with it—"

Hope suddenly pushed herself up to stand, taking a moment to regain her balance, and reached for her bag.

"What are you doing?"

When Polly looked up, she was startled to find that Hope's eyes were full of tears. "Please stop."

"What?"

"Just, please, stop," Hope said, blinking quickly. She drew a trembling breath. "I'd just rather not get upset right now. I'm actually trying to enjoy the weekend. Because I've been really looking forward to it, believe it or not," she said, then she pressed her bag under her arm and walked away.

ELEVEN

ADAM

The hill behind the dining hall looked bigger than he remembered. Didn't memory usually work the other way around? When you were an adult, things that once seemed intimidating were meant to look smaller, less daunting, like the maple tree in his parents' backyard. But the hill was easily a hundred feet high. There were steps, too, which most students used to travel between the upper and lower campus, but for the intrepid, or the stupid, the hill had beckoned—on skates, on textbooks, on orange cafeteria trays. From the back of the dining hall, it was a steep incline to the thicket of trees at the bottom, the trails that led to the track and hockey rink and gym.

Study Sprints had been a track team tradition every semester: before the first day of reading week, at the stroke of midnight, the runners all gathered at the bottom of the hill. They were joined by a crowd of under-slept, over-caffeinated classmates. Costumes were encouraged. Boxer shorts, bunny slippers, questionable pajamas. In December, the hill was often frozen; in early May, it was usually a slick of mud. The objective was to reduce stress, blow off steam. After the past year, Adam could not have needed it more.

"Ground rules!" Troy announced. "In case anybody needs a refresher."

He was standing on the golf cart, face purple and bloated, addressing the small band of revelers he'd persuaded to come along: the group from the bouncy castle, plus Eve's husband and minus Hope. For a moment, the thought ran through Adam's head that this was extremely stupid. But screw it.

"Sprint to the top," Troy instructed. "Chug a beer. Sprint back down."

Adam's father's old line wormed its way into his ear—*you go up, you get back down*—but he ignored it.

"Who's up first?" Troy said. "Not me, because I might be too intimidating. Or Olivia, because she's a party pooper."

"Moral support," Olivia clarified.

"I'll go." Jason Haskell stepped up and wrested a beer from the case on the ground. "Good luck," his wife said, blowing him a kiss. She held up her phone and sounded the starting signal, the ringtone of a rocket launching. Haskell took off to a round of claps and whistles. He was still in shape, and kept up a respectable pace. Chugged at the top, spiked the can.

"Forty-eight years old," Troy narrated as Haskell jogged back down. "He looks like a goddamn movie star. Who's confident enough to follow that?"

"I'll get it over with," said Eve's husband, displaying the same stoic amiability with which he seemed to approach everything at a reunion that wasn't his.

"If you hurt yourself, I'll kill you," Eve said, handing him a beer. When he started uphill in his laceless sneakers, he almost lost his footing, but soldiered on gamely. Adam smiled, felt that old adrenaline humming inside him, the buzz he associated with running. Back in high school, when his gym teacher first recruited him for the track team, Adam hadn't been interested. Track seemed too tame. But after checking out a practice, he realized it was exactly the outlet he'd been needing. A way to stay in motion. To burn off energy and avoid being at home. And he was good at it—senior year, he broke the district record for the eight-hundred-meter. He could have been really good if he'd cared more about winning.

"Look at this guy," Troy crowed as Eve's husband returned to the bottom, pink-faced and puffing slightly. "Not even an alum and he killed it."

"Or it killed him," Eve observed.

"He's fine," Troy said, and Adam gave the guy an appreciative thump on the shoulder. "Who's next?"

"You are," Eve shot back.

"Okay, but don't say I didn't warn you," Troy said, hopping off the cart. He did a few exaggerated squats and lunges, to heckles from the crowd. Then he said, "Stand back, everybody," and jumped gracelessly back behind the wheel, revved the engine, and drove straight up the hill.

"What the fuck?" Haskell said, but Adam just started laughing.

Eve protested, "Cheater!"

At the top, Troy executed a jerky three-point turn. Olivia filmed it on her phone. Then he chugged his beer and maneuvered the cart back down. "Jesus," he said, collapsing on the wheel. "I was driving and I'm winded."

They booed. They clapped. Laughed. Pelted him with pine cones. The details didn't matter. There was something satisfying about seeing people be exactly who you expected them to be.

"Oh, what the hell, I'll go," Eve said, kicking off her sandals. She danced up the hill, yelping in her bare feet. At the top, she raised her beer over her head. "This is ridiculous!" she shouted, but managed to get some of it down, dumping the rest on the grass. Back at the bottom, she flopped on her back and did a few lazy snow-angel-like motions, her long sweater pooling beneath her. "It's so stupid it actually feels good," she said.

You go up, you get back down—Adam remembered how dismissively his father had said it. How he'd turned and walked away. His brothers had trailed behind him, probably just relieved to be on the right side of his anger, while Adam clung to the tree, paralyzed, for how long? One hour? Three? He watched his family eating dinner through the dining room window, his brothers sending him furtive glances as the sky grew dimmer, then fully dark. Finally, his mother came out and stood at the bottom of the tree, half scolding and half begging. *Get down right now*, she whispered, so Adam did, clinging to the trunk, snot-faced, shorts damp, bark scraping the insides of his thighs.

Fuck him, Adam thought.

Then he noticed Greg looking at him strangely. "Is that you?"

He blinked, wondering if he'd spoken out loud. "Definitely not."

"It is," Greg said. "Are you going to get it?"

"Get what?"

"Your phone," Greg said, and at this Adam registered the distant buzzing in his pocket and fumbled to answer. *Andrea would like FaceTime.* When he saw her face, he broke into a rubbery smile. "You're here," he said.

She laughed. "Hello to you, too." Her face was slightly pixelated, but Adam could see the scene exactly: living room couch, feet tucked beneath her thighs. Her cheeks were warm, her feet cold.

"I miss you," he said emphatically.

"Looks like somebody's having a good time."

"I am. But I still miss you."

"We miss you, too," she said. "I let the kids stay up a little late."

He realized he had no idea what time it was. He felt one-in-the-morning drunk, but his phone said 10:42. Still, it was late for the boys.

Troy yelled, "Herman! Dalton! Who's up?"

"Up?" Andrea's eyebrows lifted. "Are you being summoned?"

"Study Sprints," he said. "It's a dumb thing we did in college."

She was peering into the phone, a slight furrow between her eyes. His own face, in the corner, was a pale, sweaty moon. "Where are you?"

"Behind the dining hall," he said. "There's this hill where we used to—"

He heard a burst of applause and looked up to see Greg crouched low to the ground, like a sprinter getting into the blocks. Adam whistled loudly. "That's Greg," he told Andrea. "My freshman-year roommate. Remember him from the last reunion?"

"Of course," she said. "A surgeon, right?"

"His parents both died last year," Adam said.

"Oh—" She sucked in a breath. "Oh my God."

The rocket sounded and Greg took off, bounding smoothly up the hill. At forty-eight, he moved with an impressive ease. It was part fitness, Adam thought, part indifference. Troy hollered, "Attaboy!"

"And that's Troy," Adam said. "Remember Troy?"

"How could I forget?"

"He's a changed man. He wanted me to tell you."

At the top, Greg thrust his arms in the air, triumphant. Then he dove onto the ground and rolled all the way back down, tumbling with abandon, and was greeted with boisterous cheers. Adam stepped away from the noise, closer to the trees. "He's been in therapy," he said. "Troy."

"Oh," Andrea said. "Good for him."

"He says it's really helped."

"Dalton!" Troy brayed. "What the fuck?"

"It sounds like I should let you go," Andrea said. "But just a second—the boys want to say good night." She swiveled the phone, and there they were, where they always were, working on The Tunnels, an imaginary universe of interconnected roads and bridges that suddenly felt so obviously symbolic Adam thought he might cry.

"Hey, Dad!" they called and waved.

"Hey, guys," he said, a sharp pinch in his throat. "I miss you."

"We miss you, too."

"How come it's so dark?" Zachary asked.

"I'm outside."

"In a forest?"

He smiled. "Sort of. I'm standing near some trees."

"Is it dangerous?" Sam asked, and it socked Adam in the chest—how they'd been living for the past fifteen months, how much fear they'd taken in.

"Not dangerous," he told them. "It's beautiful. Lots of trees. And stars. Lots and lots of stars. Sort of like camping. Remember when we went camping? In the backyard? We need to do that again. Real camping this time."

"Dalton! Are you wimping out or what?"

"Say good night to Dad," Andrea said, and then she was back on, repeating, "Sounds like I should let you—"

"I really wish you were here," Adam said.

A light laugh. "That's sweet," she said.

"Seriously, though. Why *aren't* you?"

Andrea hesitated, speaking carefully. "You know the boys were sick—"

"But you weren't coming. You were never coming. Which is crazy. This is crazy. I don't know what's even happening anymore. I don't understand what the fuck we're even doing!"

He watched her stand up swiftly and walk out of the living room, the details of their house flashing behind her shoulder—a glint of the mirror in the dining room, the bright blobs of the boys' watercolors taped to the walls. "I don't think now's the time to talk about it," she whispered. "I think you've had a few."

"That means I don't miss you? I'm telling you how I feel—"

"You're shouting," she said. "We'll talk tomorrow. Okay? Call me in the morning," she said, and like that, she was gone. Adam stared at the screen, his heart thudding. He was angry that she wasn't there. That he had to lie about it. That he'd become so comfortable lying about it. That he'd stopped being able to talk to her, his wife, whom everyone could talk to.

"Everything okay?" Troy called out, and Adam realized that the group had gone quiet, and they'd heard every word, and it must have been pretty bad for Troy to sound so concerned.

"All good," Adam said and rejoined them. It was Greg who reached out to pat him on the back, which made him want to fucking weep. "Let's do this," he said and shook his arms loose. He did a few jumping jacks to get the blood pumping, lighten the mood. These people would expect a show from him and this at least he could deliver. He grabbed a beer as Olivia raised her phone. "Ready, set—" At the sound of the mechanized blast, Adam didn't hold back. He sprinted up the hill as fast as he could, relishing the hard clap of the ground against the soles of his feet. The dull echo in his shins. It felt good to push his body. At the top, he was barely winded. He cracked the beer and drained it, then paused for a moment to take in the view. On the other side of the dining hall, he could see the top of the bouncy castle, the turrets and spires in silhouette against the night sky. He crunched the can and stuffed it in his pocket and looked down at the bottom of the hill, which was murky, lit only by the headlights' beams. When he started his descent, he didn't fuck around by slowing to a jog, but ran full speed. He felt light and strong, his sneakers pounding the dirt, breath rattling in his lungs. The ground was a blur of deep greens and shadows. He registered the moment he might have pulled back but ran past it, legs hurtling forward, feet landing a beat behind the rest of him, until his momentum overtook him and he pitched forward into the dark.

POLLY

Polly watched Hope rushing around the perimeter of the quad, chin down, bag clasped against her side. She was incredulous—they'd finally started talking about something important, and Hope just took off? She knew her old friend avoided conflict, but was she no longer able to talk about anything remotely uncomfortable? Anything real?

Polly wished Hope knew. She felt hurt—irrationally, unfairly—that Hope didn't.

But as Hope's form grew smaller, still hurrying—desperate to get out of sight, because she'd hate to be seen looking frazzled—Polly's indignation softened a little. Maybe she'd been too hard on her. She knew how much this weekend meant to Hope. An argument at the reunion was the last thing she would want.

Hope ducked around the side of the chapel, then disappeared from view. Polly looked back to the sea of faces beneath the tent, but whatever camaraderie she'd felt earlier had slipped away. She couldn't imagine wading back into the party—but if she left, where would she go? There was the dorm, but she didn't want to be alone there. She had drunk far too much to drive anywhere. She looked for Adam, but he'd gone off with Troy and apparently had yet to return.

Unwittingly, her gaze traveled from the pristine white canopy to the old brick buildings on the opposite side of the quad. They were lit from the inside, windows gleaming under the darkened sky. The three stained glass ovals emerged gradually, sharpening into focus while the rest of the quad receded, like one of those old Magic Eye posters. The windows stared at Polly, and Polly stared back.

The last time she'd set foot inside Thompson Hall, she had just spent almost twelve hours on the Greyhound from Port Authority to Portland, then switched to a local bus, which dropped her off in front of the 7-Eleven in Sewall shortly after noon. The bus had been warm, but when Polly stepped onto the sidewalk, freezing air coiled around her, slithering down the collar of her jacket and stinging her cheeks. What had been rain in New York had hardened into sharp hairpins of sleet. She was still dressed for the prior evening's class, an attempt at looking professional: black pants, pilled black sweater, and black flats, one sole coming unglued. She had no hat or gloves, not even the fingerless ones she'd worn in college. Hope had always groaned about the inadequacy of Polly's winter wardrobe; this time, at least, she had an excuse.

As she walked up College Avenue, she minced along the slippery patches. Snow seeped into her shoes. She passed the phone booth where she'd once called Hope collect after waking up in a stranger's apartment. It hadn't been all that long ago, but they hadn't yet had cell phones. She'd just gotten lucky that Hope was home. Ten minutes later, her roommate was pulling up in the Jetta, and Polly climbed in the front seat, piecing together a patchy account of what happened. Seven years after graduating, Polly could text or call and reach Hope in seconds. So much had changed.

By the time she'd made it to the marble archway, Polly's hands were swollen, her knuckles stiff. She tugged down the cuffs of her leather jacket to cover her wrists. The quad was more or less deserted, the combined effect of the bitter weather and the anticipatory lull before a Friday night. When she passed two girls huddled under coats and backpacks, Polly gave them a smile, feeling a sense of kinship that took her by surprise.

She'd stepped into Thompson Hall and swiped her hands down her hair, snow melting under her bare palms. Then she'd started for the stairs, still believing for one more minute that coming here hadn't been a terrible idea, when she heard "Polly?"

It was Linda. She had forgotten about Linda. It was a Friday afternoon.

Polly waved. "Oh, hey."

"I thought that was you." Linda was sitting behind the desk in the department office. At first, she sounded happy to see her, then Polly watched her face change, surprise shifting to a maternal kind of concern. "What brings you back?" she asked.

"I was just in the neighborhood," Polly answered, keeping her eyes on the wooden cubbies behind Linda's shoulder, faculty mailboxes she'd filled as a work-study student what felt like a hundred years ago. She couldn't bear to look at the candy jar on Linda's desk, the expression on her face. "It's good to see you," Polly said, then waved again and kept going, beelining up the stairwell, and not stopping until she was knocking on his door.

"Come in," McFadden said. She found him typing at his desk, then he looked up. "Polly?" He stood abruptly, with a look of alarm. "What are you doing here?"

It had been a mistake: Polly saw this instantly and clearly. But she tried to sound casual, even flirty, a tone that so many years later it pained her to recall. "Well, hello to you, too."

He crossed the room and shut the door. "Are you insane?"

Her pulse throbbed in her wrists. "I emailed you. You didn't write back. I thought something might be seriously wrong. I thought you might be dead or something—"

"So you *showed up* here?" he said, glancing toward the closed door. Then he pinched the skin between his eyebrows and lowered his voice. "Sorry. You're—you just caught me by surprise. Have a seat."

He gestured to the chairs, and she sat on one of the stupidly uncomfortable hard-backed ones. She kept her knees locked, backpack clamped to her lap. In her soaked flats, her feet were numb, her exposed skin an angry pink.

"I got your email," McFadden said, returning to his desk. "And I intended to reply." He ran a palm over his head, the same freckled head she'd stared at in a hotel bed only four nights before. "To be honest, Polly, I didn't know what to say."

Polly waited, pulling on the inside of her lip with her teeth.

"I'm afraid you may have gotten the wrong impression," he said finally.

"Really?" She laughed nervously. "You invented a reason to come see me."

McFadden winced a little, then let his eyes rest on the stained glass window. But instead of appearing thoughtful as he considered what to say next, he looked tense. "Let me ask you this," he said. "Have you ever felt as if you were acting the part of someone else?"

"No," Polly said. An honest answer. For better or worse, she had always been herself.

"Well," he said. "That's rare, I think. Very rare. And fortunate. Because it can be very disorienting." He looked at her directly. "The thing is, in New York, I wasn't myself."

Polly's body was a riot of contradictions. She couldn't feel her toes, but her scalp prickled with heat. His words were painful, but at the same time she believed them, because it suddenly struck her as ludicrous that any of it had happened—that she'd slept beside him, that he'd taken off her shoes and held her feet.

When he spoke again, his voice was quiet but firm. "That wasn't—it isn't—who I am," he said.

He went on to say other things then, but she was only half listening. Her ears were humming. The room was shrinking. Each word was another cupful of water added to an overflowing bucket. *Out of context. Hard to resist.*

"You have your whole life ahead of you," he concluded. "You wouldn't want to be burdened with a dinosaur like me."

Age is irrelevant, she remembered, and her old self would have said it, but that person was gone. Instead, she made a pathetic attempt to keep her dignity. "That's true," she said. "I wouldn't."

"Very wise," McFadden said, with a weak laugh. He didn't acknowledge the tremble in her voice. "But I'm sure you didn't travel all the way here just to drop in on my office hours," he added and smiled at her. "Right?"

The smile was hopeful. And, in hindsight, maybe a touch fearful. Had it been a different time, Polly could have blown up his life with a few forwarded emails or a social media post, but back then she felt powerless. Stupid. Grateful, that he was letting her pretend she hadn't come all that way just for this.

"I'm on my way to visit my old roommate," Polly said, which she so wished were true: that she was going to see Hope, who would piece her back together, remind her of her worth.

McFadden's expression sagged with relief—surely not because he believed her, but because she was willing to play along. He stood and walked toward her. "Friends?" he said, and then he was shaking her hand and she was letting him and she was escorting herself back downstairs.

More than two decades later, Polly felt that old shame alive inside her, a dormant virus that had been waiting to flare up. When she stood up and started walking, she felt apprehensive, but defiant, as if she'd accepted a dare. She stuck to the perimeter of the quad, like Hope had, but circled in the opposite direction, past the marble archway and the music building, ultimately stopping in front of Thompson Hall. In college, the door had been unlocked at all hours, but now it was sealed shut.

Polly cupped her eyes, peering through the clear pane of glass. There were no lights on, but as she stared into the shadows, the contours of the lobby became visible in the dark: the wooden bench, the painting of the emeritus professor the building had been named for, the door to Linda's office, though it wouldn't be Linda's office anymore. Polly could make out the poster on the door, black with rainbow letters: THIS IS A SAFE SPACE. The same one hung on the door of her shared office in New York.

On that long-ago Friday, she had dashed past Linda's doorway, pushed her way out of the building, and gulped the freezing air, missing her friends so much she couldn't breathe. Then she'd walked across the quad, losing her footing on the ice but staying upright, and didn't stop moving until she reached the 7-Eleven, where she bought a hot coffee and held it in her frozen hands while she waited on the bench for the first of two buses that would take her home. Sitting there, Polly decided never to tell anyone what happened with McFadden. Not Adam, not even Hope. Because if she never spoke about it, she could erase it, step over it like a crack in the sidewalk. She could leave here and never come back.

When the glass on Thompson's door had grown steamy from her breath, Polly turned back to the quad. Night had fallen, but the lanterns under the canopy made the tent look like a floating island. Then a pair of headlights swept across the grass, and a golf cart jerked to a stop. Polly saw Adam riding shotgun, Greg Herman at the wheel. She didn't see Hope, though. She scanned the crowd again, more carefully, then dug her phone from her pocket and typed: where did you go?

THIRTEEN

HOPE

In the mirror of the bathroom in the old student union, Hope was alarmed by her appearance. The fluorescent lights showed everything: the circles beneath her eyes, the brown sunspots on her jaw. Her hair was messy, makeup smudged. Wrinkles had appeared in her under-eye concealer, like hairline cracks in a vase.

Staring at her reflection, she admonished herself to pull it together.

This was her reunion. She'd been waiting for this, and now she was wasting it.

It was supposed to be a return to normalcy.

I hate to tell you, but I don't see that happening.

If we just go back to how things were before, then what was the point?

But Hope disagreed, seeing no harm in putting this awful year behind them. She felt no need to relive it and reflect on it. She'd gotten through it, gotten her kids through it, and just wanted to move on and enjoy the weekend, but nothing felt like she'd expected. Polly was upset with her, and Adam had taken off.

She pressed her fingertips to the sink ledge. Drew a breath.

Probably she was being oversensitive. Expectations were too high. Drinks too strong. She was just out of practice, like she'd told Ashley at the inn. Polly was being Polly, and Adam would be back.

Then her phone chirped, an incoming text, and she fished it from her purse.

Where's his rabbit, Ethan had written.

Hope immediately assessed the entire situation. It was 10:33 p.m.: Izzy was at her dance and it was two hours past Rowan's bedtime and he was still awake. She knew he would be inconsolable without Gray Rabbit, and Ethan would be getting frustrated. She recalled the intake session with Ellen, she and Ethan perched on small plastic chairs in her rainbow-colored playroom. *Rowan is a sweet, smart, adorable boy*, the therapist had said, before proceeding to detail her concerns—emotional regulation, sensory regulation, impulse control. Hope had nodded, kept nodding, recognizing the truth in what she was saying. Feeling worried, but equally determined. Ethan, though, looked bewildered. His hands dangled helplessly between his knees. If Rowan was all emotion, Ethan was cerebral. Intellectual. Sometimes he looked at their son like he just didn't understand him, and though Hope wished he would try harder, in that moment her heart went out to him. When they left the session and buckled themselves into the car, she said, *Well, I like her. I trust her. We'll just follow her advice.* Ethan stared straight ahead, at the basketball hoop at the end of Ellen's driveway. *I can't deal with this*, he said quietly. *I don't want to.* Hope asked, *What did you say?* but he started the car and drove home and she'd chalked it up to the stress of the moment and they never spoke of it again.

She returned to the phone, typing sloppily.

Try bhind sofa

Or under trapoline

And tell Ro I love him!!!

Then she heard footsteps in the hallway and ducked into the stall, the lightweight door swinging shut with a bang. She sat and stared at the shiny green metal. Another memory swam up before her: the Xeroxed notice taped to the backs of all the bathroom doors. Information about the sexual assault hotline, the names and numbers of peer counselors who could be phoned at any hour. She'd stared at that list for four years, knew every name on it, but had never heard of someone calling it. Surely, though, people must have called all the time.

Now, on the back of the door, there was a guide to proper handwashing. A reminder about indoor masking. A thin, tentative scritch of graffiti: *Are we all doing ok?*

The letters pooled. The footsteps had receded. Hope stepped back out and splashed her face with cold water, then realized there were no paper towels, only one of those air dryers that never worked properly but were better for the environment, because everything now was both better and worse. She patted her cheeks dry with her hands, drew another breath, and unzipped her purse; this, she thought, was why one should never be without one. She dug out her cosmetics bag and set to work, sharpening her eyeliner and reapplying her concealer. She rubbed her front teeth with a square of wine stain remover. Ran a brush through her hair, sending a few loose strands drifting into the sink.

Then she confronted her reflection—*remain present in the moment*—and gave herself a smile. She exited the bathroom and walked back through the deserted student union. Past the darkened school store, where rows of mugs and sweatshirts slumbered behind a metal grate. Past the empty coffee bar with the chalkboard sign: STAY SAFE! Her gait was a little unsteady, but when she pushed open the double doors, the air felt good on her warm skin. Then her phone sounded again, and she braced herself for Ethan, but it was Polly.

Where did you go?

It could be hard, in a text, to gauge a person's tone—concerned? Annoyed? Emojis could help, but Polly didn't use emojis. Not that it mattered. Hope felt relieved to hear from her, and childish for walking away. She started to write back and let her know she was coming, when she heard a faint, crackling sound from the side of the building. She turned to find Grady cowering sheepishly behind the rows of landscaped petunias.

Hope laughed. "What are you doing?"

He had a red Solo cup in one hand, a vape pen in the other, the guilty expression of a kid who got caught with his hand in the cookie jar.

"Are you *hiding*?"

"Kind of," he said. "This place is bringing out the worst in me."

"So I see."

He stepped around the flower beds. "My wife hates that I smoke these things," he said, making his way over to the steps where Hope was standing. From the other side of the railing, he offered her the pen.

"What even is it?" Hope frowned. "A cigarette? Pot?"

"Like a cigarette. There's nothing to it."

"I don't know the first thing about it," Hope said, but pinched the pen warily between two fingers. "These are for teenagers, aren't they?"

"You're never too old, Stokes," Grady said. "Just inhale."

Hope put the pen to her lips and took two puffs. The smoke burned her throat. It tasted faintly like mint. "Well, I guess I can cross that off my bucket list," she said, but when she went to hand it back, the sky swayed, and she grew light-headed.

"Shit," Grady said, as Hope sank to the step. She sensed him rushing to the front of the building and up the stairs as she leaned her forehead against the railing. In her ears, there was a tinny, high-pitched ringing. Then Grady was kneeling in front of her, handing her his cup.

"Here," he said. "Have some water."

Hope took a drink. It wasn't water. But the sting of gin awoke her senses. She lifted her head, pressing her palm to her cheeks.

"Are you okay?" Grady said.

"I think so," she said. "Just embarrassed."

As her vision solidified, she saw the worried look on his face. "Do I need to call the paramedics?"

"I'm fine. Really. I just got a little dizzy."

"Campus security?"

She managed another laugh. "You mean Troy? I'll pass."

Grady sat back on his heels. "I'm taking you at your word. Your husband won't come after me, will he?" he added, and the very idea of Ethan rising to her defense struck Hope as sadly hilarious.

"He won't know, don't worry," she said. "And he isn't here anyway."

"Right," he said, and they went quiet. Grady smoked. Hope took another sip of gin. On the landing, a table had been picked over, only a scattering of gift bags and a cheerful banner left behind. WELCOME BACK, CLASS OF 1995 (WE MADE IT!!!)

"So are you having fun, Stokes?" Grady asked.

"Oh, definitely," Hope said, then paused. "I mean, for the most part. Are you?"

He exhaled. "To be honest with you, there aren't that many people I really care about seeing."

The line hung in the air, suspended on the thin tendril of smoke. Then he turned to her and smiled, his old smile, the one he'd send her across a room toward the end of a party. Funny how, in an older face, someone could look for a moment exactly as they had when they were young.

He took a final drag, then stood and offered his hand. "Come on," he said. "Let's walk."

The sky was dark, but still lighter than the trees, a smoky-gray color that reminded Hope of bonfires. As they crossed the road in front of the student union, she heard waves of chatter—louder now, looser. But before the tent came into view, Grady veered left, skirting the back of the library, and Hope followed without discussion. It felt good, to just not talk. When they reached College Avenue, Grady turned away from town, in the direction of the sleepy side streets, the old fraternities and professors' houses. The noise of the party was growing faint behind them. They crossed the street together, then he stopped on the corner. "Should we see how badly they've wrecked the place?" he said.

Cutter Drive: the street his fraternity had been on. Hope nodded and said, "I bet it's not so bad."

As they turned the corner, the sounds of the reunion disappeared completely. Hope heard only the clip of her boots, the swish of Grady's sleeve. It felt like being nineteen again: the sweet smells of pine trees and alcohol, the scuff of the pavement, the jolt that ran through her when his hand grazed hers. *Happiness*. She'd forgotten it was so tangible, a symptom like any other.

Then Grady stopped abruptly. "Holy shit," he said.

For a moment, Hope didn't recognize it. The old fraternity house now resembled a bed-and-breakfast, the porch that in a past life had been a mess of keg cups and stained futons now furnished with cushioned porch swings and Adirondack chairs. HULL HOUSE, said the placard by the door. Hope had read about it in the alumni bulletin, a new residence for students looking for a more studious, low-stimulus environment, what in the nineties they'd called a *quiet dorm*.

"The inside probably isn't so different," she said. Grady was already mounting the stairs. "What the fuck," he said, rattling the handle, then led Hope around to the side of the house, squeezing behind a row of trash cans to access a screen door she hadn't known was there. He patted the top of the door frame until he found the key. "Voilà," he said, then unlocked the knob and entered the house with the flourish of a teenager, as if the place still belonged to him.

Hope's prediction had been wrong: the living room, former home of foosball tables and musty couches, had been gut-renovated. It now looked closer to an open-concept office, equipped with balance ball chairs and flat-screen TVs. The house was clean and uncluttered, presumably unoccupied for the summer, but still bore traces of the spring semester. The wall that had once been crowded with framed photos of fraternity brothers was now papered with signs about safety protocols and campus resources, an online forum about inclusivity, a workshop on self-care.

"Come on," Grady said grimly. Hope followed him through the living room, past the kitchen, and down the basement stairs. She felt the memory of those stairs in her stomach: the sensation of inching down the narrow stairwell clogged with people, submerging into the humid barroom with its thumping music and sticky floors, scanning the crowd until she made eye contact, waiting for the moment when the night would wind down, people passing out or pairing up.

"This place is tragic," Grady pronounced. The bar had been ripped out, and the cracked tile buried under a neutral synthetic carpet. "Does anybody at this school have any fun anymore?"

"I'm sure some of them do," Hope answered.

He turned to her, smiling a little. "Stokes," he said. "Thank God you're here." Then he took her hand, and Hope felt a splash in her gut. As they walked back upstairs, his fingers remained threaded in hers. Casually, almost inadvertently. When they reached the first floor, Grady kept climbing to the second, a wide hallway with rooms on both sides. "This one was yours, right?" Hope said, pausing in front of the second door on the left.

"Stokes." He shook his head. "How the hell do you remember that?"

Hope's mind raced with all the details she remembered: the life-sized poster of U2, the glass paperweight shaped like a football. The Irish flag that drooped from the ceiling above his bed like a wind-filled sail. Then he took a step toward her. He opened his palm and pressed it against hers. When he bent to kiss her, it felt immediately familiar—the height of him, and the way she had to lift her chin to reach his face.

Then he leaned back, studying her, as her heart thrashed in her chest. "You okay?" he asked, and touched her cheek. He kissed her again, longer this time, and Hope didn't even consider breaking it off, because it felt too good, and because it had happened before, and once the line had been crossed there was less reason to stop.

He fumbled for the doorknob, and the door swung open, banging against the wall. The room itself was shockingly small—had it always been this size? Within seconds they were standing by the bed. Grady dropped to the edge, hooking a finger through Hope's belt loop, while she said, "I can't believe we're here, can you?" He tugged her lightly toward him, running his hands over her hips. "These beds are tiny! Can you believe it? Did we actually sleep in beds this tiny?" she rambled, until he murmured, "Will you be running commentary the whole time?" Then she laughed, and stopped talking, because he was unbuttoning her blouse. Her chest was warm, probably blotchy. She wanted to suck in her stomach, but worried it would be obvious. He lay back on the bed, drawing her down beside him, and she sighed. "Grady," she said, trying to meet his eyes. His expression was slack, almost solemn. He rolled on top of her, the full warm weight of him. When he parted her legs with his knees, Hope heard herself moan. She tightened her legs around his, as a hard ache of longing unfurled at her core.

Then there was a faint slam from downstairs, and Grady jumped up off the bed. "What the fuck was that?"

Hope was frozen in place. "Probably just the wind," she said. "The wind, blowing a door closed. We probably left it open." But the moment was gone. Grady glanced around the room, pulling his fingers through his hair, as their surroundings sank in. The hard foam mattress, the walls speckled with torn poster corners. He looked at her—wearing only a bra on top, pants unzipped and boots on—while he stood there with belt unbuckled but otherwise fully clothed. "Stokes," he said, with an expression she couldn't read. "We better get back out there, huh?" Then he ducked into the hall.

Hope pulled her clothes back on hurriedly, panic spiking through her, buttoning her jeans with shaky fingers and tugging her cardigan around her shoulders and locating the purse she'd dropped. She opened the door, paranoid that he might have left without her, but he was leaning against the wall, scrolling on his phone. He looked up and slid the phone back in his pocket. "All set?" he said.

As they retraced their steps, back down the hallway and the stairs, they didn't touch. Hope's heart was slamming, but her limbs were numb and prickly. She didn't know what she should be feeling. Upset that it had happened. Upset that it was over. Mortified, remembering that moan. Yet as long as she was still with him, there was the chance things could go in a different direction—he could brush her elbow, take her hand again— but outside on the porch, he pushed his hands into his pockets, glancing right and left, then started back the way they had come.

This was a different sort of silence. The zipper on her purse rattled every time it bumped her hip. Grady's pace was so brisk that she had to hurry to keep up. They turned onto College Avenue, and as they neared the quad, Hope could see the lamp-posts illuminated at even intervals, white lights blooming in the dark.

They continued, saying nothing, until they were facing the back of the library from the other side of the street. Then Grady paused. "We should probably split up, huh?"

Hope managed a nod. "Probably."

"I'll head over first." He touched her shoulder and smiled his old smile. "It's good to see you, Stokes," he said, then he was walk-ing away, chest forward and chin up. As if what just happened hadn't clung to him at all. Hope waited a minute or two, then followed, crossing the street and stepping onto the lit path. By the library, in a gap between two glowing lamps, she hesitated. She watched Grady ease back into the scene. A palm clapped on his shoulder, a drink thrust into his hand. She felt hollow. She searched the crowd for her friends. There was Adam, having re-turned as promised, still sitting on a golf cart. Polly was talking with Greg Herman, one arm crossed at her waist. Hope wanted to tell her what had happened, hear her put it in perspective. *I'm pretty sure that in real life, this won't matter at all.*

"Hope?"

At the touch on her shoulder, she jumped and spun around.

"I didn't mean to sneak up on you!" Olivia said, waving both hands. "Just me!"

"Oh—sorry. It's my fault."

"What are you doing all the way over here?"

"I just needed a minute," Hope said.

"I get it," Olivia said. "It's a lot, emotionally, isn't it? I'm surprised we're not all walking into walls." She looked a little cloudy, pushing her hair off her face with both hands. "I just left my kids back at the inn, even though they're not remotely tired. My daughter ate about a hundred cookies."

"My son has a hard time sleeping, too," Hope said, her eyes filling suddenly with tears. She hoped Olivia couldn't see them in the dark.

But Olivia didn't seem to notice, hooking Hope's elbow and steering her toward the party. She commented on the weather— *I remember Maine in June being chilly, but this is balmy!*—and how glad she was that she'd brought sneakers, because after lockdown she realized heels were actually barbaric—*when I first put them back on, I thought, how did women* ever *live like this?* As they approached the tent, Hope slowed down.

"Actually, Olivia, I don't feel so well all of the sudden."

Olivia took an involuntary step back. "Oh?"

"Not, you know, sick-sick. I think I'm just exhausted. It's a lot—like you said. Emotionally." She managed a smile. "I think I'd better call it a night."

"Oh," Olivia said and looked genuinely sorry. "Well, we'll

miss you. But it's probably wise to get some sleep. Rest up for tomorrow."

"Absolutely."

"I'll save a seat for you at brunch," Olivia said, hugging the air, then moved on. Hope watched for another second, then turned and walked quickly back toward the inn. She tucked her chin, pinching her sweatered elbows. Her eyes were watering, her purse still banging against her side. As the red door came into view, she heard a knocking sound and realized it was her teeth chattering, even though Olivia was right, it wasn't cold out. It wasn't until she made it to the lobby—empty, thankfully, at nearly midnight—and rushed upstairs to Room 207 and shut the door behind her that she started crying and couldn't stop.

FOURTEEN

ADAM

Adam lay on the grass in front of Fiske Hall, staring up at the sky through the webbed branches of the trees. His ankle hurt, but not that badly. The worst part had been the moment right after the fall, when his chin smacked the ground. He'd remained still for a minute, assessing the damage, and listened to the footsteps scrambling up the hill. Gently, he'd circled his wrists and run his tongue across his teeth. Everything seemed to be intact, but when he stood, pain scissored through his ankle. A sprain, maybe, Greg had said, prodding at it, and insisted on driving him back to the tent. Adam assured them all he was fine, even made a show of hopping into the golf cart. He might pay for it tomorrow, but for now he barely felt a thing.

A sleepy pall had settled over campus. Adam was vaguely aware of the grass grazing the back of his neck, a rock pressing into his spine. In the past year, he'd often have a few beers in the hour between eleven and midnight, but it had been a while since he'd been drunk like this. The moon was a bright sliver: *waxing crescent*, his boys would identify, correctly. The sky was a crazy spill of stars.

"Seriously," Polly said. "Where could she have gone?"

She'd been stuck in this loop ever since they'd made their way back from the party: Hope had taken off early, and Polly didn't know where she was. They'd been talking—arguing, it sounded like, though the details were hazy—and Hope walked away and hadn't come back.

"I know she hates talking about politics," Polly said. "But it wasn't even about politics. It was just reality. I mean, what the fuck else is there to talk about?"

While Adam's drunkenness had thickened, turned sluggish, Polly's was still alert and buzzing. She was sitting upright against a tree, eating Twizzlers she'd dug out of her car. In college, they would have both been smoking Marlboro Lights—they'd only smoked when drunk or emotional, and tonight qualified on both counts—but in the absence of cigarettes, Polly was determinedly chewing.

"Maybe it's because I said that Foxy is a Masshole," she said. "I mean, he was. *Is.* He was nicknamed Foxy, for Chrissake."

Adam laughed, but it took effort, no longer buoyed by the easy happiness of when he'd first arrived. This happiness was squeezed under layers. The ankle. The alcohol. The conversation with Andrea. He would call her tomorrow, first thing, to apologize.

"Try to let it go," he told her. "It'll feel different in the morning."

"It just doesn't make sense," Polly said. "Hope would never leave the reunion. She lives for reunions."

Adam thought of Hope's expression in the bouncy house earlier, that forced smile. "Maybe she wasn't having fun."

"Hope? How is that possible?"

"Maybe she got tired and went to bed."

"Not without telling us," Polly said. "That's your thing."

Adam managed a drowsy smile. "There's a name for it now, you know," he said, but she was chewing again, not hearing him.

"And she didn't text me back," she continued. "I know she read it, though, because I saw the thing that said she did. What's that about?"

"Karma for ignoring her texts for ten years?"

At this, Polly stopped and laughed. At least the loop was broken. Adam looked at the sky, trying to imagine what Andrea would say. *It must be exhausting being her.*

"Maybe Hope's just not happy," Adam said.

"Then why doesn't she say so?"

"Because she's Hope," he said.

"Right," Polly said, then lapsed into silence. He heard her tearing up a fistful of grass. "I feel bad that she was upset. But I just don't get her anymore. All she wants to talk about is stuff that happened thirty years ago. I feel like I barely know her, and she acts like we're still close," she said, but sounded more subdued.

"I guess you still haven't told her about McFadden," Adam said. The thought just fell from his soft, spongy brain out of his mouth.

This time, Polly didn't freeze up. "No," she said. "I haven't. I did try once, years ago, but I couldn't. And then it just got weird—like that whole part of my life existed in this vacuum."

Adam stared up at the trees, the rock beneath him like a finger prodding his spine. "So tell her now."

"She'd just be mad I didn't do it sooner."

"You told me. I didn't get mad."

"You never get mad," Polly joked, but the memory of that dinner still caused an ache in Adam's chest—Andrea six months pregnant, flushed and glowing, sitting in a busy restaurant in New York.

"I wasn't even *planning* to tell you," Polly said. "But McFadden had just died. Remember?"

He did. The guy had collapsed while running, seemingly out of nowhere. Not unlike Adam's father. In his early sixties, and otherwise healthy. The kind of death that rattled Adam to the core.

"I went back to his office tonight," Polly said then.

It took Adam a minute. "Wait—you did?"

"I tried," Polly said. "I think I just needed to see it. Then I couldn't even get inside. But at least I didn't spend all weekend avoiding it."

Adam concentrated on a single branch to steady his line of vision. The sky was flooding, the stars dissolving into liquid points. He remembered being up on the roof, freshman year, how the stars swam up to meet him, so clear he'd thought he might reach out and touch them.

"I almost didn't come this weekend," he told her.

"Really?" He sensed her turning toward him, the angle of her voice shifting slightly. "Your kids were that sick?"

"It wasn't the kids," he said. "It's Andrea. She isn't doing well."

Polly took a beat. "You mean the stomach bug?"

"I mean in general."

"But you said she was—"

"She isn't," he said. "She barely leaves the house."

"Oh," Polly said, in soft surprise. He could practically hear her trying to connect the dots. "But what about the weekend with her friends? The yoga thing?"

It was so absurd, the thought of Andrea going away with her friends, of Andrea going anywhere. "There was no yoga thing," he said. "She barely leaves the house. She doesn't want to. Or she can't. It's like she's stuck."

"Oh," she said. Then, "Holy shit, Adam."

He couldn't see her face, but he could picture it—a long, troubled kind of Polly look—as he attempted to collect the loose strands of his thoughts. "It was stupid of me to assume it would just get better. I should have gotten help sooner," he said, the branch thickening as his eyes blurred. "I really fucked up."

"Everyone thinks they fucked up," Polly said matter-of-factly. "Reentry is a big deal. It's unprecedented. You can't be too hard on yourself. And this isn't that uncommon. You're not the only one."

"Yeah," he said, though he knew it wasn't common. Not like this.

Adam's eyelids were growing heavy, and suddenly he was struggling to keep them open. When he gave in, he felt himself plunge backward, the jumble of sky rushing inside his head. Polly's voice sounded smaller, as if she were at a greater distance. "You know what Hope says," she said. "You can only do what you can do."

Adam wanted to smile, but he couldn't. Besides, Hope's line might be trite, but it was true. *You can only do what you can do*—but he should have done more. He could still. For now, though, his head was spinning and he let his thoughts detach and loosen, imagining how he'd wake up in the dorm early tomorrow morning to go running—his old route through the woods at the bottom of the hill behind the dining hall, the spongy path carpeted in brown pine needles—as the sun rose, and his head cleared, his ankle healed, and his hangover burning off like a fog.

III

FIFTEEN

POLLY

At first, the sound of the ringing phone mingled with the hammering rain. Polly rose onto one elbow on the thin mattress and groped the floor beside the bed, where the bare wood was silky with dust. She closed her hand around her phone and brought it to her face, squinting—8:22. Her eyes burned, the contact lenses she'd neglected to take out the night before now like chips of glass. *Unknown Caller*. Since when did robocalls start at 8:22? There was also a text from Adam—Going for a run—sent at 7:45, because Adam was insane.

Gingerly, Polly eased back onto the pillow. Her whole head throbbed. Using her phone as a mirror, she peeled the lenses from her dry eyes then blinked into the rainy gray light leaking through the shades. It was a room just like every other in Fiske, a room like the one she and Hope had shared freshman year. Back in New York, Polly would have struggled to picture it, but lying here in the half dark, she remembered it in surprising detail. Hope's purple duvet cover. Her milk crates stuffed with sweaters. Her posters of Monet waterlilies, the Robert Doisneau one of the couple kissing. On the windowsills, the flowers arranged in Boone's Farm Strawberry Hill bottles. The wall above Hope's desk had been collaged with photos from high school dances, slogans clipped from magazines. Polly hadn't had much to contribute, but Hope had enthusiastically helped her hang up her wrinkled tapestry and posters of Jane's Addiction and The Smiths.

Picturing that room, Polly was filled with an unexpected calmness. Despite the parts of college it hurt to remember, their room had always felt cozy. Homey. After what happened with McFadden, everything about Walthrop had felt somehow tainted. But she had loved it, parts of it. She'd forgotten how much.

Then the night before came crawling back: Hope had left the party and never returned. They'd been arguing about something—US politics in 2021, or campus politics in 1992? Polly's grievances were all blending together. She couldn't remember what she'd said to make Hope walk away, only her own growing frustration—a need for Hope to acknowledge something, to pop the bubble her friend now lived in. From outside Thompson, Polly had texted her, then she and Adam had left the party a while later, but Hope had never written back.

Polly pulled up the message, marked as read, just as her phone lit up again. *Unknown Caller*. This time she answered it. "Hello?" she said, tongue thick as felt.

"Hello." A woman's voice, splintery with static. "Is this Polly?"

"Yes?"

"It's Caroline."

Polly's mind drew a soft, slow blank.

"Caroline Wheeler. Charlie's mother?"

"Oh—right. Sorry." Then nerves bolted through her and she sat up straight, forgetting she was in a bunk bed and smacking her head. "What's wrong?"

"I'm sorry to call so early," Caroline said. "I just thought you'd want to know. I don't know how to put this exactly, but . . . we can't find Jonah."

Polly's body was instantly charged. "What do you mean?"

"He went outside last night," she said. "To make a phone call, we think. But it seems, well, he never came back."

Blood pounded in Polly's temples as she tried to process what the other woman was saying. "What?" she said. "What—where's Charlie?"

"He's here," Caroline said, a touch apologetically. "The phone call was taking a while, so he went to bed. He figured Jonah would let himself back in. But this morning, Tom noticed the door to the guest room was open and the bed hadn't been slept in . . ."

Polly's gaze darted around the room—the empties on the windowsill, the gift bag on the dresser, green sweater tossed on the back of a chair. "I mean, could he get back into the house?" she said. "Did he have a key?"

"Oh, we never lock it," Caroline said, which for some reason made Polly bristle. "I was hoping maybe you'd heard from him—"

"No. I haven't heard from him," she said sharply. She felt angry—at Charlie, for not making sure Jonah was settled in before he went to bed. At Charlie's parents, for letting this happen on their watch. At herself, for not calling Jonah after he hadn't replied to her text. "Where could he have gone?"

"We're guessing the woods behind the house," Caroline said, and Polly pictured the trees that met the edge of their lawn, a thicket of dense green. "It's easy to get turned around in there," Caroline added. "They're bigger than you'd think."

"That's comforting," Polly clipped, and closed her eyes, trying to reel herself in.

Then she heard a light rap on her door, and Adam saying in a loud whisper: "Pol? Is that you?"

"Unlocked! Come in, please!" she called, then asked Caroline, "So what do we do now? Is someone looking for him?"

Adam opened the door but remained in the hallway, dressed in running clothes—shorts and Walthrop T-shirt—all soaked with rain. "Looking for who?" he asked, and Polly mouthed, *Jonah*.

"Tom's already out there," Caroline said. "Charlie's about to join him."

Polly bit her tongue. Why wasn't Charlie already searching? And why didn't his mother seem more upset about what was happening? Maybe in Maine, it wasn't so alarming to disappear overnight, but Jonah was a city kid. He'd never a spent a night outdoors. Even at Elmwood, they'd lived in cabins with hot showers and laundry service.

"We just wanted you to know," Caroline was saying. "He'll probably turn up any minute, but we weren't sure if you'd want to—"

"Of course. I'm coming." Polly snapped, then pressed her fingertips into her eyes. "Sorry. I'll be there as soon as I can."

She released her eyelids, setting off an explosion of tiny sparks, and hung up. When her vision cleared, Adam hadn't moved a muscle. Drips of rain were rolling from his hair down his face.

"Jonah's missing." Just saying the words made her chest cleave in two. She swung her feet to the floor and stood, too quickly, giving herself a head rush, then steadied herself on the bedframe. "They're out looking for him. I need to get there," she said, scanning the room for her clothes.

"Whoa, whoa," Adam said. "What did she say?"

"He went outside last night to make a phone call," Polly said, reaching for her rumpled sweater, "and his friend apparently went to bed. Jonah never came back. They think he might be lost in the woods behind their house."

"Okay." Adam nodded once and rubbed a palm down his face. "So he probably just went for a walk. It probably got dark faster than he expected. He had a joint and fell asleep."

He sounded confident as he posed this theory—it was what Adam might have done, had done, at Jonah's age—but Polly was picturing her son in his hoodie and headphones, roaming the woods at two in the morning. No streetlights, no storefronts, nothing like the perpetual daytime of New York. It was one of the things that had amazed her most when she'd moved to Maine at eighteen, how dark the nights could get.

Her nose stung, and tears rushed to her eyes. "We should never have come up here," she said, turning to Adam. "Why the fuck am I even *here*?"

"Pol," Adam said. "Come on. It's not your fault."

She wiped her nose with the heel of a shaky hand. "You should have seen him when I dropped him off. I knew he didn't want to be there. He looked so miserable."

"So maybe he just needed a minute to himself last night," Adam said. "He's probably waking up right now. It hasn't been that long, and it wasn't that cold. We'll find him," he said, and for a minute Polly let herself be comforted by his story. It was possible, she thought. She could imagine it. Jonah ducking out to smoke, needing a break from Charlie, with whom he no longer had anything in common. Needing a break from the fancy house, the four cars. She pictured him leaning against a tree, taking in the fullness of the sky, the stars skimming the bluish treetops and the smoke wreathing the branches as his eyelids grew heavy. She could almost imagine the exasperation that would come after the relief when he was found.

SIXTEEN

HOPE

She woke up hurting. At first, the pain was physical, a vise of pressure on the crown of her head. It crawled down her spine, seizing her lower back, then curdled in her gut, another in the collection of aches and ailments hidden beneath the surface, like the root of her cracked tooth.

Her eyes opened, and for those first few moments, it felt like so many mornings last spring—waking up to a disturbance in her body, a floating sense of unease, knowing something was very wrong but unable to identify it. The sensation would be unsettling, yet for ten or fifteen seconds, she'd be spared remembering. Then the facts would all come crashing back.

Staring at the rain lashing against the French doors, Hope pictured the walk to the old fraternity house. The basement stairs. The fingers caught in hers.

She felt a stammering at her core—hurt, regret, disbelief—before pins and needles overtook her, currents of static swarming down her limbs.

Her phone started ringing, and she fumbled for it among the pillows. It was Ethan, still angry with her. It was Rowan, unable to manage without her. It was Izzy, somehow aware of what she'd done.

But it was Adam.

"Hope?" he said. "You awake?"

Any other year, missing the Saturday brunch at the reunion would have been devastating, but today Hope was glad for an excuse not to go. The thought of laughing along with her class-mates as they recapped the night before, groaning about their hangovers—bumping into Grady and his family over blue-berry pancakes and chatting about the rain, the class photo that afternoon—made her feel sick.

In the bathroom, she grabbed mouthwash and tissues and stuffed them in her purse. Mints for their morning breath. Advil for their headaches. These small tasks helped occupy her. Even the drive out to the island would be a job to focus on, a role that felt familiar: Polly had a problem, Hope jumped in to fix it.

Then she remembered her argument with Polly the night be-fore and was engulfed by another wave of nausea. She couldn't remember how things had escalated so quickly—one minute they'd been reminiscing about their classmates and the next Polly was picking apart everything Hope said. Still, Hope wished she hadn't let it get to her, and she wouldn't have, if she weren't so out of practice.

For now, she set all that aside. There wasn't time. Adam said they'd pick her up, and the dorm was just across the street, so she had at most ten minutes. She fished the Advil from her purse and swallowed three tablets dry. She was desperate for a shower, but the best she could do was splash her face with cold water and twist her hair up into a plastic clip, the sort she wouldn't or-dinarily wear outside the house. She grabbed her cosmetics bag from her purse and applied her lipstick in two careless swipes. Then she layered on a shirt, sweater, windbreaker, thick socks, Hunter boots—the forecast had gotten it all wrong: this was more than just rain, it was a torrential storm—and grabbed her umbrella. Out in the hall, she moved quietly past the closed doors, creeping down the stairs instead of taking the elevator, but when she smelled coffee, her heart sank. She'd hoped the lobby would be empty, didn't feel up to greeting another person. To her relief, she discovered the coffee maker gurgling on the sideboard, but no one was there.

Hope opened the door and faced the sheeting rain. She had maybe five more minutes until they got there. The umbrella would be more trouble than it was worth, so she stuffed it in her purse, yanked up the hood of her jacket, and dashed across the street to a near-empty Coffee Barn. She felt too queasy for a latte but grabbed three bottled waters, then filled a waxy bag with scones and muffins. By the time she'd splashed back to the inn, Ashley had appeared.

"Morning," she said. She was over by the coffee maker, holding a box of store-bought doughnuts, wearing jeans and a hooded sweatshirt, her hair pulled back in a thick ponytail. Without a mask on, her face looked different than Hope had pictured, fuller, more youthful. She must not be much older than Izzy.

"Good morning," Hope said. She shut the door but remained just inside it, dripping onto the floor.

"Doughnut?"

"Oh no, thanks." She clutched the bag of pastries at her side. "I'm just waiting for my friends to pick me up."

Ashley nodded, lining up the doughnuts on a doily-covered tray. "Real washout, huh?"

"It is," Hope said, gazing across the street. The white tent that

yesterday had been crisp and hopeful was now soaked and abandoned, like a wilted circus. It came to her then, the line she had
forgotten about Maine weather: *Dress for all four seasons in a
single day!*

Then Ashley said, "It's a shame about your reunion," and to
Hope's horror, she felt a pinch in her throat, a prickling in her
eyes. She considered what would happen if she just told Ashley
about the night before, blurted out the whole messy, humiliat-
ing story—the argument with her friend, the meltdown in the
bathroom, the run-in with a guy she'd gone out with twenty-five
years ago, although "going out" was an exaggeration of the truth.

"Sounds like it'll clear up later," Ashley said, and then Adam's
Subaru was pulling up out front. As Hope opened the door to
the inn, Adam lowered his window a few inches and shouted
over the rain: "Can we take your car?"

Hope gave him a thumbs-up. "That's them," she told Ashley,
as if to prove they weren't invented, digging her key fob from
her purse.

"Good luck," Ashley said, her tone so kind that for a moment
Hope felt, absurdly, that she would miss her. She thanked Ashley, unlocked the car with two bright beeps, then pulled her
hood up and pinched her jacket closed beneath her chin as she
ran across the lot.

Polly was already climbing into the backseat, Adam riding shotgun. Hope slid behind the wheel, exclaiming, "This
weather!"

"Thanks for driving. My backseat's a mess," Adam said. It
went without saying that Polly was too upset to get behind the
wheel. She seemed to be wearing the same clothes as the night
before, with the addition of a Walthrop rain poncho, probably
from the gift bag.

"No worries," Hope said. "Let me just clear these windows." She turned on the car and blasted the defrost. "Who's hungry?" She distributed the waters and passed around the damp bag of pastries.

"Thanks, Hopey," Adam said. He twisted the cap off a bottle and chugged half. His face looked rumpled, his eyes a little bloodshot. There was a gash beneath his chin. On the phone, he'd said he'd just come back from a jog. Hope would have found this implausible if Adam hadn't always been this way, able to wake up after a night of drinking, run it off, and start again.

Still, of the three of them, he appeared the most fit for human company. In the rearview mirror, Hope saw Polly facing the window, shoulders huddled in thin plastic. She pictured Polly in the leather jacket she'd worn in college; she'd been chronically underdressed for Maine weather. Then she remembered Polly's text from the night before, the one she'd never answered. She'd started to, then run into Grady, and back at the inn she was too upset to formulate a reply. She'd fallen asleep with the phone beside her cheek.

But Polly didn't mention the unanswered message, or ask where Hope had gone. It was no longer the point. Instead, as the steam inched off the windshield, Hope shifted into problem-solving mode. "So, have we heard anything else?"

"Not yet," Adam said.

"What happens when you call his phone?"

"Straight to voicemail," Polly said, and Adam added, "It probably just ran out of juice."

"Do you use a phone tracker?"

"No," Polly said, glancing at the mirror. "Do you?"

"For Izzy? God, yes," Hope said, then wished she could un-say it. She was trying to empathize with Polly—teenagers causing trouble!—but might have inadvertently sounded critical. "I mean, she resents me for it, so I don't recommend it," she added. "I'm sure it's just the battery."

Polly returned to the window, looking pale.

Adam guzzled the rest of his water, then said, "I'm guessing he just went for a walk last night. He decided to camp out. He wasn't thinking it would cause everybody so much worry."

Hope nodded. "I agree."

"And it's an island," he continued. "You can't get too lost on an island."

"Right," Hope said. But despite what he was saying, Hope thought Adam looked worried, too. Hope wasn't that worried. From what she knew of Jonah, this wasn't so out of character. It certainly wasn't out of character for Polly. By noon, Jonah would have turned up, and the drama would be over, the whole story a funny adventure Polly would be describing at the lobster bake that night.

"I'm sure there's a simple explanation," Hope said. "Let's go find him." She turned the wipers on high and they whipped back and forth as she steered carefully away from the inn. Turning onto College Avenue, she couldn't help thinking about Adam's famous disappearance freshman year—it seemed an obvious story to tell, a natural comparison to make, yet none of them did.

Ledgemere Island was thirty minutes from the college, past the tennis courts and football field and down Route 19. It was a busy four-lane road, the kind of ugly commercial stretch one wouldn't expect to find in coastal Maine. Car dealerships, gas stations, a strip mall with a T.J. Maxx, a Dress Barn—when was the last time Hope had seen a Dress Barn? The sign for the island was pasted to a busy intersection, so small that Adam, her navigator, almost missed it. But once she turned, the landscape softened, the sky opening up and the four-lane road shrinking to two. Buildings grew sparse: a lumberyard, a smattering of prefab houses. A restaurant called the Salty Dog—the kind with umbrella-topped picnic tables, serving fried seafood in red plastic baskets—sat on pylons just before the bridge.

In college, absorbed in life on campus, Hope had tended to forget the ocean was so close by. But Adam used to like driving out to Ledgemere, and during Parents Weekend, families mobbed the island, marveling at the sunsets and descending on the seafood baskets. It was a scenic drive, but harrowing in this weather. Occasionally, and without warning, the road would veer precipitously, the forty-five-mile-per-hour speed limit dipping to fifteen. The wipers sliced quickly across the windshield, the trees blowing sideways in the wind.

Inside the car, it was mostly silent, except for the persistent drumming of the rain. Hope wished they were talking, but knew how bad weather could make people quiet. Plus, they were hungover, and worried. It would be insensitive to talk about anything but the situation at hand. Polly was curled up on the backseat, holding an uneaten muffin. Adam made the occasional comment on the rain, looking at the sky and back at his phone, as if making sure the two were in agreement. Hope tried to concentrate on the road, her wet jeans pasted to her thighs, her rubber boot hovering over the brake pedal.

"Watch out here," Adam cautioned, as they approached the bridge. On a normal day, this turn onto the island was quietly breathtaking—the trees parting, the wooded road breaking into open sky and water—but today it felt nerve-wracking. The ocean was steel gray and choppy, the rain pelting it like needles.

"Just ignore him," Adam said.

It was only then that Hope registered the driver breathing down her neck. A pickup truck with a huge silver grille, a Maine license plate. When the solid line turned broken, he went zooming around her, so close it made the car shudder.

"Asshole," Adam said. "Just take your time."

"I'm good," Hope said, holding the wheel at ten and two. She knew locals could get impatient with out-of-staters, especially ones driving shiny SUVs with private school stickers. She had a flash of her fender bender last fall, the shock of contact when her car collided with the one in front of it. *How could you not see it?* Ethan had said. *Weren't you paying attention?*

"How far down, Pol?" Adam said, with a glance over his shoulder.

"Keep going," Polly said. "It's out toward the end."

The road was narrow, lined with trees and docks and cottages that in better weather must be picturesque but today looked soggy and sad. Adam consulted his phone again, while Polly returned to the window, leaving Hope defenseless against the memories nibbling at her brain. Grady leaning down to kiss her. His finger tugging at her waist. That moan. *Remain present in the moment*, she reminded herself, thinking maybe she finally understood the point.

Then the dashboard lit up with a call from Izzy. Hope jumped as if she'd been caught, then clicked the steering wheel and assumed as normal a tone as possible. "Good morning!"

"Mom?"

Her voice through the speakers sounded loud but far away. And sleepy. She'd probably dragged herself out of bed because Rowan was awake.

"Hi, honey," Hope said. "How's it going?"

"Why does it sound weird?"

"I'm driving. And it's raining. You're on speaker," she added. "Everything okay?"

"Rowan wants to say hi," she said, then Hope's little boy was on the line.

"Mommy?"

Hope heard it right away—the tremble in his voice, like a fault line. She checked the clock. Nine thirty: he would have been up for about half an hour, getting hungry, remembering she was gone.

"Morning, Ro!" she said gaily, overdoing it.

"Where are you?"

"You know where I am, silly! Remember? Back at my old college," she said, driving past a dilapidated ice-cream stand.

"But I need you," he said.

"Izzy's there," she said. "And Dad."

"But it's an emergency."

This could mean anything, of course. He was overtired. Or nervous. His waffle was too hot, too mushy, too cold.

"What's the emergency, Ro?" Hope asked.

"My tummy," he said.

"Well, did you eat breakfast yet?"

"No."

"You're probably just hungry!" she said. "Tell Izzy there are chocolate chip waffles in the—"

"But I need *you*."

"I know, Ro," Hope said, smiling. She believed a person could hear when you were smiling. "But I think you really need breakfast. Where's Dad?"

"Asleep."

It wasn't so late for a Saturday morning, but Ethan knew Izzy was on her own. Was he that oblivious? Or that self-centered? At a certain point, what was the difference? The tick of anger had returned, swelling beneath her skin, but she couldn't let it show—Rowan was too sensitive, and her friends were in earshot, and after last evening, she wasn't sure she had the right.

"I'll go make sure he's up," Izzy said, and Hope silently thanked her, but Rowan was still sniffling. Maybe he could hear the rain falling, the windshield wipers' frantic swishing, sense the tension on the other end of the line.

"Mom?" he said. "When will you be home?"

"Soon," she told him. "Very soon. Sunday. Today's Saturday, and I come home Sunday," she repeated. "One more day."

"Can we FaceTime?" he asked, and his voice dropped out for a second. As they drove deeper onto the island, the signal was getting weaker.

"I can't right now, honey," Hope said. "I'm in the car. With my friends."

There was a static-filled pause, then Adam said, "Hey, Rowan. Hey, buddy."

As Hope had feared, the unfamiliar voice caught Rowan off guard.

"Mommy?" His voice wobbled dangerously. "Mom, where are you?"

"I'm right here, Ro," she said.

"Mom. I think I'm in the orange zone."

Inside her damp clothes, Hope's body flushed with heat. She wished she could pull over to the sandy shoulder, hug him through the speakers. Of course he was having a hard time—it was the first time she'd been away from him in years! What had she been thinking? She should have brought them. She felt selfish and helpless and, shamefully, embarrassed—Rowan was on the brink of melting down, and her friends could hear every word.

"Okay," she said. "So how can we get out of the orange zone? How about we do a breath together—"

Then Polly was sitting forward, gripping the sides of Hope's headrest. "Here's our turn."

Hope saw only a post office, a mailbox, a drenched American flag. "Where?"

"On the left. Just past the post office."

"Mom?" Rowan said. "Mommy?"

"Hold on, Ro," Hope said, as she spotted the sign for PRIVATE DRIVE half hidden in some trees. When she braked sharply, Adam sucked a breath through his teeth.

"Mom?" Rowan was crying in earnest now, the sound cutting in and out. "Mommy?"

"I'm here," Hope told him. "Right here, Ro. Let's do a breath. A candle breath." She swung her car onto a one-lane road, darkened by a canopy of branches, shedding drops of rainwater the size of quarters. Then Izzy was back on, reporting, "Dad said he'll be down soon," but what she said next was garbled. Something about shoes. Lucky Charms.

"Iz, you're breaking up a little," Hope said. "But I'll call you in a little while. Okay, Ro? I'll check on you very, very—"

"No!" he shrieked. "Don't go!"

The car bounced over rutted puddles and the trees all spilled together, and the thought ricocheted through Hope that the past fifteen months had been so unnatural, so unbearable, none of them had any idea how to function anymore.

"Izzy," Hope snapped. "I'm in the car, in the middle of something, and it's pouring. Please go get Dad."

Her daughter paused. "What's going on?"

"Tell him Rowan needs help, and I'm not there, so he'll have to deal with it," she instructed, as Polly said, "It's this one," and Hope stepped on the brake and Polly pointed to a small sign that said, of all things, TRANQUILITY.

Izzy's words scrambled again, but Hope made out, "Where are you?" and "Is something wrong?"

"Nothing's wrong," Hope said, clutching the wheel as they bumped down a muddy driveway, choked on both sides with waterlogged pines. "I'm on the island near the college. Remember Polly's son, Jonah? He's staying with a friend out here and wandered off, so we came out to find him." She felt Polly's eyes in the mirror, but as soon as she glanced back, she looked away. "He's going to be fine, though. Nothing to worry about. Just get Dad and let him know Ro needs him," Hope said. "And give Ro a hug for me. Tell him I'll check in later. Okay? I love you."

Despite the choppy audio, Izzy clearly sounded startled as she said, "Love you, too."

Hope pressed the wheel to end the call. No one spoke. Her heart was galloping, the wipers flashing back and forth. She felt exposed despite all her layers. Sagging branches scraped the sides of the car and squeaked like chalk. Then the driveway ended, the disheveled woods giving way to a gorgeous property, a meticulously landscaped yard and in-ground pool. She pulled up to the wide front porch, the voices of her children still hovering in the air around them, and shut off the engine. The wipers froze midstroke. "Okay then," she said, as raindrops rushed to pebble the windshield. "Here we are."

SEVENTEEN

POLLY

At first Polly had assumed she and Adam would be driving alone to the island. She didn't want to drag Hope away from campus. But Adam insisted Hope would want to come, and Polly knew it would help to have her there. Hope could get uptight about little things, but in a true emergency, she would stay practical and level-headed. In the car, Rowan's call had clearly rattled her, but a minute later Hope was smiling warmly, greeting Caroline at the front door. "Good morning!"

"I brought reinforcements," Polly said. "This is Hope and Adam."

"So sorry to barge in like this," Hope said.

"No, not at all," Caroline said. She was dressed in black leggings and a loose white button-down. She wore no makeup, but her skin was shining, and her damp hair smelled faintly like mint. Polly tried to resist feeling annoyed that she'd taken the time to wash it. "Come in out of the rain."

Polly stepped over the threshold, her cheap poncho rustling, while Hope hung back, saying, "Where should we leave our wet things?"

"Oh, right here's fine," Caroline said.

Polly looked up in surprise. "We're going out looking, aren't we?"

"Oh . . . are we?" Hope looked to Caroline for clarification.

"We could," Caroline said carefully. "Although Tom's already out there. And Charlie. The two of them know those trails inside out . . ."

"So maybe we wait until they get back," Hope said.

"They might come walking up with him any minute," Caroline added.

"Really?" Polly said, with a blunt laugh. She had the urge to turn around and run back outside, across the yard, and into the woods.

From the porch, Adam caught her eye. "Makes sense, Pol. Give it another few minutes."

"I made coffee," Caroline added, and Hope said, "Oh, that was kind of you," and though Polly despised the idea of chatting over coffee while her son was missing, it was true that at any moment the boys might appear. She unzipped her soaked leather boots, while Hope positioned her rubber ones neatly inside the door. Then Polly shucked off her dripping poncho— her sweater gave off a mixture of sweat and beer and cigarette smoke—and followed her friends across the giant off-white living room, accented with shells and driftwood, into the kitchen. Adam was clearly limping. When he and Polly left the dorm that morning, he'd shrugged it off, but now Hope said: "Adam! You hurt yourself doing that stupid run, didn't you?"

"It's nothing," Adam said, but remained upright, leaning against the counter, as if to prove a point.

Hope settled onto a high-top chair at the granite island while Caroline poured coffee. Her hands were thin and fluttery, like restless birds. "Three, right?" she asked, and Polly stubbornly replied, "None for me," as she perched on the edge of the chair next to Hope's and watched the kitchen window. The sky above the woods was bloated, the rain falling in sheets. She was still upset at herself for not following up with Jonah the night before.

Caroline set a mug in front of Hope, and when the smell hit Polly, she realized how depleted she was. In the car, she'd been too distraught to eat, but her head was killing her; it felt as if her skull had been scraped dry. To be so hungover felt like a betrayal—the body should sense that there was something more important going on and ease up on the punishment, but no. Coffee would help.

"You sure?" Caroline said, as if sensing her change of heart.

"Actually, I might have some."

Caroline nodded, as Hope said, "This is perfect. Thank you."

"So how long have they been looking?" Adam asked.

"Tom's been out about an hour," Caroline said, pouring another cup. "Charlie, maybe forty minutes."

"And no word yet?" Polly asked.

"Not yet," Caroline said. She handed a steaming mug to Polly, then took a seat on the opposite side of the island. "Don't read too much into that, though. There's lousy service in the woods."

"Wait—" Polly was about to take a sip but stopped. "There is?"

"You know that map of cell coverage across the United States, the one from the commercial?" Caroline said. "All that red? We're this stubborn little speck of white." She winced, pinching together her thumb and forefinger. "There's a battle on the island right now over putting up a cell tower."

Polly remembered the shaky signal in Hope's car, and the signs by the road with the drawings of phones X-ed out in red. "How is that even possible?" she said. It seemed insane—that such a place could exist in 2021, that this was the place where her son had disappeared.

Seeing her stricken expression, Caroline added, "Overcast days are sometimes better."

"Are they?" Adam asked.

"That's Tom's theory." She shrugged lightly. "But he swears by it."

"Well, at least there's one upside to this weather," Hope joked, but Polly's dread was deepening. Not only was Jonah alone in the woods, he had a useless phone.

"Think of it this way, Pol," Adam said. "That means it's probably not the battery. He might be having trouble with service. So as soon as he finds reception, he'll call."

But he didn't sound as convinced as he had earlier. All morning, he'd been trying to reassure her that Jonah had just rambled into the woods and lost track of time, and his commitment to this theory had helped keep Polly above water. Now she said, "Or it means he needs to call for help and he can't."

Adam grimaced, shifting his weight from one socked foot to the other.

"Or," Hope put in, "it could mean they've already found him. And they just can't call to let us know."

Polly stared at the granite counter. Hope was good at staying positive in a crisis, but this attitude wasn't helping. *He just wandered off*, she'd said on the phone to Izzy, as if he were a six-year-old at the zoo.

Then Adam's phone buzzed, and as he pulled it from his pocket, a look of concern crossed his face. It must be Andrea. Polly suddenly recalled something he'd said about her the night before. She wasn't doing well. She hadn't left the house in—was it months?

Then Hope looked around the kitchen, saying, "Caroline, this house is beautiful. Have you been here long?"

Even Caroline looked slightly embarrassed. Given the situation, it was a silly thing to ask—and for Hope, surprisingly obtuse—but Polly decided not to care. At least Hope's chatter would keep them from sitting in awkward silence while they waited for someone to walk through the door. She asked about the property, the real estate market on the island; she was fluent in this language, though Hope had already proven she could talk to anyone. In the Chinese restaurant with Polly's father, she'd kept up a lively stream of conversation, while Polly's eyes remained glued to her cold lo mein.

Now Polly concentrated on her coffee, attempting to block out their voices. She pictured Tom and Charlie out searching the woods, the drenched trails that would all look the same to her son. Then her thoughts jumped to a different search, like a needle skipping on a record—it was last summer, shortly after the stay-at-home order in Brooklyn had been lifted. Polly was alone at almost midnight, because Jonah wasn't home. Not that this was unusual. He usually slipped in around one. He was out with Nicholas and Xavier—boys Polly loved, boys who had spent countless hours raiding her kitchen and playing video games on her TV. Polly no longer knew where they went or what they were doing, but she trusted them, and she never entered Jonah's bedroom without permission. For some reason that night, though, she opened the door. She walked slowly around the perimeter, surveying the contents like artifacts in a museum. The skateboard propped under the window. Laptop case smothered in stickers: *Bernie, Legalize, There Is No Planet B!* She tapped his keyboard and the screen flared to life, a row of open tabs, *GHG emissions solarpunk capitalism DIY Bicycle sustainability Reddit climate anxiety Green New Deal ActNow.* The wall above the desk was smothered in photos, recent ones Polly had never seen: a gallery of faces. Jonah didn't usually photograph people, but after the loneliness of the past year, this impulse made sense. There was Nicholas in front of a bodega, sucking on a cigarette. Xavier sweeping his long hair away from his face. A girl Polly didn't know, with cropped bangs and a septum ring. And Jonah—this surprised her most. He hated having his picture taken, but there he was next to Xavier, both of them masked and staring into the camera. And sitting with the nose ring girl on a bench in Fort Greene Park, her leg draped over his. Studying the pictures, Polly had the strangest feeling, not unlike the passing grief she felt when he got a new tattoo, an awareness that her son's life existed more and more apart from her own.

The back door slapped open, bringing with it a blast of damp air, and Tom stepped inside. Alarm flew through Polly's chest. "You didn't find him?" she said, though he was clearly alone.

"Not yet," Tom said. His face was red and wet, his windbreaker sloughing drops of rain. He scraped his feet on the doormat, nodding at the strangers in his kitchen.

"Where's Charlie?" Caroline said.

"Owls Head," he said, clarifying for the rest of them, "Different trail. He may have better luck."

Polly asked, "And if he doesn't?"

"Still plenty of other spots to try," Tom said. "Lots of nooks and crannies. These woods are part of the island trail system. Bigger than you'd think."

On the phone that morning, Caroline had said the exact same thing, but Polly didn't find it reassuring this time either. "I mean, should we call someone? The island police?"

"They probably require twenty-four hours," Hope said, as Caroline handed Tom a cup of coffee, and Polly wanted to scream. They were all avoiding the obvious, she thought: the woods were on an island, and an island was surrounded by water, but this was too terrifying to say out loud.

Instead, she got to her feet and said, "I'm going to start looking—" just as the front door opened, and she spun around. But it was only Charlie. He approached and stood just inside the kitchen doorway, blond hair plastered darkly to his brow. "You didn't find him either," Polly said, her heartbeat thickening in her ears.

"You checked Owls Head?" Tom asked.

"All the way to the lookout."

Polly closed her eyes. "I can't believe this is happening."

"I'll head back out," Tom said, downing his coffee.

"I'm going, too," Polly said, but Hope touched her elbow. "Are you sure that's a good idea? Maybe you should stay, in case he calls—"

"He can't call, Hope! There's no fucking service!" Polly snapped, then pressed her fingers to her temples. "Sorry. This is just so stressful."

"Of course," Hope said quickly. "Totally understandable."

Adam set his mug on the counter. "I'll go. Pol, you stay here."

"What about your ankle?" Hope asked him.

"It's fine," Adam said, and maybe Polly should have objected to this plan, but she was so reassured by the prospect of Adam looking—someone who knew Jonah, someone Jonah had met and liked—rather than these near-strangers, that she didn't. Not that it would make any difference.

Then she noticed Charlie looking anxiously at his mother. "Charlie?" she said, just as Caroline asked, "Honey, what is it?"

Charlie glanced at Polly, then back at his mother. "I think his backpack's gone."

Polly stiffened. "What do you mean?"

"Yesterday he had this orange backpack—"

"Right. He had all his stuff in it."

"But now it isn't here."

Her pulse was flooding her whole body, as she tried to absorb Charlie's meaning. "You mean you think he left? He left and took it with him?"

"Yeah," he said, plucking uneasily at the clump of bracelets around his wrist. "I mean, I guess. He could have."

"But why would he do that? Did he say anything? Was he—"

"Let him finish, Pol," Adam said gently.

Charlie looked again at his mother, then his father. "He was talking about the environment," he said. "The one percenters. The climate deniers. But I mean—he's always talking about stuff like that," he added, and Polly felt annoyed at Charlie, protective on her son's behalf.

"Was he upset, though?" she pressed. "Did something happen?"

Charlie dropped his eyes to the floor, mumbling, "I don't think so."

She asked Tom and Caroline, "Did he seem okay to you?"

"He was a little quiet," Tom said.

"But we don't really know him," Caroline reminded her, and Polly couldn't help hearing a critique of her own parenting in this. She'd left her son with a family who hadn't seen him in four years, who barely even remembered him. She pictured him standing in the driveway before she left, the look on his face. It was deeper than disappointment, as if he'd been tricked.

Then Charlie, eyes still downcast, said, "He was talking about this survivalist stuff."

Polly's heart turned over. "What?" she said, and appealed to Adam. "What is that?"

"You mean wilderness survival?" Adam asked Charlie.

"Yeah," Charlie said. He squeezed the back of his neck. "Going into the woods with just, you know, the basics. Water. Shelter.

Fire. He's been reading about it. He seemed really into it," he said, cheeks swimming with red. "I didn't think he'd actually go and do it, though."

Polly felt the eyes of the room on her, probably waiting for her to come unglued, but suddenly it was all making sense: Jonah's sudden enthusiasm about this trip, the backpack he'd insisted was all he needed, his comments when they drove onto the island. *Life stripped back to the essentials.*

"Well, let's not panic," Hope said, but Polly wasn't panicked. As the facts settled and aligned inside her, the picture sharpened into focus, and the logic of it had a steadying effect. Jonah had been planning this; the fact that he'd left on purpose made it far less likely that he was injured or lost. Her mind moved to more practical considerations. How far could he have gotten? Was he camped out or in motion? She pictured that sagging backpack and wondered what was inside. Did he have food? Money? She remembered the twenty he'd stuffed in his pocket at the Quick Mart.

Then a phone rang, and a flame of hope ignited inside her, but it was just Hope's cell. It was probably her kids again, calling to say how much they missed her. On the phone in the car, her son had been begging her to come home—*It's an emergency. I need you.* Polly, in the backseat, could hardly bear to listen.

EIGHTEEN

ADAM

It wasn't like back in college, when he could party late into the night and spring back into shape the next day. Adam had gone for a jog that morning, thinking he could shake off the night before, but made it only halfway around the quad in a light drizzle before a headache kicked in, and his ankle started hurting. Then the rain started falling harder, and he'd ended up hobbling back to Fiske in a downpour. By the time he peeled off his sock and shoe, the ankle was tender and swollen—he'd made a lame excuse not to drive to the island—and as he walked swiftly into the backyard, wearing his soaked running shoes, the pain was only getting worse.

He noticed Tom register the limp, glancing down at his feet once or twice. "I'm not sure what happened," Adam offered. "The end of last night's a little hazy."

Tom offered a sympathetic laugh but didn't press for more. Adam appreciated this. At eighteen, a drinking injury was reckless and stupid; at forty-eight, it was vaguely emasculating. In silence, the two of them single-filed into the damp woods, Adam following Tom's lead. The rain had finally let up, but the air was raw, and the chill seeped through his windbreaker. Despite its proximity to campus, everything about the island was a few degrees more extreme: colder, grayer, more exposed.

"Up ahead here, the trail splits," Tom said. "We can spread out."

"Sounds good," Adam said agreeably. In truth, he was desperate to be alone. Ever since he'd heard about Jonah, he'd been trying to stay level-headed, assuring Polly her son was okay, and mostly believing it. But as the hours passed, some anxiety had been rising to the surface. Worry about Jonah. Worry about his boys. He wanted to apologize to Andrea for last night, but in the dorm, it had been too early. In the car, he had no privacy (he'd felt bad for Hope, trying to console her crying son on speakerphone), and at Charlie's house they'd exchanged only a few messages before Tom walked into the kitchen. Boys are fine, Andrea had texted. Happy and hungry. She hadn't referenced the night before except to ask: How's the head?

"Here we go," Tom said. He drew up short and gestured to a small clearing with single hash marks on one side, double on the other. "How about you take that one," he suggested, pointing to the obviously gentler trail.

"Will do," Adam said. He was in no position to argue.

"There's a nice little cove at the end," Tom said.

"A good place to crash for the night?"

"I guess it depends. How motivated do you think he is?"

"To be honest, I wouldn't know," Adam said, but as he remembered the unhappy, angry teenager Polly had described the night before, he thought Jonah might be plenty motivated. Not that it would make him any better equipped to spend a night alone in the woods.

Tom squinted into the trees, then tapped the phone in his left jacket pocket; they'd traded numbers, because he claimed you could sometimes get a signal near the water. "If you find him, try calling," he said, then tapped the pocket on the right, where he'd stashed the walkie-talkie Caroline had given him. "And if they hear from him, I'll come find you."

"Got it," Adam said.

Tom gave him a salute. "Good luck," he said, then took off. His stride was swift and unhesitating, hard boots cracking through the undergrowth. He was the kind of father who could protect a family—hell, protect a whole island, Adam thought.

He watched until Tom was out of sight and he was surrounded by only the natural clamor of the woods, the chittering birds and snapping twigs and big, soft trees dripping rain. When he started to move again, the pain in his ankle was more emphatic. The ground was unforgiving, muddy and uneven, laced with gnarled roots and matted with damp purple leaves.

Walk it off, his father would have told him. He didn't tolerate pain—like feelings, it was an indulgence of the weak.

Adam tried walking it off. Mind over matter, stay in motion: this approach had propelled him through his twenties and the better part of his thirties. He picked up his pace, letting the sharp smell of wet pine fill his lungs. But his stress was a slow boil. Maybe Andrea's anxiety had been contagious. Or maybe this was just a symptom of being older. A father. A father during a pandemic. Adam had never been an anxious person—how had Polly described his college self? *You were the happiest person I knew.* But maybe he just hadn't been dealing with the hard stuff. When he walked away from campus, freshman year, he'd felt liberated. Now, as he pressed into the woods, his thoughts were racing, fears inflating, like those magic capsules the boys got at birthday parties. Drop them in water and they'd expand into spongy dinosaurs, scorpions, hammerhead sharks—then Adam was remembering the shark attack last summer. Not far from the island, the first in the history of Maine. Over the past several months, he'd heard other stories like this, rebellions of the natural world. Some were terrible, some beautiful. The bioluminescent waves on the shores of California, the snowy owl that alighted in Central Park. He and the boys had watched videos of them on YouTube.

At the thought of his boys, he stopped and checked his phone.

No Service—he was hit with a fresh swell of panic. What if Andrea needed him? What if something happened to the boys and she called and couldn't get through?

He clutched his phone and kept going, stumbling over a knotted root. Up ahead, through the thin stems of the tree trunks, he detected glimmering threads of silver water. He could smell it: briny, like salt. He crossed a makeshift bridge of rotting logs, then the trail narrowed, merging with a patch of leathery shrubs so overgrown he had to part them with both hands.

The cove was a shallow inlet extending fifty feet from shore, a crescent of smooth brown rocks with a thin fingernail of sand. Fog clung to the tops of the trees like skeins of wool. The rain had slowed to a sprinkle, barely disturbing the water, which was sedate after the storm. There was no evidence of Jonah, or of any other person, not even a single boat on the horizon. In the distance, Adam saw only a scattering of small islands, patches of brown earth and huddled green trees.

Standing there, he was struck by the persistence of the natural world. The immediacy of it, the pleasure of planting feet on rock. The planet might be under attack from the changing climate, but there it was, carrying on, in this quiet inlet. He pictured his boys clambering across the beach, crunching over the heaps of kelp to collect sea glass and driftwood, dunking their feet in the bracing water, crabs nipping at their toes.

He lifted his phone, the screen glazed with moisture. *No Service.* But Tom had said reception could be better closer to the water, so Adam stepped onto the rocks. He slipped almost immediately—his entire foot, his wrong foot, dunking in a slimy tide pool, pain like the twang of a string. Teeth clenched, he pulled off his sneakers and wet socks and tossed them onto the sand, then inched forward in his clammy bare feet. The rocks were slick with algae, barnacles welded to their undersides like rows of bumpy molars. Without support, Adam's ankle felt unstable. He stepped carefully on the flat parts, over and around the shaggy manes of kelp. They reminded him of those prehistoric creatures—mastodons—he and the boys had learned about last spring.

When he reached the rock farthest from shore, Adam scanned the open ocean. There were no boats, only those ragged little islands. In the swollen surface of the water, the reflection of the woods was a single mass of rippling green. He consulted his phone—lo and behold, one flickering bar. He dialed and heard a weak ring.

"Adam?"

At the sound of his wife's voice, a wave of comfort moved through him.

"Adam?" she said faintly. "I can barely hear you. Are you there?"

"I'm here," he said, as a gust of wind blew off the water. "I have bad reception. But it's good to hear your voice."

"Where are you?" She sounded nervous. "Is something wrong?"

"Kind of," he said. "Remember Polly's son? We met him in New York?"

"Jonah," she said. "The photographer."

"Right," he said. Another damp breeze, and the line fizzed, as if the air had sluiced through the phone. "Well, Polly drove him up here, and he was staying with a friend, out on this island—"

"Adam? Adam, I can barely hear you."

He shifted slightly, using the phone like an antenna, trying to tap into some magic frequency in the haze. "How about now?"

"Better. But I missed the last part. He did what?"

Adam held the phone against his face, shielding it from the wind. "He's staying with a friend. On that island near the college. But he took off last night. So we came out here looking for him—" He stopped then, feeling a tightness in his lungs.

"Adam?" she said. "Are you okay?"

He was not okay, he thought, they were not okay, but what came out was: "I'm just worried about him."

"I understand," she said. "But he couldn't have gone too far, right?"

It occurred to him then that this news might feed Andrea's anxieties about reentering the world, but it seemed to be having the opposite effect. She sounded calm and grounded. Maybe because the situation wasn't theoretical. Maybe because she could hear the degree of worry in his voice and sensed he couldn't take on hers. Adam pictured the seesaw on the playground he brought the kids to, the one that had been wrapped in caution tape for most of last year, how while one person flailed in the air, the other stayed planted on the earth.

"How's Polly?" she asked.

"Pretty scared."

"I'm sure. I'm glad you're with her."

His eyes were watering, and he scrubbed his face with his palm.

"Adam?"

"Yeah," he managed.

"I lost you for a minute. Are you there?"

How to explain to her the sorrow that was rushing to his head, squeezing his chest? Because for the first time in over a year he wasn't with his family, wasn't directly responsible for them, didn't feel the pressure to keep himself together. Because he was on the receiving end of his wife's reassurance, which he so wanted but could no longer trust.

"I'm just standing by the ocean," he said. "Thinking about how much the boys would love it."

Andrea went quiet. She probably thought he was blaming her for not turning this trip into a family vacation, was waiting for this conversation to become a reprise of the night before. But he didn't blame her for anything. He just missed her.

The line quavered, and he pressed the phone to his ear. "About last night—" he said, but she interrupted: "Here come our boys."

He heard them a moment later, a sleepy chorus of two. "Hi, Dad."

"Hey, guys!" He gave his eyes one final swipe with his hand. "How are you? I miss you."

"We miss you, too," Zachary said.

"What are you up to?"

"Mom's making monkey bread," Sam answered.

"Mom's specialty." Adam smiled. "What else have you been doing?"

"Drawing."

This was Sam again: the artist, the dreamer.

"Yeah? What'd you draw?"

"Castle," he said. "With moat and pirate ships and dragons."

"Hey—guess what? I was in a castle last night. A bouncy castle."

"But it didn't have a moat and dragons."

"It didn't," Adam said. "You got me there."

Then he heard a low, clucking sound and looked up to see a column of brown ducks gliding across the cove, a mother and four ducklings.

"Hey, guys," he said. "Guess where I am right now? I'm standing by the ocean."

"Which ocean?"

Zachary: the scientist, seeker of facts.

"The Atlantic. On the Maine coast."

"No, I mean, which zone?"

When Adam laughed, he felt his chest inflate. "Sunlight zone. Definitely sunlight," he said. "Up near the surface, probably full of crabs and shrimp and lobsters. I'm watching a family of ducks right now. And there are these kelp mountains—when I get home, I'll tell you all about them," he said, and then he heard the sound of brush crackling on the shore. He pivoted, expecting to see Jonah emerging from the woods—hungry, exhausted, maybe a little sheepish—but it was Tom, waving hard to get his attention. He held up the walkie-talkie in one hand and cupped his mouth with the other, shouting: "They heard something!"

NINETEEN

HOPE

Hope had gone upstairs claiming to need a bathroom, but really needing to use her phone. She'd silenced it in the kitchen because they were talking about Jonah, and although she was trying her best to be supportive, she'd seen that it was Izzy calling, probably because her own son was still having a hard time.

She hurried down the upstairs hallway, a horseshoe overlooking the living room on three sides, practically eye level with the skylights and cathedral ceilings. The hardwood was slippery under her socked feet. In her still-damp jeans, Hope's thighs were conspicuously swishing. The denim felt like it had shrunk two sizes. She glanced into the open bedrooms. In one, she saw a desktop computer, surfing posters, a carpet littered with socks and sweatshirts. In the next, a double bed and a stack of blankets, seemingly untouched. She found the bathroom and shut the door, relieved, but the image in the mirror above the sink made her recoil.

If this weekend had been a series of mirrors, in each she'd looked progressively worse. That morning, she hadn't had time to apply concealer, and her face was blotchy and bare. Her frizzy hair had drifted loose from the plastic clip. Worse, there was a patch of angry red in the middle of her chin: beard burn, she realized with horror. She'd been so rattled earlier that she hadn't even noticed. As her fingers flew to touch it, the night before rushed back in—Grady's hands in his pockets, the silent walk back to campus. *It's good to see you, Stokes.*

The walk of shame: the phrase swam up from somewhere in Hope's deepest well of college memories. How on weekends she'd wake up in Grady's room, the smell of alcohol and sweat rising from his pores. He'd be sleeping heavily beside her as she stared up at the ceiling and the belly of that Irish flag, needing to pee but not wanting to use the bathroom down the hall because if she bumped into one of Grady's fraternity brothers he'd make a comment—*Get any sleep, Stokes?*—and smile in a way that made her feel special but also awkward. She'd laugh it off and steal across the quad in her not-trying-too-hard outfit from the night before (good jeans, tight-but-not-too-tight black shirt, L.L. Bean boots) back to the dorm, where she'd wash off her makeup, and she and Polly would tie their hair up in ponytails, reeking of cigarettes from the party, and make their way to the dining hall to eat.

Thirty years later, the phrase traveled through her like a dart. *Walk of shame.* It sounded ugly, but back then it had seemed lighthearted—a shared joke. She'd once tried explaining this to Izzy, after she'd heard the term in a teen movie from the nineties.

Mom, it's patronizing, Izzy said, incredulous. *It's slut-shaming.*

Honestly, it was a different time.

Did it only apply to women?

I don't think so, Hope said, but she was guessing that it did.

Regardless, if it was about a guy, it wouldn't be about shame. It would be, like, a badge of honor, Izzy said. Hope had thought that she was overreacting, but she was probably right. Izzy and her generation could be exhausting—so quick to take offense;

it felt sometimes like they were *looking* to take offense—but she was in many ways smarter about the way the world worked. Or how it should.

Alone with her reflection, Hope was thankful her daughter couldn't see her. She dug into her purse, then realized she hadn't brought her cosmetics—she must have left them at the inn. She threw open the door of the medicine cabinet—sunscreen, bug spray, Tylenol, Zoloft—then shut it and faced the mirror. The scrape was visible, and there was nothing she could do. She pressed her fingertip to the red patch and watched it bloom, her chin filling with color.

A clear thought rose to the surface: *I'm so unhappy.*

It was painful to name it. She'd worked so hard for it not to be true.

Her eyes filled, two tidy pools that rose but didn't spill over. Then her phone started chirping, and she grabbed it from her purse. Izzy.

"I was just about to call," Hope said. "I couldn't pick up before. How is he?"

"How is who?"

She let out a short laugh. "Rowan."

"Oh," Izzy said. "Dad has him at OT."

Of course. Ellen's. Eleven on a Saturday. Hope couldn't remember the last time she'd felt so detached from the family schedule.

"He's been okay," Izzy said. But Hope could hear some tension in her voice. Maybe, Hope thought, she was fed up with the constant focus on her brother. Or Ethan's blind spots were more glaring without Hope there. Or it was something else, something worse, a lurking threat it hadn't yet occurred to Hope to worry about. Her mind flew through the past twenty-four hours—the therapy appointment, the dance. "Did something happen last night?"

"What was last night?"

"The dance," Hope said. "The social."

"Nothing happened," she said. "We stayed forty-five minutes then went to Lacy's boyfriend's."

Hope hadn't even known Lacy had a boyfriend, but let this go. "Well," she said. "I know it hasn't been the easiest weekend, and I appreciate you helping with Rowan—"

"It isn't a big deal."

"And I won't forget the iPad—"

"This isn't about the iPad," Izzy said. "It isn't even about me. It's Jonah."

"Jonah?" Hope paused. "Polly's Jonah?"

"Did they find him?"

"They're still looking for him. Why?"

Izzy drew a slow breath then released it. "Please don't get weird about this, because it's probably nothing, but I follow him on Insta."

Hope braced her fingertips on the sides of the vanity, studying her reflection for some clue as to how to respond. "Meaning . . . what? You communicate with him? You're in touch with him?"

"I'm not in touch with him. I just follow him."

"Since when?"

"Since—that trip to New York, I guess."

A beat of worry had started sounding in Hope's chest. How old had Izzy been when they visited Rockefeller Center? Twelve—seventh grade. Hope hadn't known she had an Instagram account. Their deal had been that Izzy could get one when she started high school; then, in eighth grade, she and her classmates were all so isolated that Hope let her sign up early. She'd monitored Izzy's privacy settings, been grateful she had another way to connect with her friends. Now she pictured Izzy on the phone two nights ago, the quick spasm of her fingers, her smile caught in the pale glow of the screen. She remembered something Jen said once on Moms' Night, after her daughter had been caught chatting online with the thirty-two-year-old—*She may be stuck in the house but I swear the most dangerous place she can be is that phone.*

Hope would pursue this later. At home, after Jonah was found. For now she said, "Is that why you wanted to know if he was coming?"

"What do you mean?" Izzy asked.

"The other night, when I was packing, you asked if he was coming. To the reunion. Did he contact you or something?"

"Mom—no. He doesn't know I exist," Izzy said. "But he posted something this morning."

"Are you sure?" Hope said. "There's basically no cell service."

"Well then, he found a hot spot. Because he did."

Hope's emotions were in competition: relief that Jonah was okay—he was out in the world, on Instagram of all things—but deepening alarm at the tone of her daughter's voice.

"It's a picture," Izzy said. "Of the ocean."

"Okay," Hope said. "That's logical. He's on an island."

"He's standing on some rocks or something—"

She nodded at her reflection. "That makes sense."

"Then there are a bunch of hashtags," Izzy said, hesitating. "Just keep in mind that his posts can be kind of intense."

"Intense?" Hope said. "How so?"

"He's just really—passionate about things. He's an artist. And an activist, kind of. But you might think his stuff is a little dark. Or, I don't know, provocative—"

"Izzy," Hope said, pushing her knuckles into the edge of the sink. "Whatever it says, I can handle it."

"Okay," Izzy said. She sounded unsure, but when she began reading, it was in the same measured tone she used when calming Rowan. "#Maine. #Woods. #Ocean. #Island. #LivingOn TheEdge. #JumpingOffPoint. #WhatComesNext?" She paused for just a beat, then said, "#MaybeThisIsWhereItEnds."

Hope watched her own eyes in the mirror. She'd always had the ability to remain centered in a crisis, grow quiet on the inside and focus on what needed to be done. Sophomore year, when Polly called her crying after waking up in a stranger's apartment in downtown Sewall. Freshman year, when Adam reappeared at their door after finding out his father was dead. When Rowan was a toddler, and he fell off a balance beam at one of those indoor playgrounds. At five, when Izzy disappeared in a Nordstrom for several minutes and Hope threaded through the racks methodically, systematically, vaguely aware of other shoppers joining in the search. It was only later, after Izzy had been discovered lying in a bed in the furniture department (*like Corduroy!* she'd said proudly) that Hope had hidden in the bathtub and sobbed beneath the sound of rushing water, thinking about what might have been. In the moment, searching the store, she'd risen above the situation, certain that Izzy was safe; it was unimaginable that she wasn't.

But when she heard what Jonah had written, a ripple of panic broke the surface. Her face grew warm, her cheeks flushed, though her expression didn't move. "When was this?"

"Around ten thirty," Izzy said. "I started checking after you said he was missing. Like I said, though, he sometimes posts stuff like this. It doesn't mean it's literal. He could be speaking metaphorically—honestly, it could mean anything." But

Hope could hear the fear in her voice. "I just thought someone should know."

"You did the right thing," Hope assured her. Her temples were pounding. *Maybe this is where it ends.* She reminded herself that Izzy was right—it could mean anything. The end of the island. End of the pandemic. End of a long night in the woods. She reminded herself this was Jonah. He was edgy and artistic, an activist. *It could mean anything.* Hope repeated this, like a new mantra, as she rushed back downstairs.

TWENTY

POLLY

Polly had not expected to find herself alone with Charlie's mother, but after Hope went upstairs and Adam ventured into the woods, there she was: six hours away from home, in a stranger's kitchen, having no clue where her son had gone.

Without Hope there to carry the conversation, the two of them had fallen into an awkward silence. Polly sat at the kitchen island, uselessly refreshing her phone, while Caroline kept busy rinsing the dishes and cleaning the counters and brewing a fresh pot of coffee. Watching her, Polly felt ashamed for getting so impatient that morning.

"I'm sorry about all this," she said abruptly.

Caroline brushed her hands over the sink. "No need to apologize."

"No, really. This whole weekend—I know this isn't what you signed up for," Polly said. "I probably shouldn't have even brought Jonah up here. He was just so excited about the idea. He seemed so happy."

Caroline gave a small shrug. "That's all any parent wants."

It was one of those things Polly knew to be true, but the past year had narrowed that knowledge to a fine point. Your child's happiness: the only thing that mattered. Yet how little control over it any parent had. Polly had always prioritized Jonah over everything else, trying to make up for what she hadn't gotten from her own mother, what he wouldn't get from his missing father. She'd supported his decisions, encouraged him to talk to her about anything, loved him exactly as he was. But it hadn't been enough.

Caroline sat down, holding two refills, and set one in front of Polly. "Charlie really struggled, too," she said.

"Oh—" Polly said. "I'm sorry." She wouldn't have expected this of Charlie, who seemed so healthy and well adjusted, though she'd stopped being surprised by candid revelations like this. She'd been on the receiving end of many such moments over the past year, people stepping out of their assigned roles—the customer service rep from the electric company who confided in her about the grandchildren she was desperately missing, the pizza delivery guy who told her about his sister-in-law who'd had her leg amputated, the Zoom meeting in which the dean showed up with a screaming toddler on her lap and vented about how impossible it was not having child care. What did it matter? Everyone was just a human being and the world was upside down.

"We thought it would be better for him, being up here," Caroline said. "He's always loved the island. But he was so far from his friends that I think it was actually harder. He got so anxious."

Polly nodded, thinking of her students, the anxiety that had traveled through them like a brush fire, compelling them to turn their cameras off, write her apologetic emails at two in the morning, students who receded more and more as the year ground on, sometimes disengaged, disappeared.

"We tried different medications, but you know, it can take a while to get them right," Caroline said, wrapping both hands around her mug. Now that they were still, Polly noticed her cuticles were badly bitten. Her wedding band was surprisingly subtle, thin as thread. "He got fixated on the future. SAT scores and extracurriculars and getting into college. He was obsessed with what would happen next."

"And what is?" Polly said.

"Stanford."

"Oh." It was not where Polly had imagined the story going. "Well, that's great, isn't it?"

"It was his top school," Caroline said. "And his top criterion? To get as far away from New England as possible. Because he hates it. That's what he told us."

She smiled ruefully, and Polly felt bad for her, but appreciated her honesty. She'd assumed that Charlie's mother had found a kindred spirit in Hope, but maybe she and Polly had more in common than she'd thought.

"It was an impossible time," Polly said. "And this place is so beautiful. I'll bet he finds his way back," she added, trying to sound confident, but the words caught in her throat.

Caroline reached across the table and squeezed her fingers. "They'll find Jonah," she said, and this sudden kindness brought Polly to the edge of tears. How had they all gotten by for so many months without such moments? Comfort of strangers. The press of flesh on hand.

"Thanks," Polly said, swallowing some coffee to dissolve the thickness in her chest. The rain had finally slowed, dripping from an unseen gutter, but the clouds looked wrung out, leached of color.

"So what's his plan for September?" Caroline asked.

Polly appreciated what she was doing, pivoting the conversation toward a future that felt solid and certain, and though she could have easily sat there worrying about the present, she let herself follow Caroline's lead. "Art school," she said.

"In New York?"

"Right in Manhattan." In fact, Jonah had applied only to colleges in New York; it hadn't occurred to her until just then how lucky this was. "He got interested in photography at Elmwood, actually. Remember they had that darkroom?"

"I remember the stains."

"God, right." Polly laughed. Jonah had worn them proudly, a fashion statement, chemical spatters on his frayed T-shirts. "After camp ended, he started taking classes on weekends," she said. "But he quit last year. He quit everything, basically. He got so withdrawn. So . . . joyless. I had no idea what to do for him."

"It was an impossible time," Caroline reminded her.

"I know," Polly said. "It was just—we've always been so close."

"I take it his father's not in the picture?" Caroline asked.

It was a question, like Polly's relationship status, that she normally resented. She had a ready answer (random guy, one-night stand) that was usually disarming enough to shut down further inquiry. But she'd invited the topic, and something about this unfamiliar kitchen and this kind stranger made her want to keep talking.

"No," she said. "It's always been just the two of us."

Outside the window, the gray sky was smudged with black shapes, as if it had been scrubbed with a hard eraser. She looked down at the veins on the back of her hand, a map of crooked blue. "He was an old teacher of mine, actually. A professor."

It was a shock to hear herself say it, as if she'd flung a grenade into the room.

But when she looked up, Caroline's pale eyebrows had lifted

only slightly. "Oh," she said, and there was no judgment in her tone.

"I wasn't his student at the time," Polly went on. "I mean, in college I was, and we were close. Not in a weird way . . . well, Hope always thought it was weird. But nothing happened. I was his student. It was later, in my twenties, that we met up again."

She'd been twenty-six years old. She was no longer a college student—in fact, she was teaching college students. On the face of it, this was fine. Yes, he was married, but their emails weren't inappropriate, at least not in the beginning. Over time, they had grown longer, and more personal. Now and then he'd make a reference that felt suggestive, not about her directly, but something adjacent to her, the romance of winter in New York City or a line from a book that reminded him of something she'd once said.

More than the content of those emails, what Polly remembered was the rush she felt upon seeing his name on the screen, like a crackle of static in the dark. These days, weeding through email was a chore, her inbox clogged with bills and ads, but back then people emailed actual letters. Their exchange had felt like a secret story, a current that was alive and simmering, hidden beneath the surface of her life.

"He told me his marriage was ending and said he had a meeting in New York." She paused and allowed herself a self-deprecating laugh. "It's all so cliché, isn't it? A naive young student and her older male teacher—her *English* teacher, no less. I don't know what I was thinking."

"You trusted him," Caroline said, and Polly was grateful for this woman's compassion toward her young self. Despite everything, Polly had always resisted thinking too poorly of McFadden, wanting to believe there was a real connection between them, but over time she'd felt less and less capable of seeing their relationship with clear eyes. Had his attention in college been well intentioned? A recognition of her potential? Or had he been manipulating her from the start? She couldn't know, but whenever she had flickers of sympathy for him, she recalled that final conversation in his office. How deliberately he'd spoken, skirting all responsibility, avoiding an apology, choosing words that implied she was to blame.

"It was only one night," she said. "Then I wrote him and he didn't write back. He didn't want anything to do with me, so my plan was just to move on and pretend the whole thing never happened, but a few weeks later—"

It was a box Polly never opened, the scene in the cramped bathroom in the shared apartment in Astoria. Tangled hairdryer cords, mildewed pink tile. Crumpled instructions in the bowl of the sink, bouquet of damp sticks from Duane Reade, racing heart. They hadn't used protection, a fact that until that moment she hadn't let herself acknowledge. McFadden didn't seem worried about it, and Polly foolishly followed his lead.

"And what did he say?" Caroline asked.

"I never told him," Polly admitted. Her mouth was dry, but her head felt oddly light. "That probably sounds terrible. But I knew he wouldn't want to hear it. Not to mention he already had a kid—in college. And I was hurt. And stubborn. And embarrassed."

The person she'd wanted to confide in was Hope. And she'd tried, once, just like she'd told Adam. After teaching a section of freshman comp one night, she'd called from the part-time office, where there was free long-distance, staring at the crowded, lonely city out the window. When Hope answered, she'd just gotten home from work and was giddy. Ethan had been offered the job in Philadelphia. He was on his way over. Hope was making chicken. Polly remembered how, in college, Hope was always feeding people. *Why do you have to cook for him?* Polly snapped. *It's just chicken*, Hope said with a laugh. Polly closed her eyes, listening to the sounds of Hope's apartment, the clicking of her shoes and the opening and shutting of her kitchen cabinets. She wanted so much to tell her but didn't want to let her down. Maybe she didn't want to admit that Hope had been right. Instead, when Hope asked what she was doing that night, she led with an attempt at humor—she'd bought a test, on a whim, then thought it might be defective and went back for another— but Hope's reaction stopped her. *Oh, Polly.*

It was unmistakable, the disappointment in her voice. The pity.

When Hope started bombarding her with questions, when and who and how it happened, Polly couldn't bring herself to tell her the truth. *A random guy in a bar*, she said. *Oops!*

At least you're taking this seriously, Hope said, and Polly had felt furious and small. Hope with her perfectly decorated apartment, her dull boyfriend with his dull job and dull chicken. Hope, whose life was unfolding exactly as expected and who would never make a mistake like this.

When Hope said she'd come to New York, go with her to the clinic, even help her pay for it, Polly told her no. She'd be fine on her own.

After that night, a new idea had taken hold, a new version of her future: maybe this pregnancy hadn't been a mistake. Maybe this was exactly the sense of purpose her life had been lacking, a decision she would make entirely on her own. She put off the appointment, then put it off again, and as the days went by, she moved through her life with this possibility inside her, carrying it in her mind like a cupped palm filled with water.

"From a practical standpoint, it was kind of nuts," she said. "I had like fifty dollars in my bank account and was living with two strangers. But I just knew I could do it. I can't explain it. I'd had a lousy father myself, so a partner didn't seem strictly necessary. And I had my mom, in the beginning." She felt emotional, remembering how Diane had risen to the occasion. When Polly told her she was pregnant, and by whom, she didn't get upset. She let her cry and promised it would be okay. She helped convert Polly's old room into a nursery. She urged Polly to ask him for money but, when she refused, backed off. She watched the baby when Polly was teaching. She stopped drinking, at least around Jonah. Those had been their best years together; it made her cancer diagnosis, when Jonah was only four, particularly unfair.

"We still live in that apartment," Polly said. "Jonah barely remembers her, but they were close. Once, when Diane was really sick, I heard him ask her about his father, and she told him he was dead. Maybe she was out of it because of the pain meds—or maybe, after dealing with my father coming and going ever since I was little, she thought she was doing me a favor. I don't know. Then she was gone, and I couldn't ask her, but I never told Jonah any different. And now he actually *is* dead. Otherwise, there's no way I'd be back." Her eyes prickled with tears—of sadness, or relief. "I realize it's weird I'm telling you all this. Believe it or not, you're actually the only person I've ever told. Except Adam, but that was only—"

Then Polly heard the sigh of a floorboard behind her. She spun around, expecting to see Jonah—quickly computing what he'd overheard—but Hope was standing in the doorway. She looked unraveled. It was more than the tense, muted sadness from the night before. Her skin looked mottled, her face fallen, all pretense of cheerfulness gone. Polly didn't know how long she'd been there, and all Hope said was, "I just talked to Izzy," and handed Polly her phone, open to a screenshot of an Instagram post. Polly pinched the screen, holding it close to her eyes, so she could make out what it said.

TWENTY-ONE

ADAM

Adam recognized the picture right away: the cliffs at the end of the island. In college, sitting on those jagged rocks—smoking a joint, letting his feet dangle above the crashing surf—had felt daring and dramatic. Now he saw the place, like everything else in the world, through the eyes of a parent. As the two cars pulled up by the cliffs—Tom and Charlie in the Jeep, he and Hope and Polly in the SUV, Caroline back at the house in case Jonah turned up—Adam's anxiety came storming back to the surface. He needed to find this kid. Needed for him to be okay.

"It's huge," Polly said, despair in her voice. The five of them had converged by the weathered bench that marked the trailhead.

"This trail runs a half mile east and west," Tom said, indicating the overgrown path that wound tightly among the rocks. "So we'll split up."

"Divide and conquer," Hope said, but faintly.

Polly raked a hand through her hair. She had her sunglasses on, though the sky was a flat, milky white. "What about those rocks down by the water?"

"Charlie and I can check them out," Tom said, setting a hand on his son's shoulder. The poor kid looked sick to his stomach. Adam wished he could be more help, but it was all he could do to conceal his own panic. He thought of his own boys, rosy-cheeked but cozy, snuggled in bed with Andrea—then let his eyes close. He squeezed his hands in and out: paper rock paper rock. When he opened his eyes again, Hope was watching him.

"I'll go this way," Adam announced, and before anyone could propose an alternative, he'd started down the path heading west.

The pain in his ankle was now a shrill, sustained note, but Adam didn't mind. There was a clarity about it: pain that was specific. Pain he understood. He walked quickly in the direction of the rocky staircase, wet pebbles scattering beneath his sneakers. The path was muddy, crowded with spiny rosebushes and stalks of purple lupine, hairy bursts of seagrass scratching at his knees.

"Jonah!"

His shout sank like a penny in a well, swallowed by the dull pounding of the waves. It had been almost two hours since Jonah's Instagram post. Polly had kept trying to reach him, but her texts went unanswered and calls went straight to voicemail. Adam pictured the photo—not unlike one Jonah might have shown him and Andrea that day at the museum—beat-up sneakers meeting the edge of the cliff. It had been shot from above, a tumult of dark green waves. The toes of Jonah's Chuck Taylors. A mossy scrim of rock.

"Jonah! Are you out there?"

No response, except the urgent cawing of a seabird. The sound of its cry was strangely human. Adam watched the bird flap by, close enough that he could see its bright yellow feet, hear the feathery, effortful pumping of its wings.

"Jonah?" he called louder. "Can you hear me?"

Adam thought he must be getting close to the staircase, but

the farther he walked, the more he questioned whether he was heading in the right direction. Whether he hadn't invented the staircase completely. He wished he still had that foolish sense of invincibility that had carried him through four years of college, through his twenties and thirties, the energy that had spiked through him the day before, but it had deserted him.

"Jonah!" he hollered, voice cracking. "Where are you?"

Then he saw a sign nailed to the trunk of a stubby, wind-twisted tree. STAIRCASE TO THE SEA. Adam had never known this spot had a name. In his head it was more secluded, a magical secret he'd discovered, but when he looked down, there they were: five granite slabs, a rough approximation of a set of stairs hurtling toward the waves.

But Jonah wasn't there. The steps were empty, smothered with graffiti, the ocean thumping hard against them and kicking up spray. For a minute, Adam just stared at the rocks. He'd been so sure that he would find Jonah, that he would rescue him and this would all be over. His face was damp; his lungs burned. The water and sky were a monotone white—disorienting, vaguely nauseating. Then, in his peripheral vision, he caught a flash of color in the fog and started running.

TWENTY-TWO

HOPE

Adam had walked in one direction, Tom and Charlie in another, leaving Polly and her together on the path. Polly was leading, the clearance so narrow they were forced to walk single file. She moved at an anxious clip, as if striding down a city street, while Hope hurried to keep up. She was still reeling from the conversation she'd walked in on in the kitchen. She'd overheard only the final minute, but it was enough to understand that McFadden was Jonah's father. She was stunned, and confused, and devastated that Polly had never told her.

"Is this definitely the place?" Polly yelled over her shoulder. The wind off the ocean whipped her hair around her ears.

"It must be," Hope said, tightening her jacket around her waist. "Caroline seemed sure of it."

"Where is he, then?"

"He's here somewhere. We'll find him."

"I can't see a fucking thing," Polly said.

It was true: the path was swollen with wildflowers and rangy bushes, most of them at least shoulder height. Beyond them sat an expanse of brown and gray rocks, desolate from every angle. The air had grown warm and soupy, even though the sun was still hidden, the horizon line undetectable except for a faint ribbon of pink.

"We'll find him," Hope repeated. "He's definitely here some-where."

She was attempting to stay focused—her job, as ever, being to keep Polly from coming apart—but her thoughts were racing. How could she not have told her? When Polly got pregnant, she was in New York and Hope was in Philadelphia, but they talked all the time.

"'Maybe this is where it ends,'" Polly said. "What does that even mean?"

Hope elbowed past a shaggy dark green bush, splashed with beach roses, like sloppy pink corsages. Jonah's post had been scary, but Hope knew that no good could come of speculating. During the past year, lying in bed at night and letting her mind race with what-if scenarios had only made things worse.

"Try not to think about it," Hope advised.

"How do I do that?"

"I just mean—don't read into it yet. It could mean anything." She shoved her sleeves up to her elbows. She was sweating, sharp pinpricks under each arm. "Izzy said his posts are often kind of different. Artistic. It could be a metaphor or something—"

"What if he's on those rocks? What if he's down there, hurt? Or unconscious?"

"He isn't," Hope clipped, like snapping off a thread with her teeth. "And if he did go down there, just to climb on the rocks or something, Tom and Charlie will find him. The trail isn't long. What did Tom say? A half mile? And actually, up ahead, it's less overgrown, I think—"

"God, I can't take this."

"We'll find him. We know he's—"

Polly spun around so fast they nearly collided. "Jesus, Hope, would you stop?"

Hope pulled up short, too shocked to reply. They were standing inches apart, close enough that she could see the beads of sweat on Polly's cheeks.

"Just acknowledge that this is upsetting and let me be upset," Polly said.

"Okay." Hope raised both palms. "Sorry."

Polly jammed her sunglasses on top of her head, brushed her eyes with the heels of her hands.

"I get that this is stressful," Hope said carefully. "I'm just trying to be optimistic—"

"You're doing it again!"

"What?" Hope said, startled.

"The thing you do!" Polly said. "Smoothing things over. Insisting that everything's okay."

Hope's heartbeat was a bright, alert flutter, like a moth inside a jar. "I don't think I'm insisting everything's okay. I'm here, aren't I?" she said, with a light laugh. "I'm just trying to stay positive about the situation—"

"It's not just this situation, Hope. It's every situation. It's the house where Jonah's staying. It's the end of the pandemic. It's the food at Walthrop—I mean, it's *everything* about Walthrop. Laura Rhodes and her boyfriend. The women's studies major! It's like you think it was this perfect place."

"Actually, I don't," Hope admitted, then attempted to continue walking, stepping around Polly and through a patch of bushy weeds. "Let's just keep going," she said, pressing her hair behind her ears. "This is the last thing we should be talking—"

"Right. Because we never talk about anything real."

"Like what?" Hope bit back. "Politics? How everything's terrible and miserable? I'm sorry if I don't choose to be upset every single minute."

"It's not just about politics, Hope," Polly said, practically stepping on her heels. "It's anything about our actual lives. All you talk about is things that happened back in college."

"It's a reunion. I thought that's why we were here," Hope said, but her body was at odds with itself, the desire to stay in control in conflict with the heart banging loose in her chest. "And we *have* talked about our actual lives," she couldn't help adding. "We talked about Jonah and your teaching—"

"Yes, and then you ran away!"

Hope went silent, flooded with the memory of hiding in the student union, then stepping outside and finding Grady standing there—the familiar banter, the concern on his face as he knelt beside her, the secret thrill as they walked away from the party. She felt sick with loss. Then she surprised herself by saying, "If you hate it so much, why did you even come?"

"I didn't want to," Polly said. "Believe me. If it wasn't for Jonah, I wouldn't have."

"Right." Hope pushed her fists into her thighs. "Because God forbid you actually spend time with us."

"That isn't what I said."

"No—it's fine. It's how it's always been. I don't know why I ever thought it would be different. I've always cared more."

"Hope. That isn't true."

"It is true." She was walking faster now, gaining momentum and rightness. "You never call me. If I never called you again, I'm not sure you'd even notice," she said, then wished she hadn't, because she didn't want to believe it, and the fact that she'd said it meant she might.

"Our lives have just become completely different," Polly said.

"So?" Hope said. "They've always been different. That doesn't matter."

"It does, actually."

"Why? Because you think my life is easy and yours is hard?" Hope knew this wasn't the time or place, but suddenly she was vomiting words and couldn't stop. "Your life has *always* been hard. You choose for it to be hard. If you didn't have some drama going on, you wouldn't know what to do with yourself."

"And neither would you!" Polly snapped. "Because then you couldn't fix it!"

"Did I have a choice?" Hope whirled around, causing Polly to nearly crash into her, and flung her arms wide. "Look at where we are!"

She wished right away that she could take it back. There was a line and she'd crossed it. Polly's face was furious and teary. "I guess your life is perfect, then, right?"

Hope gave a choked laugh. "My life is far from perfect."

"Then how come you never talk about the hard parts?"

"I tried, actually, last night," Hope said, though it had been a weak attempt, dropping a hint and hoping her friend would catch it. "I guess I'm just not very good at it. And I don't like to complain about—"

"It's not complaining, Hope! It's being honest!"

"Honest? Really?" Hope's laugh this time was almost a shriek. "I heard you," she said.

Polly's mouth was still open, but she closed it, her jaw tightening below her ear.

"How could you not tell me?" Hope said. Embarrassingly, her eyes filled with tears.

Polly looked toward the ocean, gripping her elbows. Her mouth was a pale, straight line. "I didn't tell anyone."

"You told Adam!"

"But that was only recently, when he and Andrea were—"

"You told *Andrea*?" Hope said in disbelief. "And you told Caroline, and she's a complete stranger! I'm your best friend!" On the inside, she felt indignant, but her voice came out sounding wounded. "Before you say it, I get that things aren't the same between us now. I'm not clueless. But back then, it was different."

She couldn't bear to look at Polly, staring instead at her mud-spattered boots. She felt turned inside out, neck flushed, eyes stinging. It was mortifying, to care so much.

"It was after the reunion," Polly said. "The five-year. He and I met for coffee. You probably don't remember."

Hope remembered. Of course Hope remembered. Polly had arrived on campus ridiculously late on Friday night, then Saturday morning, she was gone again.

"After that we started emailing," Polly said. "For a while. Over a year."

"A year?" Hope said, mind reeling as she did the math—what had she been doing then? Working at the PR firm. Living in her first apartment. Meeting Ethan at a party thrown by a friend from work, a girl she'd long since lost touch with. Ethan, the co-worker's neighbor, was a grad student dressed in a wrinkled shirt and thick, smudged glasses. He was a mess, Hope assessed, but he was smart and ambitious; he was working on his doctorate in history. He told Hope he wanted to be a college professor. *Oh, I loved college so much*, Hope said.

"And then McFadden came to New York," Polly continued. "He asked me to have dinner. It was one night." She paused. "I just didn't think you'd understand."

"I would have!" Hope said automatically, though honestly

she wasn't sure. She'd been enamored with her own life, certain of her future happiness—painful, now, to think of it—and getting frustrated with Polly, who bumped her way through the world with no real sense of caution or consequence, whose cool indifference had become harder and harder to understand.

"Here's the part I've never told anyone," Polly said and looked her in the eye. "A few days later, I came up here."

"Where?"

"To campus," she said. "To surprise him."

It took a few moments for this to sink in. The fact that Polly had taken a trip to Walthrop without Hope knowing—had this experience of college that was so far outside the one they'd had together—made her feel sad, strangely left out.

"I hadn't heard from him, and I was starting to freak out," she said. "So I showed up at his office."

"And?" Hope said, but she was filled with dread.

"It was terrible," Polly said bluntly. "He made me feel stupid. Like I'd misread the entire situation. Like it was my fault, even though it wasn't. But I accepted it, because I was young. And he was my teacher. Or had been my teacher. And that's why I never came back," she said. "But for you and Adam, it's different."

Then she turned around and resumed walking, her leather boots splashing in the shallow puddles. Hope was tongue-tied, charged with feelings she had trouble naming, but they boiled down to simple things: sadness that she hadn't known what Polly was going through. Regret that Polly hadn't felt she could tell her. Anger at McFadden for walking away unscathed. *Oops!* her friend had said in that long-ago phone call—Hope had been bewildered at the time, but she considered now what was behind that glibness. How alone she must have felt.

"Last night," Hope told her, "I was with Grady."

Polly stopped and turned back, facing her. "What?"

"I didn't sleep with him," Hope said. "But when you couldn't find me, that's where I was." She folded her arms across her chest, felt her heart pound against her wrists. "I'd rather not hear what you think about him, because I feel awful enough—"

"I wouldn't do that," Polly said softly. "Are you okay?"

"No," Hope said. She tried to laugh, but it came out as a stifled sob. "But it's not about last night. Things at home—" Then her eyes swam with tears, and she found she couldn't speak.

"Oh, Hope," Polly said, taking a step forward.

"My marriage—" The word alone was enough to make her voice break. "It isn't working. It isn't happy. It isn't . . . anything, really. Ethan has no time for me—I mean, I guess it's sort of always been that way. Except now I don't think he even likes me. He might actually resent me. And I'm so careful—like this weekend, I knew he'd be annoyed that I was leaving, so I waited to tell him. I managed every detail. I'm always *managing* everything," she said. "It's exhausting. And it's lonely." She wiped the back of her hand across her nose. "I told myself it was the stress of last year and now, you know, things would get better. But actually I think it just dragged our problems into the light, and now I can't stop seeing them. And I don't want all of this to affect our kids, but I'm sure it is. Izzy actually asked to see a therapist," she said, and as she did so, the reason became obvious to her for the first time.

Water blurred into sky. She felt Polly reach for her hand, squeeze it. Hope squeezed back.

"Sorry," Hope said, pressing a fingertip to the corner of each eye. "I realize there couldn't be a worse time for this. Don't worry about me. Let's just keep going." She fumbled in her jacket for a tissue. Then Polly's phone rang, and she grabbed it from her back pocket.

"It's Adam," Polly said, and Hope froze as she read the message, watching her face collapse with relief. "He's with Jonah. He's okay."

TWENTY-THREE

ADAM

It was the backpack Adam saw first, like a bright splash of coral in the haze shrouding the edge of the cliff. For that first instant, fear blasted through him, and he sprinted awkwardly across the rocks. Then he saw Jonah, sitting cross-legged next to the pack. He was hunched over his lap, headphones clamped on his ears. As Adam slowed down and drew up behind him, Jonah looked up in surprise. "Hey."

"Hey," Adam replied, catching his breath. "Mind if I sit?"

Jonah hung the headphones around his neck as Adam lowered himself to the ground, stretching the throbbing ankle out before him.

"I'm Adam," he said. "We met a few years ago."

"Yeah," Jonah said. "I remember."

Adam studied his friend's son from the corner of his eye. The night in the woods had clearly taken its toll. The bottoms of his jeans were caked with mud, his neck streaked with dirt. He smelled like sweat, vaguely like pot. His eyes were bloodshot. Around the discs in his ears, the skin was pink and slightly swollen, as if still thawing. He'd balled up a sweatshirt in his lap and wore only a stained white T-shirt, exposing his bony elbows and tattoos.

"You okay?" Adam asked.

"Yeah." Jonah shrugged. "I mean, basically."

Adam didn't push for more. All the questions about where he'd been, why he'd left and didn't call, he'd be getting soon enough. Before he did anything else, Adam pulled out his phone and texted Polly.

Oh thank god, she wrote.

"Is she here?" Jonah asked.

"She's here," he said, sending Polly their location. "She's coming."

"How mad is she?"

Adam paused then said, "She's pretty upset."

A seagull soared by, flat as a boomerang. Jonah watched it. Maybe Adam should have been more pissed off at the kid, after all the worry he'd caused Polly, but his heart went out to him. He was skinnier than he'd been on that New York trip, but there was a heaviness about him. Adam pictured his Instagram post, the sneaker toeing the steep drop-off, and wondered just how dark that moment had gotten.

"Sorry about your reunion," Jonah said.

"Don't worry about it," Adam told him. "It's nicer out here, to be honest."

He heard muted music and thought it might be leaking from Jonah's headphones, then spied a lobster boat in the distance. The music sharpened or muffled as the wind shifted, carrying a wisp of classic rock. The sky had started lightening, but a veil of mist still hung on the water, the scattered islands more like suggestions of islands.

"I used to come out here in college," Adam said. "When I was about your age."

"Yeah?" Jonah said, but didn't sound all that interested. Why would he? The college, the reunion, his mother's friends who were now pushing fifty—it probably all felt completely removed from his life. At eighteen, Adam hadn't felt any connection to his parents' generation; the past seemed irrelevant. But Jonah, and his own sons, would never know the luxury of that misconception. They had already lived through something historic, catastrophic, all the ways it would impact them still unknown.

"It feels good out here," Jonah said then. "Kind of removed from reality."

"It does," Adam agreed. The cliffs felt ageless, the rocks like slumbering giants. Even when Adam was young and stupid, he'd had the sense to be awed by this place. In retrospect, that feeling was part of what kept drawing him back there. Sitting at the end of the island, the world seemed majestic and mysterious, and lifted whatever unspoken tension had been building up inside him.

"But it's only a matter of time until these islands are all underwater," Jonah said.

His tone caught Adam off guard. Jonah didn't sound vehement, or even particularly grim. This was the world he lived in. When Adam was an ES major, and even in law school, the climate hadn't felt so urgent. His interest felt more personal; he hadn't borne a sense of responsibility to the larger world. He remembered the article that had sent Andrea reeling, the child looking into the camera with such matter-of-fact sorrow. The challenge, he thought, was to avoid denial without drowning in despair.

The boat turned, and the muffled tune grew sharper. The Eagles, "Take It to the Limit." Jonah picked up a flat brown rock, palm-sized, and examined it. His fingernails were coated in chipped gold polish. "So you're an environmental lawyer, right?"

"I am."

"And you live in the middle of nowhere?"

Adam chuckled. "That's what your mom said, huh?"

"She said you took off and moved to the woods." Jonah shot him a quick look. "Don't get me wrong. I'm not knocking it. I totally fucking admire it. Not kneeling to the big corporations. It's the only way to not be complicit."

Adam thought about his house on its two unruly acres. His life wasn't truly remote, not in the way Jonah meant; he could drive to the McDonald's in Keene in twenty minutes, and sometimes did. But *in the middle of nowhere*—in some sense, he was.

"It's a small town," Adam told him. "I don't want to oversell it."

"But you chose it because you needed an alternative, right? Because your old situation wasn't working?"

"Something like that," Adam said. "We were looking for something simpler." It was bittersweet, remembering all the conviction they'd felt about their new life. For so long, Adam had avoided dealing with hard things; then he'd met Andrea and naively assumed he wouldn't have to.

"I respect that," Jonah was saying. "If the system doesn't work, go outside the system. The whole idea of working just to make money, to pay back student loans and buy mass-produced shit. I mean, what's the point?"

"Now you sound like your mom."

"Yeah." Jonah pressed the rock into his open palm. There was a new intensity about him, as if some inner flame had been ignited. "I just don't want to spend two-thirds of my waking hours doing something that doesn't add any value to the world. I don't want to be a passive person."

Adam felt that tightness in his chest again. He admired this kid's passion—his idealism, even his anger. He watched as a seagull went coasting by, its shadow running across their laps like spills of ink.

"From what I hear, you're not being passive," Adam said. "You're going to art school, right?"

"In theory," Jonah said.

Adam glanced at him. "I remember your pictures. They were really good," he said, then the phone in his lap buzzed.

Two mins. How is he?

Adam tapped back: Tired but ok.

"That's your mom," he told Jonah. "She'll be here any minute."

Jonah nodded but didn't reply. He was looking out at the water, weighing the rock in his hand. "I think Polly was hoping if she brought me up here, it would make me care about all the shit I'm supposed to care about," he said.

"I think she's just worried about you," Adam said.

"Maybe." He tossed the rock over the edge, too far down for them to hear the splash, then grew quiet again. "I know I should have called," he said finally. "This weekend got fucked up."

Adam waited, sensing that if he just listened, Jonah would keep talking. He tracked the lobster boat as it gained speed, navigating toward open water.

"This kid I came up to visit," Jonah said. "We used to go to camp together. He was like this nature prodigy. I remember he built a fire on one of our overnights—like literally rubbed fucking sticks together."

Adam offered an appreciative laugh.

"From what he posts, you'd think this guy was a fucking Eagle Scout or something," Jonah went on. "So I thought he could teach me things, you know? Like actual skills to become a useful member of society. Maybe I should have run it by him before I got here. I guess I thought he'd be less likely to say no in person. But right away, I could tell he wouldn't be into it. He's nothing like he seems online. All he talked about was college. Stanford. I think his commitment to the environment was mostly about looking good on applications." He picked up another small rock, gray with a single thick band of white, enfolding it in his hand. "So I decided to just take off. I mean—what the fuck, right?"

Adam nodded, mentally filling in the blanks—the sheeting rain, the impenetrable dark.

"It was rough," Jonah said. "I won't lie. I couldn't see my hand in front of my fucking face. And there was no service, and then it started pouring. In the morning, I was too embarrassed to go back, so I just kept walking." He squeezed the rock until the tips of his fingers turned white. "At first, though, it was amazing," he said. "To just walk into the woods and keep going. It felt like I had some ounce of control over my own life." He glanced again at Adam. "Not to sound completely cheesy."

"Not cheesy," Adam said. If he told Jonah he knew that feeling well, the kid probably wouldn't believe him, but he did. It was biking away from his house when he was thirteen and splitting his eyebrow open. It was flying around the track in high school. It was taking off from campus freshman year then waking up on the roof, alone, sensing the nearness of the edge. It hadn't been a conscious thought, but the knowledge had moved through him, at eighteen, how easy it would have been.

Then he heard Polly's voice. "Jonah! Adam!"

Adam pushed himself to his feet and spotted her half running down the path, Hope on her heels. He started waving like an air traffic controller. "Right here!"

"Jesus Christ!" Polly cried out, veering off the trail. She clambered over the rocks, arms out to steady herself. Jonah stood up and stuffed the headphones and sweatshirt into his backpack, dropping the striped rock on top.

"Jonah," she said, and he cradled the pack against his chest, as if bracing for punishment, but when Polly reached him, she gripped him in a tight embrace. After a moment, he pressed his face into her shoulder, and she just held him. The rest would come later, Adam thought.

When Polly stepped back, she took Jonah by the upper arms. "You scared the shit out of me," she said.

"I know," he said, his head hanging. "I'm sorry."

"Are you okay?"

"Yeah."

"Are you really?" she said. "Please. Please talk to me—"

"I'm okay," he said, looking up at her. "I am."

She scanned his face, hands on his cheeks, as if inspecting him for damage. "You must be starving."

"I can't tell. I might be."

"We'll get you something. And we need to tell Tom and Charlie—"

"I texted them," Hope said.

"Thanks," Polly said, and her voice caught as she looked at Hope, then at Adam. "Give us just a minute, okay?"

"Take your time," Adam said.

Jonah hitched his backpack to both shoulders, and Adam was reminded of his boys strapping on their packs for the first day of in-person kindergarten, the unaccustomed weight nearly making them tip over. He watched Polly and Jonah making their way slowly back toward the path, Jonah leading, Polly holding one strap of his backpack like a balloon that might float away.

"You coming?" Hope said.

She'd stopped, and was giving Adam a questioning look. Her eyes looked washed out, as if she'd been crying.

"I need a minute too," he told her. "I need to call Andrea. If I don't do it now, I'm afraid I'll lose my nerve."

Hope nodded, but she didn't press for details.

"We'll head back soon," Adam assured her.

"It's fine," Hope said. "I don't care. If you need me, you know where to find me." She looked around and smiled faintly. "It's so beautiful. I should have come out here more often." Then she turned and picked her way back across the craggy rocks, stepping deliberately from one to the next.

Adam waited until she'd arrived safely on the path, then limped his way back to the Staircase to the Sea. He lowered himself to the slab on top. The surface was still damp, but getting warmer. It was low tide, and the foamy waves crawling over the pebbles at the bottom of the steps made a light sizzling sound. The rocks themselves were covered with graffiti. Twenty-five years ago, there hadn't been nearly as much, but it was still benign stuff, people's names and couple's initials. Adam heard the drone of a speedboat and glanced up to see it go streaking across the cove, trailing a wrinkled ribbon of churned-up water. Then he looked back down at his phone. He knew what he had to say: it was difficult but simple. He loved her. He was worried about her. They needed to get help.

He watched as the final chops from the speedboat broke, slapping and sloshing against the rocks. The sun had broken through the mist, and the light on the ocean sparkled like popping flashbulbs, clusters surfacing and disappearing as the tide dipped and rose. To capture it would, he knew, be impossible, but he held up the phone and turned it to video and panned slowly back and forth.

TWENTY-FOUR

POLLY

It was a survival exercise, Jonah told her. To disappear into the woods, relying on virtually nothing except the natural world. When he sensed Charlie's hesitation about the idea, Jonah decided to venture out on his own.

"And it didn't occur to you to tell him what you were doing?" Polly said. "Tell *anyone*?"

They were sitting on the bench back by the trailhead. Jonah's hands were on his knees, elbows locked, squares of nail polish reduced to dull gold chips.

"That would sort of defeat the purpose, Polly."

"What purpose? Scaring everyone to death?"

"Being genuinely out there. On my own. Without a net—"

"I don't care," Polly said. "That wasn't fair to them. Or to me."

She was angry, but her anger was hard to sustain. She was too relieved to have her son beside her, and too worried about what it all meant.

"I know I should have called," Jonah said, staring at the ground. "I just couldn't."

"But you had reception—"

"I don't mean the cell service," he said, cutting her off. "I just needed to be away."

Polly pictured the huge house in the woods, the gleaming

cars. She knew Jonah had been counting on this weekend, and even if his expectations were unrealistic, it had let him down. "I know Charlie's wasn't what you were expecting."

"It's not Charlie's." He spoke with surprising fervor. "It's everything. Life. School. New York."

She paused, recalibrating. "I'm not trying to minimize it," she said. "But I really think it will at least start to feel easier. Soon you'll be in school—"

"I haven't made art in over a year, Polly."

"No one's made art in over a year!" she said. "And anyway, is that even true? Haven't you been taking some new pictures? Of your friends?"

Jonah stood up then and took a step toward the water, kicking at a rock. "*Fuck!*" he shouted. He kicked another, sending it plunging over the side. "Fuck! Fuck! Fuck!" Polly was startled, but she didn't intervene. He stopped and faced the ocean, hands laced on top of his head. "I'm sick of life just happening to me! I'm sick of reading about all the horrible shit going on and feeling too helpless to do anything about it. The world shuts down, people die, and now things are supposedly getting better but no one really knows that for sure. And meanwhile, the planet is dying but people ignore it or refuse to admit it and the country is still full of fascists and everything is still fucked up. So it's like, if I pass a class, fail a class, do art, don't do art—who cares?"

"That isn't true."

What he was saying—this strain of despair—felt new. Felt electric. It made her nervous.

"Plenty of things matter," she said. "If anything, it's even more clear now *what* matters—"

"That's what I'm saying. There's shit going on that's actually important."

"This is important, too. This is your future—"

"It's hard to care about my future when the world could end tomorrow."

"The world could always end tomorrow."

"Yeah," he said. "But it feels different now."

Polly stopped for a moment. What reassurance could she offer that she truly believed? When she was young, she'd felt unmoored, but her uncertainties were about where to live and what to do with her life. For Jonah—and Nicholas and Xavier, and Charlie, and Izzy, and her disembodied students, their names floating on screens—the future was more unstable than anything she and her friends had known.

Jonah released his hands from his head and threaded them behind his neck. He turned around, facing her. "I don't want to go to college," he said firmly. "I mean, I'm not going."

Polly felt a quick drop of pressure in her chest but remained calm. Remembered all he'd been through. "I get why you'd feel that way," she said. "I do. But it won't be like high school."

"I get that, Polly."

"You'll be in person, doing what you love—"

"It's not about art school," he said. "Or any school. I just—I need to do something else."

"And what would that be?" Polly asked.

"Okay," he said and held both hands in front of his chest, palms pressed together. "Hear me out."

If there had been no plan, or the plan had been theoretical, even disorganized, it would have been easier, but as Jonah started speaking, Polly felt her insides cave in. His friend Grace, he said, had a cousin who was part of this eco-village. An intentional community. *Self-sustaining, low-impact, micro-society—* the details came faster than Polly could absorb them. Everyone there contributes, he said, getting excited. Grows their own food, builds their own houses. He'd clearly done his research—was this what he'd been doing, all those days and hours she'd been trying not to crowd him? Listening, Polly had the sense of being carried toward a future that was already set in motion; it felt surprising but inevitable, as if she'd known this was coming all along.

"It's part of a global movement," Jonah said. "People who care about the same things. That's important. You told me that, remember?"

"Did I?"

He let his arms flop to his sides. "This is why I didn't tell you sooner. I knew you'd flip out."

"I actually thought I was holding it together remarkably well," Polly said, with a weak smile. "I'm trying to take this all in, Jonah. It's a lot."

She patted the bench, and he walked back over, sand crunching beneath his sneakers. "You're disappointed," he said, dropping down beside her.

"I wouldn't say that." But she was. She'd always supported Jonah's art, ever since he fell in love with that darkroom at twelve years old. She'd wanted him to be an artist—how many parents wanted their kid to be an artist? She'd wanted him in New York. It had felt like a plan they'd made together. But she couldn't deny that lately she'd been the one driving this plan forward, holding fast to that version of his future; it wasn't unlike what she'd criticized in Hope. Polly had been hard on her for not facing reality, but she knew how painful that could be. To let go of a certain idea of the world, because you wanted so much for it to be true.

"Where is this place, anyway?" Polly asked him.

"Not that far. Closer to New York than this. New Hampshire," he said. "I want to try it for a year."

"A year," she echoed.

"And then I'll reevaluate," he said, adding, "I just really feel like this is what I need to be doing," and Polly could tell, looking at her son, how deeply he believed this. After this terrible year, it was a way forward. He wanted to do something meaningful; it was the person she'd raised him to be.

"Okay," she said.

His eyebrows rose. "Okay?"

"It's your life," Polly said. "Your decision."

He chuckled. "It is?"

"With a caveat," she told him. "You cannot disappear."

Jonah broke into a smile, but she said, "I'm serious, Jonah. You have to promise me. You cannot just walk away like this—"

"Okay," he said and put a hand on her knee. "I hear you. I'm sorry."

Polly looked at his hand, the inked arm and dirt-lined nails. She remembered when he was a baby and she'd stare at him for hours, amazed he was hers. "I'm sorry, too," she said.

"What do you have to be sorry about?" he asked.

Right then, she made a promise to herself: she would tell Jonah the truth about his father. Not now—because her friends were waiting, and this moment was about something else—but that summer. Before he left.

Instead, she said, "I'm sorry to say you'll have to come to the reunion."

He groaned. "Oh my God."

"It's really our best option," she said, which was true. They'd said goodbye to Tom and Charlie—later, she'd call Caroline to thank her profusely—and she was too depleted to drive back to New York tonight. They could look for a hotel room, but at this point she doubted there were many left. And the fact was, though bringing Jonah to the reunion would have been unthinkable twenty-four hours ago, Polly now liked the idea of his being there. The three of them could give him a tour of campus, and show him their old dorm.

Jonah gave a resigned sigh. "How awful was it?"

"Honestly," Polly said. "Not that bad."

"Right," he said, but he laughed. She realized it had been a long time since she'd heard her son laugh. "All I know is this food better be fucking amazing." He bent to scrape his backpack off the grass, then said, "There's Adam."

Polly looked up to see her old friend making his way up from the rocks. He waved, and Jonah waved back. New Hampshire, she thought: with luck, the two of them would live close.

As Jonah looped his pack onto his shoulders, Polly said, "I have to ask you one more thing."

He stopped, giving her a wary look. "Okay."

"It's about the Instagram post."

Jonah frowned. "How do you know about that?"

"Hope's daughter."

"The one who came to New York?" he said. "Isn't she, like, twelve?"

"She's fourteen. And she was worried. We were *all* very worried—"

"Okay," he said, sagging back against the bench. "Understood."

Polly looked him in the eyes. "'Maybe this is where it ends'?"

Jonah tipped his head back, staring at the sky. "Don't worry about that, Polly."

"I can't not worry about it."

"It didn't mean anything."

"Then why did you write it?"

"Honestly—I don't even know," Jonah said. "I wasn't thinking about suicide, if that's what you're asking. I've never really thought about that. Not seriously. I was just out there on those rocks and there wasn't anyone around and it felt like—" His expression, when he turned to her, was bewildered and soft. "I mean, the world is going to end, right?"

Polly looked at her son and felt the need to say something honest. Something matter-of-fact, but comforting. That she had no idea what the future held. That she understood he was pissed off and afraid. That she was, too. That he was eighteen years old and, in many ways, this was just the beginning.

"Eventually," she told him. "But not yet."

TWENTY-FIVE

HOPE

Hope had, improbably, almost forgotten about the reunion. When she pictured what was happening on campus—classmates regrouping on the still-wet grass of the quad, posing for the Class of 1995 photo in the sunshine, trading sweaters for T-shirts, coffees for gin and tonics—she could see the scene in detail, but it felt less immediate, as though she were observing it from behind a pane of glass.

She was alone: it was the state that for the past year she'd been missing. But this solitude felt different, because her friends were there. Adam was still down on the rocks, calling Andrea. Polly was sitting on the bench with Jonah. Minutes before, he'd jumped up, looking heated, but now seemed calmer. He stood with his hands behind his head, elbows framing his face, outlined against the sky like wings.

After talking to Polly, even just beginning to talk to Polly, Hope felt a little lighter. Still, when she considered the prospect of driving home tomorrow and starting a conversation with Ethan, she felt sick with fear. It was impossible to picture. She'd been living with a familiar unhappiness; for a long time, this had been easier. Now, how to even begin? What would she say, and how would he react? What might get admitted? Or decided? And her kids—she was so worried about how this could affect them. It was terrifying, to look toward the future and not be able to imagine what would happen next.

Her phone chirped. FaceTime. Izzy's intuition was uncanny.

"Mom?" Her daughter's face filled the screen. She was sitting on her bed, a curtain of string lights on the wall behind her. "Did you find him?"

"We did," Hope reassured her. "He's okay."

"Where was he?"

"The end of the island. Where he took the picture."

Izzy let out a long breath and closed her eyes, revealing neon orange lids. "That was scary," she said, and her voice faltered. She was frightened, Hope thought. Of course she was. Because terrible things happened. Terrible things were always happening.

"Oh, honey," Hope said tenderly. "It's okay now. Thanks to you."

"It was an Instagram post," Izzy said, shrugging.

"Still," Hope said. "It was important."

Izzy opened her eyes and rubbed them, then squinted into the phone. "Wait. Where are you?"

"In the car, waiting for my friends. We're still out on the island."

"Mom!" she exclaimed. "You mean you missed half the day?"

Her reaction was so heartfelt that Hope grew teary. Now that she'd started crying, it seemed she couldn't stop. "Well, yes. But it's only one fifteen," she said, though it was hard to envision rejoining the festivities on campus. She wasn't even sure she wanted to. "And anyway, it's fine," she said. "It's been a good day, in a strange way. How are you?"

Izzy twisted a lock of hair around her finger. "Ro was having a hard time," she said. "But he did his breathing. And sounds like he did okay at OT."

"Good for him," Hope said, her heart full, picturing Rowan in Ellen's playroom, clinging to the rope ladder, naming his feelings as he made his shaky way up it. Her two brave kids.

"But how are you?" Hope asked.

Izzy paused with her hair, frowning at the phone. "Why are you being weird?"

Hope laughed. "I just miss you," she said, then listened as Izzy described the night before, and Lacy's boyfriend, who was nice enough but kind of needy and obsessed with his band and Lacy could do better.

By the time they hung up, Hope felt a bit steadier. She recalled another saying of Dominique's—*Exhale the past, inhale the future*. It was a line she didn't hate. Then she saw Adam walking up the path. On the bench, Polly and Jonah were now sitting side by side. The clouds had burned off, one sky becoming another. In the end, it was the afternoon the weather report had promised. Tomorrow, the reunion would be over, and she would go home to face whatever lay ahead.

I'm so unhappy: it was a place to start.

Adam's limp had gotten decidedly worse, or maybe it was that he'd stopped trying to hide it. He knocked his shoes against the front tire and opened the car door. "Thanks for waiting."

"Did you get through?"

"I did," he said, climbing in. He looked exhausted.

"And how's the foot?"

"Hurts," he admitted, and leaned back. "You don't have a first-aid kit, do you?"

She smiled and shook her head. "Sadly, no."

Adam turned to look at her. "You doing okay?"

"I don't know," she said. "But I talked to Polly. Finally."

"Thank God," he said, closing his eyes, and seemed to settle farther into the seat. "Be sure to tell her about the mini-reunion this fall. My house."

Hope promised that she would. They sat for a minute in an easy silence. The sunlight on the water was feverishly glittering. "I wish I could take home this feeling," she said.

"Hold that thought." Adam reached into his pocket and drew out his phone, and a minute later, Hope's buzzed. *Video from Adam.*

Souvenir, the message said.

The video, filmed down on the rocks where he'd been sitting, was only thirty seconds long. It was a panoramic shot of the ocean, the tides moving in and out like long, slow exhalations. Hope vowed that later, when she watched it, she would remember this moment as it was: sitting behind the wheel in her damp, sweaty clothes, scared to death about going home. Adam collapsed beside her with his swollen ankle. Polly, walking back to the car with her son's mud-streaked arm around her shoulder.

"Hey," Jonah said, opening up the door.

Adam said, "Hey, Jonah."

Jonah slid across the backseat and stuffed the backpack under his feet. "Sorry I ruined everybody's weekend."

"You didn't," Adam told him, and Hope said, "We're just glad you're okay."

Polly shut the door and said, "I think everybody's now accounted for." She caught Hope's eye in the mirror. "Ready to go?"

Hope slid the key in the ignition and took one last look around, casting her mind forward to the rest of the afternoon. It was only one forty-five. There was still plenty of time. They would return to the college, bringing Jonah with them. But first, they would leave the island, driving past the sleepy docks and deep woods. They'd stop for a late, leisurely lunch at the seafood restaurant on the other side of the bridge. By the time they made their way to campus, the day would be leaning into evening. The air would be cooler, and the sky darker. The lanterns inside the tent would give the world around it a bluish tinge, and Hope would marvel at how, in the changed light, it all looked different.

ACKNOWLEDGMENTS

When I started writing this book, in May 2020, it was in many ways an exercise in projection, a story that let me travel to places I was missing. It existed at 5 a.m. It felt ephemeral. I am thankful to the following people for helping it to make its way into the actual world.

Katherine Fausset, who read a very early draft and threw light on what it needed. Thank you for guiding my career so thoughtfully, for being both so honest and so kind.

Emily Griffin, phenomenal editor and passionate advocate. Leslie Cohen, Katie O'Callaghan, and the team at Harper—I'm grateful this book is in such excellent hands.

Amanda, Brian, Emily, Jeremy, Pete, Amy, Theresa, Michelle, for helping remember details of college in the early nineties. The CLAW, for advising me to find myself an empty off-season beach house. Betty Bonshoff, for offering that beach house. Kerry Reilly and Rachel Pastan, for smart and generous feedback.

The University of the Arts, for providing a sabbatical without which this book would still be unfinished. My colleagues in the creative writing program, especially Rahul Mehta and Steven Kleinman. My talented, daring, caring students.

My dad, for treasured trips to Maine and the island.

My mom, who read this book so many times, with great patience and wisdom.

Jake, for taking that walk in the woods that enabled me to see my way forward, and making space for the book to get written. It would not exist without you and Theo, whose imagination inspires me all the time.

ABOUT THE AUTHOR

ELISE JUSKA's previous novels include *If We Had Known* and *The Blessings*. Her short fiction and nonfiction have appeared in the *Missouri Review*, *Gettysburg Review*, *Ploughshares*, the *Hudson Review*, *Electric Literature*, and other publications. She is the recipient of the Alice Hoffman Prize from *Ploughshares*, and her work has been cited by the Best American Short Stories and Pushcart Prize anthologies. She lives with her family outside Philadelphia, where she is a professor of creative writing at the University of the Arts.